DUST

JUSTINE HARDY

ISBN: 978-1-7365975-5-2

Published by Batik Press

London, England

Cover and interior design by Tami Boyce
www.tamiboyce.com

MOLLY.

Recently.

Molly was sixty-five yesterday.

Her effort for the day had been to wear something that held in all the softly falling bits, but it just meant that she was constantly fidgeting in clothes that felt too tight. Now, the day after, she felt only relief as she slid back into expandable comfort.

Elasticated trousers had entered Molly's wardrobe the day she decided that she no longer wanted to worry about holding in her stomach for effect.

Standing beside a rack of stretchy-waisted trousers in Marks & Spencer, she told herself that it was just an experiment. Ignoring the flopping shapelessness of them, she told the checkout assistant that they were for an elderly relative. The woman smiled without hearing as she clicked off the tag.

Molly had not missed the look of regret in her husband's eyes when he saw her easing into that first pair.

'The glorious twang of elastic,' she announced, snapping the waistband into place.

'They look very comfortable,' Tom replied, turning away

Easy for him. His body still fitted the shape of him while she felt as though she was now falling out of all of her own seams.

No hysterectomy for him, no ridged scar for zips to chafe.

Molly pulled out the elastic on her trousers and her 'ten-gallon pants', as Tom called them. Or maybe she had dubbed them that. It did not matter. They were huge, awful and very comfortable.

She ran her fingertips over the scar, still livid even after twenty years, mounted on top of the first unzipping, her C-section scar.

Fifteen years between one scar and the next.

That was the one she wanted to find now, the first one, the proof of birth.

She could hear Tom next door in his study on the phone, his voice frightening in its pent-up control.

Molly held her breath. He sounded like a hissing cat.

That's not fair. He does not trust cats. Who can? Where's the dog?

She tried to call out, but as she did, her whole body bucked, pitching forward in the chair.

This was a pain she had never experienced.

TOM.

Ipswich. December 1990.

H e did not enjoy carol services.

Nine lessons with a lot of bad singing, a churchy version of the *Eurovision Song Contest*.

Whenever Kate was about to do anything in public, Molly started to twitch. She was beside him, shuffling about in the pew and picking things off his coat.

Kate had a solo, the first verse of one that was all wrong for her voice. 'Oh, Wobbly Dirge of Bethlehem', as Tom had dubbed it.

Actually, there were not many things that suited Kate's range.

Why humiliate her, straining an eleven-year-old's half-formed vocal cords in a register that she could not reach?

The solo opened the carol service, a privilege reserved for 'best in class' as long as they had the semblance of a singing voice.

The combined heat of pride and embarrassment made his haemorrhoids itch. He tried to readjust on the hard seat. Molly reached across to take his hand, but they were both in his pockets. By the time he had taken one out, she had turned away, her hand now flitting in a nervous wave at another parent.

KATE.

December 1990.

She was standing just inside the belfry curtains. The heavy red velvet had a mushroomy smell. Kate wanted to cough.

Not a good idea. Not now.

She held her breath, trying to swallow the itch in her throat.

She could see her mother's muzzy hair three rows away, half-way along to the left. She was waving at someone.

Why can't she brush the back of her hair? It's beautiful hair but they'll just see that she doesn't brush it properly. That's the kind of thing people notice. They'll think she's lazy. That's not fair. She's not lazy.

She looked for her father. His head was hidden by a pillar. She could see the left shoulder of his safe green coat, the one that smelt of toast and home. She knew his hair would be tidy.

The rest of the carol-service choir was stacked up behind her, shuffling and giggling.

Someone was playing with the worn, silky loops of the bell ropes.

Kate's stomach gripped.

What if they pulled a rope and the bells rang? What if the whole service had to stop because of unscheduled bellringing? What if people thought it was her fault?

She stared straight ahead, eyes fixed on the cracks between the aisle flagstoning.

Weak sun was pushing through the grey rain.

Mr Atkins, the choirmaster, stepped out in front of her.

Now it would be all right. This was how it was supposed to be.

He stood right in front of Kate, both hands raised. Ahead of her, above the altar, Jesus's face was touched by pale light. The flagstones ahead shone in the same rainwash. Mr Atkins lifted his right hand higher.

Kate took a breath.

Silence.

All would be well.

FAZLI JADOON.

Islamabad. 1990.

'Mr Jadoon, please sit down.' The man with the power to decide came out from behind his desk.

For a moment Fazli Jadoon had no idea what to do.

Every article of new clothing was uncomfortable, his shirt collar too tight, the tie choking and the shoes biting into his heels.

It was not just his clothes that did not seem to fit. There was no balance in this city, just noise and so many things he had never smelt before. Everything had been an assault as the auto rickshaw plunged in and out of narrow lanes, bursting out of them into a structured horizon that Fazli could never have imagined.

And now this man was asking him to sit down.

Should he shake his hand first?

Fazli's palms were sweating.

The man was pale, upright, his clothes tailored and well fitting. He looked natural in them, just as he did in the room, at ease in every way that Fazli was not.

Sweat slid beneath his shirt, from armpits to wrists and shoulder blades to tailbone.

The man did not try and shake his hand.

'John Sandman,' he said, picking up a folder and pointing towards a row of chairs, half a room away from his desk.

On a table between the chairs, there was a copy of the Qur'an.

Fazli tried not to stare. It seemed too obvious, the only thing on the table. It had been placed on a low stand so that it would be above everything else that might be put on the table. It was not a translation, but in Arabic, golden calligraphy glowing from the cover.

Was it to trick him into letting down his guard? Could this man really read the *mus-haf*, the pages, as they were supposed to be read?

He stopped himself. This was not going to help him, and he was still not sure which chair he should sit on.

There were five of them.

Was this another test?

John Sandman pulled his chair out from behind the desk, placing it closer to the row of five.

Fazli watched as he sat down, gesturing again towards the other chairs.

'I would like to congratulate you on your results,' he said, opening the file.

'Most kind,' Fazli replied, still distracted by where to sit.

John Sandman watched as Fazli looked again along the row of chairs and then hovered at the very front edge of one, barely even sitting. 'There is a section in your personal statement that particularly interests me,' he continued.

Fazli stared, his mind blank about anything he had written in the application.

'You wrote that you believe this is an important time to raise the standards of regional and rural medical practice to a higher level.'

'Yes, sir.'

John Sandman was about to stop him, to tell him to call him John, but he did not.

The boy was terrified. He did not need yet another challenge.

'What did you mean by that?' he asked.

Fazli was blank.

He could name this brain silence, one of the basic survival reactions to threat, the one that comes after fight and flight, there to protect the prey from the hunter by freezing all movement. He could see the explanation on the page, exactly as it had been when he had first read it, an oil smudge from someone else's food beside it in the margin. He knew, too, that all of this recall would seem to be happening in slow motion, while it was really only taking a fraction of a second.

Most important of all was that it was not going to help him.

It had to be overridden.

Taking the full length of a slow breath to steady himself, he began. 'I have been lucky, sir, to have had the very best of teachers, one in particular from your side.'

He paused. He could hear himself rushing.

'I mean from your country, sir.'

John smiled.

'He has helped me in so many ways,' Fazli stumbled on.

It was as though he could hear his teacher thumping the lectern. 'Just answer the question. Babbling tells them one thing for sure: that you do not really know what you are talking about.'

Fazli took another breath. 'This teacher, medical professor I should say, sir, he has been helping me to understand this thing. What it is that I mean is if we people are to raise standards in medicine, we have to start by uplifting the standard of teaching.'

'And do you agree with this?' John asked.

'Yes, sir.'

There was a pause, the older man watching as the young medical student fixed on the Qur'an on the table between them.

'Do you think this is possible here?' John asked.

Fazli stared.

Answer the question.

'Yes, sir. It will take some time, but unless levels are raised up in my generation, this thing will not be possible.'

'Good.' John paused. 'Then all that remains is for me to tell you that I am pleased to inform you that you have been granted a full Commonwealth Scholarship to pursue your postgraduate medical studies in the United Kingdom.'

The young man was staring straight ahead, eyes wide.

'I understand from your application that you have been offered places at two universities, and a teaching hospital as well. You will have to decide which of the courses you wish to take so that we can finalise the paperwork.' John stopped. 'Mr Jadoon?'

Fazli turned back to him.

'You do understand that you have to make the choice now? I should add that the scholarship panel has given a recommendation that you take up the place at Leeds General Infirmary.'

'Why this one, sir?' Fazli asked, freezing again as he heard himself.

Why answer with a question? This man is going to think I am being rude or arrogant.

John looked down at the file again. 'Perhaps it will help if I quote directly from their statement. "It is felt that this candidate will benefit from the biomedical research programme applied for at Leeds General Infirmary..."'

Fazli was silent.

'Why do you think they recommended this particular programme?' John asked.

'Is there any other note, sir?'

'I don't think so.' He looked back down. 'Ah, wait a minute. There is an asterisk.' He leafed through the pages. 'Yes, here we are.' He read and then shut the file. 'It seems that the board felt that Leeds General Infirmary would be the most effective research programme for you to be able to put to use when you return to Pakistan. You do understand that the scholarship stipulates that you must return here once you have completed the programme? This is the central aspect of the Commonwealth Scholarship programme.' He paused and looked very directly at Fazli. 'I would imagine the board's recommendation is that, of the three courses that you have applied for, research into diagnosis and disease prevention is going to be the most useful to you in pursuing your aspirations here.' He put the file down carefully and folded his arms.

'I am sorry, sir?' Fazli longed to pull off his strangling tie, to say what he wanted to say in Urdu.

'Excuse me, sir. Do you speak Urdu?' he asked.

'Yes, a little,' John replied slowly in Urdu.

'May I tell you about my name, sir?'

John nodded.

'It is a not a name that is used often, but my father chose it because my birth was hard. There were problems. My father sent a message with his brother to the house of the doctor in our village. He was not to be found. This troubled my father, and he asked his brother to hurry and find anyone who could help. My uncle went to the Christian mission because he did not know where else to go, as it was so late in the night.' Fazli paused.

His professor had told him to tell the story but to be succinct. He knew that he was already taking too long.

'It was a sister, a nun, who delivered me, and who saved my mother from dying during childbirth.'

He paused.

Was this man listening?

John was searching for words that he could latch on to.

'Therefore, my father picked this name. Fazli means "kind" in Arabic, from our Holy Qur'an. It is my duty to live by this name.'

John was grasping for words that he knew: something about birth and obstacles, someone helping. The last part had been easier. The boy's name meant 'kind'.

'Good.' Unfolding his arms, he rubbed his hands together. 'I am delighted that you have this opportunity.' He waved towards the door. 'Please do go back to the reception office and you will be given the forms that you need to fill in. You will need to start applying for your visa as soon as you have confirmed the course that you will be taking. I see in your notes that you have a passport already, so at least there is one less hurdle.'

'Yes, sir, that is done.' Fazli jumped up, hitting his knee against the table. As it tipped, he reached for the Qur'an.

'*Bismillah*.' He straightened the table and the scripture, stood up and held out his hand.

For the first time, he shook a stranger's hand. The grip of one palm to another felt unnatural. Fazli hoped that he would not find everything about life in Leeds as alien and impersonal as this strange act of two hands meeting and bobbing.

John stopped himself from telling Fazli that he needed to shake hands with more purpose. He also made a point never to tell anyone, ever again, that he spoke a little Urdu.

MICHAEL.

Recently.

She was late.

She was never late.

Michael slammed the door behind him.

'Can't get hold of Kate. There's still no reception. I went right up the hill. Nothing.'

'The network is down,' Omar told him for the second time.

'What's the story now?' Michael asked.

'Same story, cable damage caused by the aftershocks.'

'But they made that big announcement about having dealt with it. How does that work?'

Omar shrugged, sipping the skin off the top of his *chai*.

'Do you really like that?' Michael stood over him.

'My grandmother always made me. She said it was the best part. She didn't know why, but that didn't matter because she was right, as I found out later. It has the best part of the milk protein in it.' Omar sucked in more of the chai.

Michael looked up from his phone. He was irritated by the sippy, slurping sound, but he loathed his judgement more.

Two months in and he was still trying to find his way.

'Have you ever known her to be late?' he asked.

'No, but the delivery trucks are, every time. She can't tell us because there's no signal.'

'They weren't late last week,' Michael replied.

Omar laughed, tipping back in his chair, knocking into Michael. 'This was a miracle.'

Michael moved aside and leant over the table, forehead dropped into his palms.

Kate had laughed too, a week ago, when the trucks from Gilgit and Skardu had rolled in exactly when they were due.

Michael had heard the muffled sound of it as she pulled her headscarf across her face to mask the dust cloud whirling up from the wildly painted convoy. He had wished that he had something to cover his face too as he stood beside her with his arm across it, coughing.

The front of the first truck was a colour blaze of a demon's face. The headlights were red-rimmed eyes, the radiator grill nostrils spewing fire, the dust guard a lolling, scarlet tongue.

Kate loved the truck art, photographing the painted road warriors every time. One wall of her bedroom was a collage of the pictures—peacocks in full display; hawks swooping across side panels; lotus flowers; roses; camels crossing deserts; lush oases; an actress with a valley of cleavage, her head uncovered, flowing raven hair. Kate particularly liked that one. It was right in the centre, a huge pair of lips cut out of a *Rolling Stones* poster stuck so that they hovered just above the actress's pitching décolletage.

Kate had turned to Michael as she ducked down in the dust to photograph the lorry demon. 'It's to keep the devil away, a sort of vaccination against disaster and hell,' she said.

Every time she said something like that, he felt like the new boy all over again. It was not because of what she said, but that she had to say it at all, still explaining the way things were.

He pulled his *pakul* down over his forehead, trying to protect his eyes from the dust.

He had bought it because he had hoped that it would make him fit in. It felt right and respectful to be wearing a hat that had no brim to get in the way of a head bowing in prayer, though its thick wool made his forehead itch.

One of the first things he had noticed about Omar was that he did not wear one.

He thought that they were for old men and tourists, not that there were many of those any more, except the new breed of travellers, the 'Landcruiser-*wallahs*', the international aid and NGO crowd. They all loved their *pakuls*.

Kate did not have one. It was one of the reasons Omar liked her. She may be a tough boss, but she laughed, and she understood about family and respect without pretending that she understood more than that.

This was important.

'What are the chances they would be on time two weeks running?' Michael asked, his head still on the table.

'Zero,' Omar replied. He wanted Michael to leave the room so that he could climb up the hill and check. He might be able to get a signal. There might have been a missed call.

KATE.

December 1997.

The corridor was full of noise, bouncing off the linoleum and back down from the low ceiling.

Everyone was running.

This was forbidden inside the school buildings. The punishment meant running up and down the mile-long school drive, regardless of the weather or time of day. Kate did not run inside.

The noise and speed around her meant that the exams results had been pinned up. She was waiting, tucked away in a corner at the end of the corridor beside the phone booth. The crush would make her feel sick, so she would stay there until everyone had screamed or cried and then gone away.

She stood very still, staring at the checked linoleum. She fixed on the thin black lines around the greying cream squares, lining them up, creating a perfect, symmetrical, calming grid.

Wait, wait, not yet.

She counted the horizontal lines of her safety matrix.

Thirty-six.

'Kate!' Two friends were barrelling towards her, charging across her grid, crossing the barrier.

'You've done it—you're in!' Sarah was shouting.

'I hate you.' Joe was laughing.

Neither of them had taken A levels early. Their exams were not until the summer. For them it was all to come.

As Kate began to feel something that might be relief, she stopped it. She had been helping both of them, building revision schedules—how many hours per day, per week, how many essay practices they needed to do.

They were not sticking with the programme.

The lines in the linoleum lurched. Kate leant against the wall as her friends leapt at her. Sarah was hugging her as Joe punched the air again and again. Kate counted eleven air punches.

Their words faded in and out.

She knew she had to smile, to join in the noise. Her palms were sweating. She felt sick.

There was no exhilaration.

Smile. I have to smile.

Sarah was grabbing her hands, trying to swing her around. Kate pulled back, conscious of the sweat. She saw the confusion in Sarah's eyes.

She made herself hug her friend, trying not to stiffen as she did.

All she could feel was the rough wool of Sarah's jersey. It smelt of deodorant sprayed on to cover up cigarette smoke. It made Kate feel sicker. She forced herself not to pull back but to keep holding on to Sarah so that she would not have to say anything.

She waited to feel something—excitement, pleasure, anything.

Come on, Kate.

She pushed her thumbnails hard into her palms.

You're safe; you're in. School done. University now. Best in class.

KATE.

Recently.

Mum's birthday today, sixty-five.

She had rung Tom a few days before.

'What are you going to do for Mum's birthday?' she had asked.

'She said she would rather do something when you're back.'

'But I still don't know when that's going to be.'

'You know Mum. She wants the whole "No fuss, please" thing.'

'Oh, come on, Dad. That's code for "Do make a fuss but don't involve me in the planning". Couldn't you just take her out or do something with Susie and Mike—a film and dinner, something like that?'

'Didn't I tell you about the salmonella risotto saga?' Tom laughed. 'Starring your mother as the cook of the Borgias?'

'Yes! And you gave all the graphic detail that you seemed to enjoy a bit too much.' Kate smiled into the phone.

'You know she still hasn't apologised to Mike for nearly killing him with whatever poisoning it was. She said he needed to lose weight.'

'To his face?'

'Not quite, but she might as well have—you know that eyebrow clenchy thing she does that means "This is good for you"?' Tom laughed.

'They won't be coming to the festive rescue then?' Kate's voice softened. It was so good to hear her father's laugh.

'Unlikely.'

'Dad, I've got to go. Please put the birthday bow on Jack, get a cake. Just do something, please. And sing for Mum. Jack will bark; it's adorable, it's trad.' She closed her eyes for a moment, the lids pressed hard. 'I've sent Mum something, but it definitely won't be there in time. Will you tell her it's on the way if she asks?'

'She won't ask.'

'She might.'

Tom could sense his daughter, a tiny figure against the colossal landscape. The wind was whipping her voice away from him. He knew she would have climbed up behind the house to get better reception, out onto the hill, alone in the vast darkness.

It was four o'clock in Suffolk, nine o'clock in Gilgit. Tom longed to ask her about other things, but he hated the idea of her alone on the black hill.

The wind was building. Tom was saying something that Kate could not hear.

'Bye, Dad!' she shouted, her mouth pressed against the phone. She could see the connection bars falling to a flat line.

Tom could only hear the buzz of a lost connection. He gripped the phone against his ear, just in case.

MOLLY, TOM AND KATE.

September 2001.

It had been Molly and Tom's graduation present to Kate, a day of favourite things.

That meant a day in London doing some of the things that they had always done, things that had bound Molly and Tom together from the very beginning, and that they kept doing with Kate as soon as she was old enough, creating patterns, the fabric of memories to hold them all together.

It had been a good day, still soft with the tail end of summer warmth. People were still wearing shorts, determined to parade holiday-brown legs, jerseys tugged down against the edge of cooling air.

They walked the towpath along the Thames, crossing Albert Bridge, skipping when then reached the sign to 'break step', Kate moving ahead of Tom and Molly, just as she always had.

It had been the same formation since Kate's first crossing at four. She had asked what 'break step' meant. Tom had explained carefully that the soldiers from the nearby barracks needed to break their matching marching stride to lessen the crashing of their boots on the filigreed bridge. Kate had skipped ahead. 'Come on.' Molly had taken Tom's hand, skipping on behind their little girl.

A group of squaddies from the nearby barracks, running in a block, eyes forward, passed skipping Kate. Tom watched as every pair of eyes flicked right to clock his girl. A straggler tried not to smile as he looked. Kate saluted. The soldier winked and she blushed.

Tom thought again how very lovely Kate was. It was so difficult for him to let go of wanting to protect her from everything, always.

As they reached Barnes, they argued about lunch. Tom wanted to go to the place where he used to get drunk as a schoolboy, the pub on the green. It was the first place he had been sick from beer, the first place he had almost had sex. Going back there crushed time, and the food was good enough now to justify his argument.

Molly and Kate wanted to be beside the river.

'It's my day, and I want to look at beefy rowers,' Kate said.

The pub on the river meant Tom could drink beer, Molly eat scampi and Kate drown in rowers.

A hunk of them, fresh and pink off the water, homed in on Kate as they came into the bar. Molly and Tom argued about how much scampi and beer to order while Kate smiled down into the bar top as the men around her sweated and talked much more loudly than they needed to.

Tom passed one of the half pints to Molly. 'It's what she wanted,' he said, shouldering into the enthusiastic crowd. He lifted Kate's glass to show her that they were heading to the table.

She did not see.

When the scampi arrived, Tom did not remind Molly that she had asked him to stop her from eating fried food. She ate her food and started on Kate's, raising the plate a few times, waving to Kate as she did. When she did come to sit down, Molly ordered another portion. She ate from this plate too as Kate chatted, gesticulating more than usual, her face flushed, prettily so, Tom thought.

They walked on from the pub when all the beer and scampi was gone. Kate was still pink, and Molly was complaining about having eaten too much. Tom was softly fuzzy from the beer. He felt tenderness for Molly and her indigestion, and hot pride for Kate. It was a high day, a holiday. Why not enjoy the narcotic overdose of deep-fried fat and salt and Kate's flirting with young men?

She used to be so shy and lost. Not now. Wonderful university. Wonderful life!

The river rippled ahead of them. Seven seagulls sat in a line on worn pontoon posts, an eighth in flight, beak gaping, squawking, trying to crash one of the others from its perch.

Kate and Molly were ahead of him, their conversation a familiar buzz. Tom stopped to watch the birds on the pontoons. The scene seemed to be moving in heightened slow motion, the shrieking bird horrifying, his wife and daughter infinitely lovely.

A cyclist swerved.

'What the fuck yer doing?' he yelled at Tom.

A phone was ringing.

Tom stepped off the path, shocked but aware that his reactions were beer-slow and that it had been his fault. He raised his hand in apology as the screeching cyclist shot away.

Just beyond him Kate had her phone to her ear. So, it had been her phone ringing.

Tom raised his hand again, waving to show that he had not been hurt. They did not seem to have heard the cyclist. He shrugged at Molly. She was striding towards him, fast. His focus sharpened.

'Something's happened in America, a plane crash or some-thing. Kate says it's bad. She's upset. Come on!'

Tom looked at his wife without understanding.

KATE, MOLLY AND TOM.

September 12, 2001.

'You won't be going now, will you?' Molly asked.

'I don't think it changes my contract.' Kate was poised beside the hob, staring at the puffs of steam as they pulsed from the coffee pot.

'But they won't expect you to go, surely?' Molly looked around. 'They'll cancel it, won't they? Tom, where are you?' She raised her voice over the radio news.

Tom was hovering at the back door, listening.

'Tom?' Molly was shouting now.

Kate looked at her father, doing what he so often did when Molly started shouting. He was trying to leave the scene quietly.

Frightened Mum. Faintly cowardly though probably wise Dad.

She looked from one to the other. For the first time, they looked old. Or perhaps she felt old and they looked vulnerable.

'Can we turn off the radio?' Kate asked. 'If you want to talk about this, I'm not doing it with that constant hysteria in the background.' She looked at Tom. 'Dad, please can you come in?' She switched off the radio and pulled two chairs out from the kitchen table, the solid place where she had sat across the years, hunched over homework; writing thank-you letters, essays, her thesis; the table at which they had eaten together—always.

'If it is Bin Laden, they'll bomb the place back to the Dark Ages. That's what they're saying. How can they expect you to go into that?' Molly gripped the back of the chair that Kate had pulled out for her.

'There will be a huge flood of refugees into Pakistan,' Kate said.

'Why there?' Molly asked. 'Why not other countries?'

'Iran is unlikely, Turkmenistan...' Tom paused, trying to picture the map. 'And all those other 'stans are just as unlikely.'

'Why?' Molly snapped.

'They already have too many of their own IDPs,' said Kate.

'IDPs? What are you talking about?'

'Internally displaced people,' Tom said quietly.

'Internally displaced. That's how I'm feeling in my own kitchen. Don't you feel you have to listen to us any more? You still haven't got all the answers, Kate. You're still a child, for God's sake,' Molly wailed, turning from one to the other. 'You both think I'm being hysterical, don't you?'

Neither spoke.

Molly dropped her forehead onto the back of the chair. Tom winced at the thud.

Kate looked at her father, her eyes quiet.

Tom knew that she would go.

OMAR.

Recently.

She still gets her tenses wrong, and most of the genders but, no matter, her accent is better than most foreigners. People think she's fluent, so they're offended when she gets it wrong.

She doesn't realise, and so she doesn't apologise.

That's the part I have to do.

Omar was trying to remember the name of the *sarpanch*, the head of the village council meeting that they had just left.

A man with thick, earth-cracked fingers, he had ignored Kate, using Shina, though Omar had told him that she understood Urdu better. In a pause Kate had addressed the *sarpanch* in courtly Urdu. He had at last turned to her, and then her mistakes had begun, tumbling in one after the other.

Omar would go back later and find the man to explain that she did not actually speak Urdu as well as he might have thought.

Her mistakes had tumbled into one another as she tried to propose a girls' school to be backed by the council. She put the idea in the past tense, mixed up genders, jumbling 'he' and 'she' together. To the council members, it sounded as though she was proposing a co-ed school, an idea both offensive and dangerous to villagers who were even considering female education in the face of the Taliban's edicts.

The misunderstandings had built, filling the air. Several of the senior council members left, even before chai had been served.

Omar sighed. That was bad, particularly when everyone was already in a second language, few of them at ease with the language of politics.

Urdu was a poor compromise at these village meetings.

It didn't matter that her accent was good. It wasn't good enough. She pretended not to notice when some of them left. That was bad. She had been there long enough to know the significance of that.

When Kate left the room, he tried to explain. One of them picked at his *pagri* and then wiggled his finger into his ear with elaborate boredom and a growling sound. Some of them pulled phones from folds of shawls of thick wool, making calls, their voices loud above what Omar was trying to say. Another patted Omar on the shoulder and told him that they all understood the problem.

Omar could only look at the ground as he edged towards the door of the village council room, furious with Kate, conscious of his jeans, his city-style *kurta* and imported duck-down parka amid the muted, heavily woven layers worn by the men around him.

Half and half, neither one thing nor the other.

'May I take your leave?' he asked those still in the room.

They nodded.

Even as he closed the door, he could hear words like 'pup' and 'plaything'.

He did speak Shina, the language of his family's kitchen, of food and his grandmother's laugh.

He spat now, as far out into the road as he could, flicking up his chin to give it height. It just missed two boys running past, spinning rubberless bicycle wheels with sticks.

Beyond the boys, a shepherd clucked at his straggling herd. A twirling wheel hit one of the sheep. The shepherd struck out, catching the dodging boy's shoulder with his crook. Neither shepherd nor boy made a sound as the crook thwacked down.

Omar watched.

He had come from this, not as far into this kind of deep-rutted village remoteness, but it was all so familiar. He, too, had spun wheels with sticks, skipping away from possible beatings after each collision. Except for the time when he had crashed into the pomegranate juice seller, juice, fruit and pith flying, twenty glasses broken, pomegranate splattering everyone around.

The scene had been too bloody red for people not to react. Someone had called the guilty boy's uncle from his electrical shop, just next to where the juice seller had his stand.

Omar had been beaten in front of the juice-stained crowd, his uncle's thick leather sandal burning his back until all sound around him began to blur. His uncle had promised the watching crowd that the boy would wash all their clothes until they were as good as new.

Pomegranate juice marked in the same way as blood; the longer it was left, the deeper the staining.

There had been an attack the week before, two men running through the market place, shouting. One threw a grenade. It did not go off immediately but rolled under a stack of poultry cages while everyone watched. Chickens had filled the sky, and the boy minding the cages had two fingers blown off.

Everyone had wild, kitchen-announced theories as to the reason for the attack. The boy with two missing fingers knew that it was meant as a threat to his boss because he had not paid his dues for the illegal side of his business. The chicken front man paid the boy a large sum, ostensibly for the loss of his fingers. The boy's family bought a television that was too big to run on a car battery, and so they bought a small generator as well, even though that meant taking a disabling loan.

For months afterwards the walls of houses were dotted with sticky feathers, up above the level that people could reach with brooms and buckets.

After the juice incident, and the beating from his uncle, Omar's father had thrashed him as well because he was the one who was going to have to pay for all the broken glasses and wasted fruit.

Omar's upper back shivered at the memory of the double punishment as he watched the boys bouncing away, their wheels puffing up tiny dust clouds.

The shepherd moved on, his crook back over his shoulder, a lamb in a leather pouch at his side, bleating at it bounced on his hip.

He may have come from this, but he had stepped too far away to expect them not to treat him differently.

Even if he wanted to, he could not go back. He was the hero of the family now, the one with a smartphone and clever ideas, the one helping to pay off their loans after three generations of debt. His father and uncle greeted him with praise and blessings whenever he went home. His mother made the *pilau* that she only used to cook specially for Eid, family weddings and funerals.

He wanted something else that would not mean spending his professional life translating the errors of foreigners to his countrymen and apologising to foreigners for moments of flying spit and all the other gruntings and gas that punctuated the daily round.

KATE.

Recently.

She did not want to sit in the car waiting for him.

Too Lady Muck while he was cleaning up after her.

She would wait in the road.

Kate had known that she was getting it wrong. That had made it worse. When she was nervous, her grammar collapsed, genders flipping, tenses colliding. The fact that Omar had sensed she was worried had made it worse.

One of the elders had been staring at her throughout the meeting. That was unusual.

The more usual pattern was that she would be tolerated in the room, without eye contact. That would be disrespectful.

But the council elder had looked directly at her all the time, the tracks in his forehead lining up above thick glasses. The bridge was bound with a bulge of green tape, making them sit lopsided on the great triangle of his nose. It gave him a clownish look that did not match the eyes behind the thick, smeared lenses, milky with cataracts but still staring hard at Kate through the mist.

The room had been thick with the smell of rancid butter and thick winter clothes, still musty from hot summer months, stacked and unaired.

Kate had expected the clammy edges of claustrophobia, her old familiar, known and controllable. She had not anticipated the fear that made her leave the room.

She kicked at the dirt, her heart still thundering, her senses over-alert. Further up the road, she heard the door of the council room open. Omar stepped out and stopped.

He could not see Kate. The driver had parked away from the meeting, where the narrow road widened a little on the edge of the *maidan*.

A shepherd was passing, his flock spreading the width of the road. Sheep scattered into startled groups, the goats weaving strategically, hunting out fodder—low trees, scrub bushes, rubbish on the sides of the road. One stopped beside Kate, its lips testing a plastic bag. It started to chew. Kate ducked down to grab the bag from its mouth. The goat braced against her, the black rectangles of its eyes fixing on her like the old man in the council room.

Something was happening further up the road, animals skittering, two boys running through the herd. The goat got away from her, skipping off with the plastic bag hanging out of its mouth. The herd moved past as the two boys sped in the opposite direction, light bouncing off the silver of their spinning bicycle wheels.

She loved the chaos of it: the smell of fleeces, their oily earthiness; the woolly flow of backs as they passed; the clack of the wheels each time the boys spun them with their sticks.

Omar was looking around for the car.

She raised her hand to him. He saw but did not respond. Moving towards the car, he pulled out his phone and fixed on the screen as he reached her.

'I know I got that wrong, Omar. It was my mistake and you had to apologise. I am very sorry.'

He looked up, surprised.

MICHAEL.

Recently.

Once again, he was the one left behind.

Kate's explanation had been logical. Omar needed more exposure if he was going to start leading programmes. Of course, it was sensible for her to have someone with her whom the village elders would see as being one of their own, and who could speak both Shina and Urdu fluently.

But he was irritated. He knew that his Urdu was not good enough, and certainly not as good as he had managed to make the job interviewing panel believe. The extent of his spoken Shina was 'thank you', 'big', 'small' and 'Where are you going?' Not very helpful.

Bluffing his way in Urdu had been easy on the day. Being able to read the swooping script had impressed the interviewers more than it should have, as had his barely adequate translations. It was the day-to-day use that thwarted him. Vowels died in his mouth. He was nasal when it was supposed to be glottal, or glottal when it should be aspirated. The exuberance of tone always seemed just out of his grasp, except when he was speaking to children.

That was easy. He was unafraid of judgement, of syntax, gender, grammar or vocabulary.

If he could be at ease with children, why not everyone else?

Why mind so much what Kate thought?

When he knew that she was listening, it all collapsed. Even though she made some of the same mistakes as him, it did not help.

Kate was too like his older sister, with that ability to make him feel useless, especially when she was using her kind and understanding tone. The age difference was about the same. Kate had to be about thirty-five, seven years older than him, the same as his sister.

Sometimes, it was because she reminded him of a postgraduate teaching fellow who had taught some of his undergraduate classes. That had been the kind of crush that induced a stammering inability to speak, even to ask questions during lectures.

He remembered her for her short skirts, worn right into the cold core of winter, her long legs erotic, even in lumpy woollen tights. And always the same fluffy white hat, the pom-pom bouncing as she walked.

He had followed her back to her digs after a lecture once, just so that he could see her pull off the hat as she went inside, her hair lifting in the static.

He had longed to run up to her, to reach out and smooth it down.

Her name was Catherine, Catherine Scott. Perhaps that was it: Kate, Catherine, almost the same name.

Kate had good legs too.

Bit muscly, but good.

Why not be able to speak around her in the same way as with the cook's kid? No qualms there, just a chatty mixture of what she has been doing at school. The maths teacher is mean; the Urdu teacher is kind. Perhaps she could teach me too. The kid does most of the talking, but I understand everything.

Someone was calling out to him, the girl's father, the cook, Azad.

'Lunch?' he asked in English.

Even he won't speak to me in Urdu.

Azad watched Michael closely, trying to work out what he was saying as he replied in Urdu. As Azad turned to leave, Michael asked where his daughter was. Azad smiled. He tapped his head but said nothing.

School, of course. Should have known that.

Azad had put a table out on the veranda in the winter sun, a blanket folded over the back of a chair for Michael. His parka was thick, but the addition of the blanket around his legs made it a pleasure to sit out in the cold, bright air.

Azad returned with a tray full of dishes.

Michael stumbled through his thanks, embarrassed by the amount of food, five separate bowls and a pile of *naan*, steam puffing from the soft, fresh bread.

Azad went in to get another table for the laden tray. Michael called after him to tell him that there would be enough room.

He knew what Kate would say: 'Please let him do his job.'

Just as Azad had put the table out in the sun with the blanket, so he was now simply attending to the detail of his role.

It was the very first thing that Kate had challenged Michael about almost as soon as he arrived, as he was trying to take his bags out of the car, caught in a strange luggage wrestle with the driver.

He got up to follow Azad and bumped into him as he was backing out of the house, a table hoisted above his head. Michael grabbed one side of it, jamming them on either side of the door.

He had never been so close to Azad. The grey of his stubble and the deep darkness of the skin around his eyes surprised Michael. Azad looked older than he had realised.

He was about to say something, to apologise, but Azad pushed the table hard, shoving it through the door and into Michael. He backed away, almost losing his balance, apologising as he stumbled.

Azad put the table down and assembled the dishes slowly, adjusting each one several times. He stepped back to examine his work.

'Ma'am back what time?' he asked in English.

'I'm not sure. Depends on the roads, how long the meeting goes on. Soon, I think, quite soon.'

Azad tilted his head to one side.

'Later.' Michael simplified.

'Dinner?'

'Yes, dinner,' Michael replied.

'When?' Azad asked.

'Oh, I'm not sure, probably around seven o'clock.'

'Seven in the night?'

'Yes, seven in the night,' Michael replied tentatively.

As he sat down, Azad whipped the lids off all the dishes.

Steam rose from the food, misting the view of Mount Rakaposhi's four peaks rising in up stark, sheer lines as though bursting straight out of the fields below.

Her name meant 'covered in snow', just that.

Easy to understand.

Michael ate slowly, scrutinising the mountain and hoping that Azad would come back and take the food away soon. He liked the idea of the girl having some when she came back from school.

Azad did not come back for the plates, and Michael went on eating, now watching the road, hoping to see the dust-burst of

Kate and Omar's return. He wanted to stop feeling useless, sitting out on the veranda eating too much and just waiting for the afternoon to pass.

✍

They came back just as Michael was about to start on the last piece of naan.

Kate fell on it.

'Thank God. I'm starving.' She held out the plate to Omar. 'Come. Please come and eat,' she said, turning back to the table. 'Can I have some of this?' she asked, reaching for the half-empty bowls.

Before Michael could answer, Kate dived into the remaining food, still holding the naan plate out to Omar who stood watching from the edge of the veranda.

'I've got to get to the delivery in less than an hour.' She spoke while she ate, stooped over the table.

Michael watched her.

Yes, she's pretty masculine at times. Not surprising. Has to be, to get things done here.

He stepped away from the table.

Omar watched as well.

There had been no ease to the silence between them during the drive back from the village meeting.

He liked that she ate with her hands, but he was not going to eat with her. Not yet.

'Will you come with me?' Kate asked as she ripped the last piece of naan in two, leaving half. She pushed the plate to the corner of the table closest to Omar.

As she asked, both Michael and Omar started to speak, stopped and started again.

It was not clear who she was talking to.

She turned to Michael.

'We should leave. I'll be back in a minute.' She looked at the remaining naan and turned again to Omar, one hand raised as a question.

'I'm going to ask Azad if there is some more,' he replied to her gesture.

As Kate walked away, Michael wanted to ask Omar if there was anything that he needed to know for the delivery, but Omar was walking away as well.

Awkward, yes. There are so many occasions when it seems to be a normal conversation, but then the air turns tricky and I don't get what's going on.

Michael coughed and cleared his throat without there being anyone there for him to speak to.

MOLLY.

February 1979.

She was sitting in front of the television, clutching a pillow to her balloon belly. Even though the baby was pushing down on her pelvis, she did not want to move, as she was transfixed by the images on the screen.

A man and woman were walking across an airfield towards a plane in an elegantly choreographed sequence of despair. The woman was the taller of the two, movie-star beautiful, her fur hat rising above the crown of the man's sleek head, the matching collar of her coat just behind his shoulder. She seemed to be both beside him yet just a step behind, a graceful Amazon at his back.

A crowd was moving behind them, men in sunglasses and blazers, their heads turning, checking, in time with each other.

The woman carried a pair of leather gloves while her husband's hands were bare. An officer stooped in front of him, clasping his hand, kissing it, his mouth pressed against the man's hand. The unclasped hand hovered over the officer's head, but all that the man could do was pat the kneeling soldier with the side of the hat that he was holding.

The cortège moved on.

Another man in the uniform of the Imperial Armed Forces fell at the feet of his emperor as the group approached the aircraft, wrapping his arms around the man's legs, imploring.

The picture switched to dense crowds in the city, fists raised in triumph beneath Tehran's Azadi Tower.

It was eight years old, still as white as snow, carved of marble from Isfahan and quarried by the man they called 'the Sultan of Stone'. The emperor had commissioned the soaring, pristine Freedom Tower as a memorial for two and a half millennia of the Persian Empire. It had been financed by those that he had empowered.

Molly stared at the fevered human crush of celebratory rage.

Tom called after his morning lecture to remind her that he had a faculty meeting and that he would be back later than usual. Molly burst into tears as soon as she heard his voice.

'Oh, darling, what is it?' he asked.

'It's so moving. Are you watching? Did you see them leaving?' Molly whimpered.

'Who?'

'The Shah. They've gone,' she sobbed.

'They had to go. They would have been assassinated, the whole family, the Romanovs all over again.'

'I know, I know, but she looked so beautiful. They were so dignified. They kept looking at each other. It was so tender,' Molly whispered. 'It's heart-breaking.'

'It had to happen,' he said.

'Tom,' she wailed. 'What kind of world is our baby coming into?'

He was flipping a pencil between his fingers, staring at an unmarked pile of papers, essays on the Treaty of Versailles. He did not know what to say, nor did he want to mark the papers. He just wanted her to stop crying.

Ever since their first date, they had been arguing about the news, the state of the world and its political games. From that first time, in the woolly, wintery huddle of a Cambridge pub, their views had been big and bold, some coloured by their favourite lecturers but most by the wild hopes of a post-war generation longing to be the children of a new enlightenment.

Their views had become more muted in the face of the millions marching across Iran, demanding the end of the Shah's rule, declaring the Ayatollah as their leader, calling for the execution of the emperor.

Tom knew the truth of it. He had no idea what kind of world their baby would be entering.

KATE.

November 2001.

She was standing on a rise of ground beyond the main entrance
to the refugee camp.

The patchwork of survival changed as the light faded. Destitute
acres of flapping canvas became a sea of glowing triangles, their
outlines softened by thick dust in the air. Crude tents that offered
little shelter became thousands of tiny stage-sets in the dark, the
illuminated movement within them reassuring. The smell of onions cooking in oil was sweet in the air.

It was as ancient as the story of any tribe on the move, wise men
and woman, mothers and fathers, children, babies born in a foreign
land, all finding their way from one place to another in search of safety.

The wind had dropped into the pause after sunset.

For Kate it would be the first time in her life that she had not
been with Molly and Tom for Christmas.

She lost her balance for a moment and reached out for something to hold.

It was a story she was creating, a prettified biblical version of
what was around her, a lie for homesickness.

The scent of browning onions was rare among tens of thousands of families, so many of whom spent most of the day queuing for food. Onions were a luxury available only to those with money to buy them on the camp's black market.

There must be a tent nearby, one family who had enough to buy onions. They probably paid for having a tent so close to the gate, for the positioning that would allow easier access when the supply lorries came in and stopped to be checked. Some would be there for long enough to allow a box or crate or two to come off the back, for the right money.

Kate was still learning these rhythms of survival.

Just by standing where she was meant that she was already breaking three of the main rules for foreign staff working in the camp.

No female member of foreign staff was allowed to be in the camp after sunset. No member of staff could move around the camp alone. They had to have an interpreter with them at all times unless they were fluent in Dari.

Kate had been at the pick-up point at the right time, but no bus had come.

She had been too self-conscious to ask any of the people around her if they had seen the bus. She knew it was her fault, as she had insisted that her interpreter—a young mother—go back to her family and that she would easily find her way back from the education centre to the pick-up point.

All three rules broken at once.

She squatted on the slope as the wind came up again, dust blowing into her mouth, her nostrils, eyes and ears. She pulled at her scarf.

It would never stay on in the same way as her interpreter's. Kate tried to study how the women in the camp wore their headscarves. She would copy, but still it slipped off. She fiddled all the time, pulling it forward, untying and retying it, awkward in each attempt.

She watched as figures loomed in and out of the gloom in the distance.

The women would all be inside now, watching over their children who had been herded in with the late afternoon muezzin's call, long before sunset in the canvas city.

Kate could hear something nearby, a group approaching her, their voices rising and falling.

One of them was shouting something as they moved towards her, faster now.

Every sound was magnified: their voices, the crash of her heartbeat in her throat. She could smell them as they got closer—sweat layered with dust.

She shouted the only thing she knew in Dari, screaming a formal greeting into the wind.

They stopped in a half circle around her.

KATE.

November 2001.

'What the hell is the matter with you? The head of mission was leaning towards Kate, shouting. 'Have you any idea how stupid that was?' Ian was trembling, his cheeks flushed, spit threading the corners of his mouth.

His anger shrunk her, throwing her back to the garden at home.

She was eight.

Her new bicycle was sprawled just inside the gate.

She had been told that she could only bike in the garden, that she was never, ever to go through the gate alone.

But she had, wobbling along the road, thrilled by the feeling of speed, the cold wind of it.

A car came around the corner, skidding, the smell of burning, the horn screaming at her.

Then silence.

Kate was in the hawthorn hedge at the side of the road, the front wheel of her bicycle under the car.

A man was shouting, running down the road towards her.

It was Tom. He was picking her up, dragging the bicycle out from under the car. She was under one of his arms, the bicycle under the other. Molly was talking to someone nearby, her voice tight with apology. Someone else was shouting as well.

Kate began to cry in swooping sobs.

Tom put her down as soon as they were back through the garden gate, dropping the bike from under his other arm as he did. Kate sensed his huge presence leaning in towards her. She ducked.

Tom had meant only to smack her on the shoulder, but as she dipped, his hand caught her full in the face.

They stared at each other, silent shock circling them.

It was that same spit-spraying rage as Ian shouted at her now.

Kate knew that he was not going to hit her, even if he wanted to.

He was scared, just as Tom had been.

'Nothing happened.' She tried to keep her voice steady.

'You're fucking kidding me?' He thrust his face closer.

In that silence in the garden, after Tom had slapped her, Kate had known what she had to do.

'I'm sorry, Daddy.' She had been surprised by her own voice.

Tom pulled her hard against his chest, clinging to her, kissing the top of her head over and over. She had known, absolutely for sure, that she had done the right thing.

'I'm sorry.' She said it again now.

Ian pulled back.

'I didn't think it through.' She watched him as she spoke. 'When I left the education centre, I told Ara to go back to her family. Her son is ill; he's got a fever. She had been worrying all day.'

Ian stood with his arms folded, the edges of his nostrils filling as she talked.

'I went to the pick-up point on time. I waited. There was no bus.'

'Did you check the time?' he asked.

'Yes, last night, and this morning as well before I left.'

'Why didn't you ask someone else to go to the pick-up with you?'

'I didn't think of that,' she replied.

'Christ!' He was shouting again. 'Do you know how fucking lucky you've been?'

She just wanted him to stop shouting at her, to stop swearing. She was still shaking from what had happened in the camp, every response over-functioning. His fear smelt of acidic yeast.

The sweat of the men who had surrounded her in the camp had been different.

'Kate?' One of them had stepped towards her. 'I am Hamzad. I am the brother of Ara, your interpreter.' He extended an open hand to her, not to shake but to reassure, his palm patting the air.

Their sweat smelt of heat and dehydration.

'My sister was concerned for you. She knows that it is not right for you to be in the camp without protection. We are here for this reason. We can take you to the guard tent.'

Kate squatted so that she would not fall, her arm across her face so that they would not hear as she struggled for breath.

The young men stood around her in silence.

MOLLY.

March 1979.

S he had always known about this. It had been her childhood.

When the amniotic sac around a foetus broke, the waiting was done.

It came as a bracing heifer's roar filled the barn, her eyes rolling up. Molly's father would be scrubbing his hands and forearms, bent over a deep enamel bowl, her mother pouring boiling water from the big kettle in a smooth flow, even as the heifer bellowed.

Molly had been at her father's side so many times as he held the emerging sac in cupped palms, waiting for it to break, the amber liquid pouring down between the mother's hind legs.

She must have seen more than a hundred calves sliding down into clean straw, soft hooves pushing out through the membrane that had held them. Each time, there was that same feeling of smallness in the face of emerging life, the fully formed completeness of the calf, the hugeness of the ears, the size of the eyes, unfurling legs, eyelashes long and thick enough to count.

Each time there was fear as well, as fragile as the membrane around the new life. The further her father's hand had to go inside and the more agonised the roaring of the cow, the more fear filled the barn.

The most likely time for a death during birth was when it was a heifer, an inexperienced mother.

Christ, I'm a heifer too, an eye-rolling, bellowing, terrified newbie.

It had been such a small sound, like a knuckle cracking.

Molly stared in horror at her own waters pooling around her feet. So much.

'Fuckin' 'ell,' said a lorry driver standing behind her in the queue of men waiting to pay for petrol at the garage.

'I think we'd better get you to the hospital, love.' The woman behind the till leant over the counter, reaching towards Molly.

'Could you ring my husband?' Molly asked, sinking back against a rack of sweets.

She fixed on the fruit pastilles.

Must not faint! Concentrate. Green pastilles. My favourite.

Must. Not. Faint.

'I need his number, love.' The woman was beside her, scooping Molly from under her arms.

'I need to pay,' came another voice. 'I've got to get back on the road.'

'Shall I drive her there?' came a third voice.

'Higham 72...' Suddenly Molly was blank.

Green pastilles. Higham 72... but then what?

'I can't remember.' Molly started to cry.

'I know, love, I know.' It was the woman from the till again. 'I'm going to get someone to take you to the hospital.'

Molly could feel the woman's arms under hers, but she sounded so far away. 'You can get someone to call your husband as soon as—'

Her voice cut out as Molly felt her body being flung through a glass wall, the world splintering around her.

Now she was looking up at the vinyl roof inside an unknown car.

Like snakeskin. Odd.

'Get the towels under her,' someone was saying.

'It's okay, love. Just lift up for me. Grip my hand, hard as you like. Up a bit more.' It was the safe voice again, the woman from the till.

Molly forced herself, but she was being smashed through the glass wall again.

Someone else was lifting her, but the vinyl roof was not there now.

'Molly, can you hear me?' Another voice came at her in a rush of white. The walls, ceiling, clothes: everything was now a haze of speeding whiteness.

'Molly, I need you to roll towards me.'

Why was this voice so slow?

A face came right to her. White again.

'Why are you wearing a mask? Am I ill?' She tried to make the shape of the words, but they fell back down her throat.

A hand was under her back, a strong one. She was rolling, the world tilting.

Nothing was safe any more.

'Molly, I'm putting a stethoscope on your tummy. I'm sorry that it's cold. Can you feel it?'

'No!' It burst out of her, the first thing she could remember saying out loud since her waters had broken in the queue at the garage.

No, I can't feel anything. I have no control. Help me! Someone! Tom! Help! Help me!

MOLLY. MARCH 1979.

Her screams were silent again, crawling up from her panicking womb, stuck, unable to emerge.

TOM.
March 1979.

H e could not get his arms into the gown being held out to him. He was clenching his fists to stop his hands from shaking.

The nurse smiled at him, offering the arm openings at an easier angle. 'You'll have to wear this as well,' she said, passing him a surgical mask as she tugged the ties of the gown together, tying them at his back.

As he put it on and followed the nurse through swing doors, he could hear how fast his breathing was inside the mask.

Molly was lying on a gurney, her hair snaky with sweat.

Tom stared.

There was no colour in her face. It did not look like her.

He scrambled for something recognisable. Memory locked on to an etching in his grandmother's bedroom, a Victorian deathbed crowd of mob-capped relatives weeping around an ashen-faced figure. All around were the props of death: wreaths; bound lilies lying beside prayer books; the Bible; limp hands held to faces or clasping rosaries; a vicar, rapt in prayer, his face tilted heavenwards.

Tom wanted to laugh or be sick. He could not tell.

Lights were being turned on in the operating theatre beyond another set of doors.

Molly saw Tom, and she laughed. It was a strange and strangled sound.

'You're all dressed up for the occasion,' she wheezed, reaching out for Tom's hand.

He did not know if he was allowed to touch her. He looked around for permission.

Molly caught the hesitation.

'I'm one of Dad's heifers—breech. They've got to get it out. Hold my fucking hand.' The words twisted away from her as she grabbed his hand.

She crushed his fingers, the strength terrifying as her back contracted, snapping her up from the bed and then dropping her back down.

'Dad's tricks aren't going to work this time,' she whispered. 'I'm scared.'

'You're doing really well, Molly.' The nurse who had tied Tom into his gown nudged him aside. 'We're going to give you the epidural now because we need to get baby out.' She took Molly's hand out of Tom's. 'And I need you to come with me,' she said, leading him away.

He had no choice. She was surprisingly strong.

'I'm going to be next door, darling. I'll be here all the time, right here, just on the other side of these doors,' he called over his shoulder.

As he was led away, five people in scrubs crowded in around Molly, inserting, pulling, shifting the angle of glaring lights.

'You need to stop shouting now,' the nurse said.

'I'm sorry.' Tom lowered his voice. 'It's going to be all right, isn't it?'

He stared at the top of the nurse's ear.

This was terrifying. It was all too fast.

What if she wasn't all right? Is this why she didn't want to know the sex of the baby, why she had been so insistent about not knowing, in case of this?

In case of what?

In case it dies?

In case she dies?

Tom did not realise how hard he was pressing his head against the corridor wall. He saw the purply-green spread on his forehead in the bathroom mirror a few days later as he wiped the condensation away to shave. It took him a while to remember how he might have got the bruise.

MOLLY.

March 1979.

There was no more pain. Just the humming sound of machines and limp numbness as images flashed past—her father, a bellowing heifer, her mother's blank eyes as a breech calf thudded into the straw, lifeless.

And then empty silence.

'I'm going to be sick.'

Molly's first memory of motherhood was retching very green bile into a grey cardboard bowl, the kind that equally lurid jelly used to be dolled out in at parties when she was a girl, except that this one was kidney-shaped.

Her body was on fire, as far as her chest, and from there, icy nothingness.

She could feel her ribs convulsing, her diaphragm sucking in and up, the burning acid in her throat and mouth. But when she tried to move, the whole of her lower body was a dead weight.

Am I paralysed?

Single images slipped back: her sense of herself screaming, Tom being led away, faces crowding in around her, light burning into her.

'My baby!' she shouted. 'Where's my baby?'

'Hello, Molly.' It was another one of those voices, the calm ones, pulsing towards her through the sound of her retching like the one when it all started, so long ago.

'She's doing fine, and so are you. Just lie down again. Let me have your arm.'

'She?' Molly asked.

'Yes,' said the nurse. 'You've got a little girl. Now, arm please.'

A little girl.

'I can't feel my body. I don't understand. Where's my husband?'

'He's going to be back in a moment,' the nurse said, wrapping the green cuff around Molly's arm, pumping, flicking the stethoscope under the cuff.

A cool circle on Molly's skin.

She could feel that.

She snatched her arm away.

'Where is my daughter?'

'Now, now, this isn't going to help.' The nurse pushed Molly's arm back down, her hand steady and firm.

Molly wanted to shout again, but there was something about the nurse's voice, steady, firm and safe.

She let her arm flop under the nurse's hand.

'When are you going to tell me what's happened?' she asked. 'Please?'

The nurse watched the blood-pressure monitor and picked up her clipboard without looking up. 'Your midwife did not have time to get here, so let's wait for her, shall we? Your obstetrician will be doing his rounds later, so you can speak to him as well.' She kept looking down at the clipboard as she spoke.

Why won't she look at me? Why is she talking to me like this?

She wanted to hit the nurse.

'Please...' she started, and then she began to cry, hiccoughing out the words. 'Has something happened to my baby?'

KATE AND MICHAEL.

Recently.

When she felt indecisive or confused, Kate liked to drive.

It upset the driver, and he would ignore her for several days afterwards. It was worth living with his irritation for the sense of freedom and perspective that driving gave.

He was sitting beside her now, stamping down on an invisible clutch and brake every time Kate changed gear or braked.

She knew that Michael was hanging on to the back of the seat behind her.

Ever since he had first arrived, when she had told him to let people do their jobs, she knew that he had been keeping a tally of her hypocrisies.

This was one of them, taking over from the driver rather than letting him do his job. She could feel Michael's judgement seeping around her from the back seat.

She was still uneasy about her behaviour at the village meeting that morning. Of course, it was right to have apologised to Omar, but she was fidgety enough to know that she was unsure about what to do next.

The ugly choice had been lying by omission, not admitting to the mistakes she had made with the council elders, or admitting to them, though that meant showing herself to have judged poorly in the moment.

Part of Kate felt old and tired, another part pouty and homesick.

She skimmed close to the outer edge of a corner, dust arcing up behind them as they skidded on the edge of the roadside gulley.

The driver slammed both feet to the floor. Michael swore from the back.

'It's fine,' Kate snapped, steering out of the skid.

Below them were just crags before a vast drop to the river, a mad squiggle of turquoise among the grey and dun of rock and dirt.

She wished she could turn off at the fork ahead and take the road down to the water.

It was called the Snake Road, uncoiling down the valley side to the bright water that threaded together the trees and postage-stamped fields with their heady scent of damp earth.

And all the colour—stark green, burnt orange, so many yellows, fading bronze, all the colours of home.

The colours of Mum's birthday, and then Jesus's after that.

Another birthday, another Christmas, away from home. There were so many of them now.

'Kate?' It was Michael.

'Yes.'

'Are you okay?'

'Yup!' she replied.

'Could we slow down a bit? I'm sorry, but I'm feeling sick,' he said.

'You're right. That was too fast.' She pulled across the road into a passing place and stopped the jeep. 'Do you want to get out and walk for a bit? I find it helps. I get sick on these roads too.'

59

As she was getting out, Michael said something that she could not hear. She stood by the side of the road, stretching and peering over the edge, but he did not move. She waited for a while and then climbed into the back seat beside him.

They sat, both looking ahead, fixed on the convoy of lorries charging past, buffeting the jeep.

No one moved, Kate and Michael in the back, the driver still in the passenger seat.

'Is there a reason we're waiting here?' Michael asked.

'I thought you were feeling sick,' Kate replied.

'I'm fine now.'

'Okay, we'll get going.'

The driver remained in the passenger seat.

'Could we carry on now, please?' Kate asked.

Another line of tailgating lorries surged past, horns blasting.

The driver wound down his window slowly and looked out.

Michael looked away as he opened the door and lunged out into the road.

'I know it's not ideal that I drive, but I do find it relaxing.'

'Relaxing!' Michael snapped back.

Kate was laughing. 'I know, not very relaxing for you, not for anyone. It's entirely selfish.'

Michael tried to think of how to reply.

The driver got back in and took a while to adjust the seat and the rear-view mirror. He pulled out, lurching into the road between two blocks of lorries.

Kate and Michael fixed on the road again. She flicked her eyes across, and then again, surprised that there seemed to be the edge of a smile in Michael's expression. She had caught the moment when he realised that he had spent most of the day feeling bored and useless but yet might well die on some lost stretch of mountain road at high speed.

As he thought this, he was also regretting that he had not applied to go home for Christmas.

That had been a bad decision.

ONE OF THE DELIVERY DRIVERS.

Recently.

Fourteen hours to go. Nothing left in the tin.

The co-driver who did not drive was snoring beside him, his head bouncing on the seat.

He would have to get more pills.

After the delivery.

The old chemist in Pasu was not there any more.

Idiot! Who decided to stop paying protection money when they had such a good business going?

The driver had not tried the new chemist yet. He did not know if he was stocking the same pills. He had forgotten to ask the other drivers at the *chai-khana* stop. Even if the new chemist was stocking the pills, he did not know how much more he might have to pay him for *garam dawa*, the uppers that meant that they could go without sleep for days at a time.

If he waited until Gilgit, he would definitely have to pay more.

It'd better be that local guy taking the delivery. Easy just to dump the load and head out. If it's her, she just talks—wants to know how the drive was, if there's another delivery, if I've slept.

Sister fucker! I haven't slept for three days. How does she think we make our money?

He pulled the mirror around so that he could see himself.

Both eyes were bloodshot, pale irises retreating behind tight pupils.

He fiddled around in the driver box above his head, trying to find the drops that eased the gravel feeling in his eyes.

He knew he would have to stop to put them in.

All the lorries that he had just been overtaking would stream past.

He pulled into a passing place, tilting the mirror down further so that he could see what he was doing.

Another bunch of lorries charging past agitated him, and he poked himself in the eye with the dropper.

He would just have to do battle with the same drivers all over again.

The drops stung and fogged his eyes.

Sister fucker!

Blinking and shouting, he pulled back out onto the road, horns yelling behind him.

His co-driver slept on.

Useless idiot!

Still fourteen more hours.

Then he could rest.

The idea of the uninterrupted sleep cheered him as he blasted past another lorry, swinging in just in time for another corner.

'See my arse swing!' he shouted.

His co-driver opened his eyes, shifted and drifted away again.

He reached across and whacked the sleeping boy on the shoulder.

'Wake up, sister fucker!'

The underage and unlicensed boy shuffled across the seat and out of striking reach without opening his eyes.

His curled figure reminded the driver of himself at that age, sleeping on long journeys, ignoring the amphetamine rages of the man at the wheel who was doing all the work and taking the risks. He sniffed, rubbed his smarting eyes and thought about home.

How many months was the new baby now?

He had been on the road for three weeks. The baby had been born, what, maybe two weeks before he left. His wife had said it was too soon for full sex, and she had spat loudly after he came in her mouth.

When could he plant a boy in her? Three girls, and now four with the baby. Their dowries would cripple him.

I have to put a boy into her. *Bismillah!*

He wanted to remember when he had last been inside her. She had been heavy with the girl, crouched over the rice sieve, her arms wide, shaking the grains, her breasts moving in time, tight and full with late pregnancy. He had pulled her into the rice store, away from the other children and from his half-blind mother, pushing her against the wall, grabbing her, his hands and mouth full of her stretched nipples.

He smiled.

Yes, that was a good memory.

The woman at the delivery, the *gori*, she's old, more than thirty, bony, but her breasts are a surprise, large. She tries to hide them, but I can tell.

He imagined the dark skin of his hands grabbing at her milky skin, his teeth biting tight pink nipples, her pale head bending over his groin.

The road swirled for a moment, the dust from the truck ahead impossible to see through.

Son of a whore! Not going to die today.

I should eat.

When? Where to stop before the delivery?

No bonus if it's late.

But the imprint of Kate's bending head would not go.

Stop this. Think on your mother, your honoured mother.

Her image sat down, fat on his fantasies, all in black, her form solid in the corner of the kitchen, shucking corn to roast.

His favourite.

His stomach ached.

I really need food.

Kate's breasts pushed through again.

Stop this sin, sister fucker! Think of your unborn son, the son you will plant in your wife, your good wife.

He was on an empty stretch of road, the river below clear. For a moment there was no dust in the air from other lorries. He could see the crossroads ahead, the delivery place.

There was just one jeep.

I'm the first to deliver. I won. Might is right. *Rasta ke Raja*, king of the fucking road. Me.

There were two figures beside the jeep.

He narrowed his eyes.

Sister fucker! It's her.

There were two other dust clouds coming as well from the other direction.

He accelerated.

KATE.

Recently.

She had been car sick all her life. It was another reason she liked to drive, because she stopped feeling sick when she was behind the wheel.

If Michael had not jumped out as soon as they arrived, she would have tried to explain this to him.

She knew she would have jumped out too if faced with her jaded and unsubtle behaviour.

I need to get away.

It had been more than a year since she had last spent any time away. Even then it had only been for a couple of days, to Islamabad for a wedding.

The wild and privileged of the city had been at full play for swirling days and nights of too much whisky and no sleep—fun, of course, but not a time of rest. The memory was indistinct— jaded and unsubtle.

Kate had loathed the deadened cynicism of the first head of mission that she had worked with.

She had hated having to travel with him. He complained constantly about the drivers in a sneering stream on their inability to follow any kind of traffic protocol, their failure to use mirrors, the bunny hopping as they braked. It seemed irrelevant to him that they were making do with slipping clutches, brake pads worn to nothing and loose steering columns.

Kate had despised him for his derision.

Some of the same deadness was in her now too.

Sickening.

She bent over with her hands on her knees, trying to breathe.

The dirt sparkled at her feet.

Fool's gold.

Staring at it without focus helped, for the soft glow of it.

The grinding of lorry gears cut through the hazy quiet.

She had not expected them to be on time, but here they were, three smudged clouds coming from opposite directions along the road.

One was bringing gas cylinders, bought on the black market in Islamabad, the price hiked even further by the distance. The cost would mean creative accounting. The other two were coming from Peshawar with supplies for the winter school lunch programme, financed by USAID, all accountable, all to be checked and counted on delivery.

Neither delivery would be clean on the account sheet. They would not tally as they had all been skimmed somewhere between departure and delivery.

Kate had factored in a twenty per cent loss on the gas cylinders, and about the same on the food, maybe even higher. Gas cylinders were sealed liquid gold as winter came in. She had asked for a guard to travel with the delivery, but the seller had refused, insisting that his driver was better than any guard.

The driver would just be doing what his boss had ordered, dropping off some of the cylinders in Gilgit to the highest payers, those prepared to pay yet another premium on top of what Kate had already had to pay in advance.

Kate stood up again and watched as the gas lorry turned in ahead of the other two.

Take the hit or don't get the gas.

She knew she would have to explain all of this to Michael soon.

He was always watching.

When anxiety thrummed through fitful nights, she would convince herself that he had been sent to spy on her, to build up a body of evidence that would make it look as though she was in some way operating on the sly.

In the relaxing muscle of the early morning, the cycling fears faded into what she knew. It was the same every time—the squeaky-clean newcomer would arrive, full of ideas, shiny with highly polished principles, quick with the judgements, light on the evidence and understanding.

She knew that he felt underused.

He's trying his best. They always do. Standard newbie, except that he's not a newbie any more. Definitely time to talk.

Kate straightened up as the first truck turned in, wild red eyes for headlights, flaring nostrils across the grill, a great tongue, grotesquely wonderful.

She laughed and took pictures, one as the dust was still whirling around the truck, another as it began to settle, the tongue emerging more clearly, wildly red and unrolling.

The driver hopped down and stretched, his body shuddering with exhaustion.

KATE. RECENTLY.

Kate raised her hand.
She asked him how the drive had been.

TOM.
March 1979.

H e bent over the clear, plastic incubator.

It was like a tiny, see-through coffin.

She had monitor pads on her chest, a tube between her minuscule pink lips and another one in her nose, held in place by a piece of surgical tape. Everything attached to her looked oversized, the tape huge on a face no bigger than an apple.

The nurses had put a white cotton cap on her. She looked like a little old man, older than time, the oldest thing Tom had ever seen.

He wanted to reach in and pull the tubes out of her, to take off the monitors and gather her to him, enfold her, absorb her through his skin, body and soul so that nothing could ever hurt her again.

He pressed his hands against the plastic, willing her to open her eyes.

'It's a shock, love. I know.' A warm hand rested on his shoulder, the nurse on duty, her quality grounded, the rustle of her reassuring as she moved.

He longed just to collapse against the softness of her.

'You can touch her, you know,' she said.

'I thought there was a risk of infection?'

'There is, but you can protect her by covering up to go in. I'll show you.' She rolled on a pair of surgical gloves, elegantly, deftly, and slipped her hands through the rubber-sealed openings at the side of the incubator. 'I've got to change her in a mo, but why don't you have a go before I do?'

Tom's hands shook as he tried to put on the gloves. She helped him.

'It's all right, love. I know she looks weak, but in some ways she's a lot stronger than you think. You'd be surprised. You won't hurt her.'

She stood at his shoulder as he pushed his hands through the slots.

He did not know where to touch her, or how.

'Go on, love,' the nurse encouraged.

He put his index finger on the bird chest. It looked huge on the tininess of her.

There was a fluttering. He could feel it, a tiny thudding.

Tom snatched his hand away, yanking it out of the incubator. He looked at the nurse in horror.

'It's her heart. It's beating. She's okay,' she said, putting a safe arm around Tom's back.

He wept, looking at his baby daughter, her eyes tightly closed, thick, fine eyelashes so clearly defined, countable. The nurse did not move but waited, her arm still around him.

MOLLY.
March 1979.

As she opened her eyes, Molly saw a baby being rolled towards her in a clear, plastic thing, a tray, a trolley, neither one thing nor the other.

A sort of human greenhouse.

What are they called?

Insulators, no. Incubators, that's it.

As she tried to lift herself up, pain stopped her.

The baby was pushed past and further on down the ward.

Molly dropped back onto the pillow, staring up at the grey tiles above.

Her mother prided herself on never having looked at a hospital ceiling. She had given birth at home every time. Molly and her brother had come without even a midwife, the younger two with a bit of help, not much though, barely any at all.

Molly had been put in the airing cupboard to keep her warm.

I was small, that's it. I was a tiny baby too. She's like me. They wouldn't have me on this ward if my baby had died. Not surrounded by other mothers with babies.

No one would be that cruel.

Molly tried to lift herself up again to see where the nurse was now.

'I wouldn't bob up and down so much,' came a voice from the next bed.

Molly turned to see a woman with hair so dark red that her skin shone. She was grimacing as she pushed her arms into an elegant little bed jacket.

'Caesar?' the woman asked.

'Yes.'

'Thought so. You've really been out of it.'

'How long?' Molly asked, words still woolly in her mouth.

'Not sure. I think you were here when they brought me down a couple of hours ago. I was a bit out of it too,' the woman said, buttoning the bed jacket.

'Have you seen your baby?' Molly asked.

'She's coming up for a feed in a minute. That's why I'm getting all dressed up.' She laughed and flinched again. 'They bring them up to the milking shed in rotation.' She nodded towards the nurse with the incubator further down.

'They wouldn't have me here if something bad had happened, would they?' Molly asked.

'Not sure. I don't think so. It wouldn't make sense, would it?'

'Have you seen your husband yet? Was he with you?' Molly asked.

The woman laughed. 'Bloody hell! Sorry, but really, bloody hell that hurts.' She curled over her swollen belly. 'He doesn't do blood. Husband number one didn't do poo. Maybe third time around I can find someone less finicky about body fluids.' She turned to Molly. 'Oh, and I'm Susie by the way.'

'Molly. I'm Molly. I'm on my first. First baby, first husband.'

The nurse was coming back, the incubator empty now. Molly lifted her hand.

'Back in a mo,' the nurse said, rattling past.

'She's always saying that. She's good, though. If you want to know something, ask her,' Susie said.

'This can't be your first?' Molly asked.

Susie laughed again. 'No way! This little madam is number four.'

'Four!'

'Yup, seems I'm a bit of a rabbit. One wave of a willy and that's me in the club. Two with the poo-hater, and now two with the blood-phobic. I just wanted a girl. Three boys and now madam. Job done. Legs crossed from now on in. No more miniskirts for me.' She laughed again, clutching her stomach. 'You know what? Stuff that, I'm not giving up on miniskirts. I'm going to wear chastity pants from now on, Evonne Goolagong-style. Big, meaty tennis knickers.'

Molly laughed and then wailed.

'Just not a good idea for a bit.' Susie waved a hand at Molly. 'Think you've got visitors.'

Tom was walking towards them, the nurse behind him, pushing an empty wheelchair.

'Hello, darling.' Tom leant over Molly, his lips barely touching her forehead as though she might break if he kissed her too hard.

She pulled away.

They looked at each other for a moment in surprise.

'This is Susie,' Molly said, pointing to the next bed. 'Susie, this is Tom.'

Tom looked at Molly and then at Susie. He smiled, pushing his hands into his pockets.

He knew he should be doing something other than standing between them, motionless, but he had no idea what it was.

Molly watched him, trying to read his posture for signs that he might be about to tell her something that would destroy her.

The nurse stepped past him.

'Hello, Molly love. We've come to take you to see your little girl.'

Molly stared at her, blinking away a sprout of tears. She reached out for the nurse's hand.

'Why can't you bring her to me like the other babies?'

'She was really early. She needs help with everything at the moment. Come and see her.' She put her other hand over Molly's. 'It's all right, love. Just come and see her.'

But Molly did not believe her. She knew that she was about to find out something that was going to hurt even more than having had her baby cut out of her. She could feel it burning from under the new wound.

'Tom?' she looked at him.

He tried to smile, his hands still in his pockets.

'Don't hold your breath when you're being moved. It just makes it hurt more,' Susie said as the nurse began to roll Molly towards the edge of the bed.

'Go on, pull the covers right back so she can get her legs out more easily,' Susie directed.

'Thank you, Susie. Good to have an old hand around,' said the nurse, her head cocked to one side at Susie.

Tom just felt grateful for people who seemed to know what they were doing.

'Could you give me a hand, love?' The nurse nodded at Tom as she slid Molly's arm over her shoulder. 'Just do the same on your side and we'll have her in the chair in a sec.'

Tom's body felt odd to Molly, as though it was a stranger pressing against her. He was rigid, his hip pushing awkwardly into her side as they lifted her.

She cried out. Tom winced.

'Easy, Molly. Nearly there,' encouraged the nurse.

For the first time, Molly softened.

That was what her father used to say to the heifers: 'Easy, girl, easy,' his hand on their rumps, soothing them, his voice gentle—a lullaby.

'Good luck,' Susie said as Molly flopped down into the wheelchair, her jaw clenching.

She raised a hand in salute as the nurse wheeled her away.

Tom was beside her, but she could not look at him. She stared at the green linoleum rolling past beneath her.

The nurse tipped and spun the chair around, reversing through the doors into the neonatal unit.

Tom was now directly in front of Molly. She could not avoid looking at him.

He reached out a hand to her.

She looked at him, her eyes empty as the nurse turned the wheelchair back to face forward. As she did, Molly knew that she should have reached back to Tom. It was too late now.

MOLLY AND TOM.

March 1979.

Molly stared through the clear plastic shell in front of her.

How could this be her baby? It was just a mess of tubes.

She felt sick. Grabbing the sides of the wheelchair, she tried to get up.

'It's a shock, love, I know,' the nurse said, putting her hands on Molly's shoulders to keep her in the chair. 'She looks very frail, but, you know, she's a lot stronger than you can imagine.'

Tom was just relieved that she was saying exactly what she had said to him.

She was good, the same steady script, the same experience played out again for Molly so that they both had the information. No one had to pass anything on secondhand. No risk of confusion. He liked that.

Molly was still staring.

As Tom was about to speak, the nurse widened her eyes to stop him.

Seconds passed. Tom longed to speak.

I want her to know that it's okay, that she's just being helped because she's so little. The tubes are frightening, terrifying, but then you get used to them. I think I find them reassuring now. I know they are making her stronger.

He could feel every part of his body tightening with the strain of not telling Molly that it was all going to be fine.

Molly looked up at the nurse.

'Is she okay?' she asked.

The nurse leant forward so that her face was beside Molly's, so that they were both at the same level as the incubator.

'Look Molly. Have a really good, close look.'

Two little lips were making an 'O' around the tube in the baby's mouth.

'What's she doing?' Molly asked, grabbing the nurse's hand. 'What's the matter with her? Do something.'

The nurse was smiling. 'There's nothing the matter, Molly. Your daughter is yawning.'

Tom leant over the incubator to look.

Their daughter's mouth opened and then settled again around the breathing tube.

My daughter is yawning.

Tom looked at Molly.

Our daughter is yawning.

Molly stared.

Both miniature hands were clenched in tight fists. One of them, the left hand, closest to Tom, began to open, each flawless, minuscule finger uncurling.

He could see each nail, the smallest things he thought he had ever seen in his life. So pure, clean and utterly perfect.

Molly could not see the tiny hand opening from where she was. She was still staring at the baby's mouth.

A bolt went through her entire body as her daughter opened her eyes, the squeezed slits relaxing a little and then separating. Her eyes were blue.

It was the bluest blue that she had ever seen.

Molly's heart shot through the plastic, right into her daughter.

'Tom!' she shouted. 'Look, look! Her eyes are open.'

He learnt further over and, for the first time, looked into his daughter's eyes.

He reached out to Molly again and she grabbed his hand so hard that it hurt. It was the loveliest thing he had felt for days.

They looked at each other for the first time as parents.

Tom saw again the sweet, soft, brown eyes that he had melted into when they had first met, their warmth welcoming him.

His were grey green.

To Molly, they had been full of something electrically indescribable as Tom had hopped up and down in front of her on a cold university quad ten years earlier. She had been longing for something softer, kinder, more poetic than the male students who seemed to have only two female theories: either that enough beer made them great lovers or that reading Erica Jong gave them a licence to no-strings-attached sex, no condoms required.

Brown and grey green had now made blue.

As Molly and Tom looked into those just-opened eyes, they felt invincible.

MICHAEL.

Recently.

Michael was standing on a warehouse pallet, trying to count the bags of rice as they were unloaded. The extra height meant that he could see right to the back of the lorry.

Kate had suggested it. She had told him that she would explain later.

Michael was not short, six foot he told himself and others, but the suggestion of standing on the wooden pallet had made him feel small.

Kate was neither tall nor physically imposing.

That was not quite right—there was that hardened strength to her that Michael found intimidating, though oddly interesting too.

She was narrow but strong, and often there was a fizzing, curled-up energy there as well that unnerved him.

He had watched her walking up the hill behind the house a few days ago. She had looked like a boy, with a bit of goat thrown in, scrambling up over the dusty scree.

It annoyed him too that she was right about the pallet. It meant that he could see the whole of the truck's interior. The drivers knew it too, and they were making a show of dragging the food sacks from the very back, before pushing one out together. They stood together on the tailgate, arms crossed.

Michael could see a pile of blankets beyond where the rice sacks had been, uniformly stacked at the very back.

'Part of the delivery?' he asked the main driver.

'No, just bedding,' the man replied, pushing another rice sack at Michael.

'Can check you please?' Michael jumbled the words.

The driver and his sidekick looked at each other.

'It is not needful. Just for sleeping,' the driver replied.

'Not correct number of sacks,' Michael replied.

Both men shrugged.

Michael looked at the two road warriors, tough as gnarled wood, small and strong, red-eyed on amphetamines. He did not want to take them on.

'Okay over there?' It was Kate, calling from the gas cylinder truck.

'Some counting problems,' Michael shouted back across the wind.

The driver and his co-pilot stood, legs apart, unarmed gun-slingers, staring down at Michael perched on his pallet. The driver flicked his chin at Michael.

'Speak with her.' He spoke to Michael as though to a difficult child.

Kate was already there, stepping up onto the pallet beside Michael.

'It looks like we're five sacks down on rice, and about the same on sugar and onions,' Michael reported.

'Fifteen sacks?" Kate asked.

'I think so.'

She turned away, stepping down from the pallet. 'Michael, could you double-check the delivery sheet on the cylinders,' she asked in English, slowly and clearly.

'Of course,' Michael replied in kind.

As he walked away, he could hear her asking the drivers for their boss's number. He turned as he reached the gas lorry. She was holding her phone in the air, waving it about to try and get a signal.

Of course, she would negotiate directly with their boss rather than shoot the messengers.

Michael was beginning to understand.

There was no signal. Kate climbed up onto the truck to try for a signal beside the two men.

They moved away from her, the sidekick pressing himself against the metal ribs of the lorry so as to be as far away from her as possible.

'Did he tell you ten per cent?' Kate asked the driver.

He looked down at the floor.

'It is ten per cent. I know this. I understand. But why fifteen sacks? This much is twenty per cent.'

The driver nudged his assistant towards the tailgate. The boy jumped down, looking back up as the driver waved him away. Nothing was said. The driver peered around the lorry side to check how far the boy had gone.

Kate waited.

Michael and the other drivers' voices sounded close, blown towards them. They were talking about Manchester United, the players, how much they earned.

The wind would carry Kate's voice away from them.

'Are you paying off a loan?' she asked the driver.

He looked up, focusing just past her shoulder.

'My daughter's marriage,' he replied, kicking at the floor.

'Dowry?' Kate asked.

'The boy's family demand a scooter, a refrigerator, a television, these things and more. He is college graduate. My daughter was only up to tenth class.' He looked down again.

'I am sorry.' Kate picked the words slowly. 'You have to find a different way for paying the loan, no?'

'What way?' he asked.

They stood looking out over the valley, side by side, neither speaking.

His hands were balled tight. How could he stop her from telling his boss about the skimming?

She watched as horsetail clouds whipped off the top of the mountains, the browns and fading greens again reminding her of Suffolk.

She wanted to go home.

And so did he.

MICHAEL AND KATE.

Recently.

'Could we go for a walk?' Kate turned to Michael as they pulled away from the delivery lorries.

'What, now?' he asked.

'Not right now, but we could stop at one of the *chai-khanas* on the way, have some tea, a walk?'

'Okay.'

What had he done?

It had seemed to go well during the delivery. For the first time, he felt that they had worked well together—as though there had been an easy understanding without everything needing to be spelled out. He had not felt that she was having to watch over him. As he got back into the jeep, he had felt almost elated.

What had gone wrong?

He fixed on the landscape without seeing it, replaying the delivery moment by moment.

It did not make sense.

Why does she want to talk to me? She thanked me when we were leaving. I stared down the gas truck driver when he was being really gross about her. He might have said it under his breath, but he meant me to hear. She had heard it too, of course. He wanted her to hear too.

Maybe she's going to thank me for that?

Did I get it wrong with the food truck driver? Is that why she came over? What could I have done differently?

Not another lecture about pitching things with the right tone.

Kate asked their driver if he could stop at the next *chai-khana*. He nodded, accelerating as he did.

He did not want to stop.

He was not a tourist driver.

Enough of this day. It was time to get home.

Kate turned to Michael.

He was still quite new to this, but he had been good at the delivery. Now she had to try and explain about the skimming percentage that they had to factor in to guarantee delivery of the goods.

I hate this, but I've got to do this while it's still fresh or he's just going to go away and overthink it. And then he'll report back to London with a big, fat dose of righteous indignation.

Fuck! What I would give for some trust between us, the three of us.

She knew that part of Michael's job was to report back to the board about her performance—to spy on her.

It was standard practice. Of course, it was the right thing to do, though the board in London would never be given the full context. For them, it was just about impact. They wanted to know that all the programmes had been implemented in all the schools, that every meal had been provided, that the bottom-line accounts added up.

Not one of them had ever asked what it took to get the number of gas cylinders needed to cook the food in all the schools. Not one of the board had been to Pakistan since Kate had been running the programme.

There was a tea stall ahead, but their driver was accelerating. Kate asked him again if he could stop. He swerved, brakes jamming, dirt engulfing the front of the stall.

The *chai-wallah* watched the show from behind large sunglasses, the end of his *pagri* pulled across his mouth and nose against the shower of dust that rose and then floated down, settling evenly on the surface of the two glasses of tea that he had just poured.

He offered them to Kate and Michael as they got out of the jeep.

They took them, smiling. Neither of them said anything about the powdery film on the top of the tea.

A boy wearing bright purple earmuffs was balanced on a stool behind the man. He flicked a horsehair whisk as dust circled the architecturally ordered stacks of glasses and teapots around him. His carefully ordered pyramids teetered on top of an oil drum, burnt black in its reinvention as a stove. The front of the tea stall was hemmed in by perfectly geometric displays of milk biscuits and packet noodles. A large basket of little, hard rounds of bread was just far enough from the *chai-wallah*'s extravagant pouring not to be splashed as he swooped his kettle over his spread of glasses.

The driver disappeared behind the stall with his glass of tea, dipping and flicking his finger to skim off the dust.

Kate pointed to a string day bed under the only tree near the stall, but far enough away not to be overheard.

'Sorry about the driver,' Kate said as they sat down.

'You were right,' Michael said.

'Not at the delivery. I meant our guy.'

Michael looked up.

'I was rude to him earlier on the way. Not clever.'

'I hadn't noticed,' he lied. 'What about the food delivery driver? What was that about?' he asked.

'About twenty per cent of the delivery was missing, and thank you for handling it so well.' She was tentative, choosing her words. 'But it was less about how much was missing and more about why it was.' She paused.

'Oh.'

Kate watched a black kite plunge, pale talons extending. It whipped up a small, squirming ball of something.

'What's your take on aid ethics?' she asked, turning aside and spitting out more dust from the tea.

'What?' he said.

'Aid ethics.'

'I know what you said, but I don't think I understand the question.'

Kate smiled at the unusual lack of bluff. 'It's just a huge ethics minefield.'

They both watched the kite as it looped back up into the blue air, the victim rigid in the hunter's talons, the animal's tiny tail stiff.

'Ten per cent is standard. That's pretty much what every supplier takes. We pay for, say, a hundred sacks of rice, they deliver ninety and they get to sell the other ten again. That gets factored in. In this case they have doubled up, and we have been skimmed twice over. The driver's boss skimmed us, and it seems that the driver skimmed off another ten per cent as well.'

'What do you mean? How does corruption get "factored in"?' Michael was sitting up very straight on the *charpoy*.

'That's the fusty academic ethics of it. Are we meant to stand up against all corruption but then risk not being able to find any suppliers who are prepared to work with us, or do we just suck up the ten per cent skim and do the work that we are supposed to do, that the donors donate to, and with increasing scepticism, not surprisingly?' She leant forward, unwinding the scarf, tugging it off and combing her fingers through her hair, her head between her knees. 'And then there is the "hiding in plain sight" bit. We could just tell these increasingly and rightly cynical donors exactly what is going on, and why.'

Michael could see the soft, pale skin at the back of her neck and the fine, blonde down at the base of her skull. He wanted to reach out and touch it.

'Come on, Michael. What would you do if you were having to make the decisions?' she asked.

He coughed and moved further along the *charpoy*. 'Did he give you a reason for the scam?' he said.

'Excuse, a reason, whatever it may be, but yes, he did,' she said.

She wondered again if the lorry driver had been lying.

'So what was his story?' Michael asked.

'That he's repaying a loan, having been shafted for a dowry by his daughter's fiancée's family,' she replied.

'Did you believe him?'

'I'm not sure. They know how uptight we get about the dowry stuff.'

'So you think he was playing you?' Michael asked.

Kate laughed. 'Not really. I told him he had to find another way to repay the loan.' She paused. 'You know there are more dowry deaths here than anywhere else in the world?'

He was about to say that he did. He paused.

'No, I didn't,' he said.

'The highest percentage in the world per capita,' Kate added. 'And so, what would you do?' she asked again.

Something shifted. When he was defensive, when he pretended to know things, she ploughed over the top of him. When he was honest and admitted that he did not know something, she softened.

She could be kind, surprisingly so.

He smiled. 'You know, I wouldn't begin to know what to do.'

'You know, Michael, neither do I.' She smiled back at him.

KATE.

November 2001.

Ara and Kate had crafted a routine.

The translator would meet Kate near the main gate of the camp each morning. At the end of the day, they would walk back to Ara's family tent, pick up her son and then walk to the main gate, the boy between them.

It was slow. The boy was three, his steps smaller than theirs, his delight in being out of the tent vast.

It gave them time to talk.

Kate found out more about Ara's flight from Afghanistan, of what it had been like to live a childhood only in war. She began to learn a little Dari, just basic things, family words, ones about survival, humour and sorrow.

Ara was always searching for new words, for more accuracy.

'You know I am called a displaced person,' she said one afternoon as they left the women's education centre. 'We all are. This is what we are called, this word.' She was striding ahead of Kate. 'I am not lost; we did not get lost. We have been cut out from the place we belong.'

'Misplaced,' Kate said, trying to catch up.

'What are you saying?' Ara stopped and turned.

They bumped into each other.

Ara had her hands on her hips, square and solid. Kate had not seen her like this.

'Misplaced means lost,' Kate said. 'Displaced means dislocated.'

Ara was staring at her.

'It means a whole load of other things as well, but dislocated is one of them.'

'And what does this word mean to you?' Ara challenged.

'Well, dictionary-wise I think it would say something like being taken away from a place. The second part "locate" means "of a place".' Kate stopped.

Ara looked at her closely.

'No! I was not taken from my place; I was forced from it.' She paused. 'This is not right either. We were violently made to leave from our homes.' She turned and started to walk again. 'Yes, this is it. We are not displaced persons. We are families who have been forced with much violence from our land.'

'I am sorry,' Kate said.

Again, Ara stopped. 'Why are you sorry? You did not do this thing to us.'

'But my country is involved.'

'Are you not proud of your country?' Ara asked.

'I am not sure,' Kate replied.

'Do you believe that this man, this Bin Laden and this Al Qa'eda, is a threat to your country?'

'That's not why I came.'

'Then why have you come to this place?' Ara was watching Kate.

She started but stopped herself from repeating what she had said to her tutor at university, in the job interview and to anyone who asked her why she wanted to work with refugees. She had been about to talk about the displaced to someone who rejected the label.

She blushed.

Ara put her arm through Kate's. '*C'est n'importe*,' she said.

'You speak French?' Kate said, delighted.

'Yes, I went to the lycée in Kabul. I learnt to argue in French. I think it is a highly argumentative language, but I have forgotten so much of it now.'

'That's fantastic. I speak some too. We can speak French and no one will understand.'

'There is quite some number of people here who speak French. Please do not make this same mistake made by so many who come to work in the camp. We are not all poor and uneducated.' Ara patted Kate's hand. '*Tu comprends?*'

Kate apologised, words tumbling into each other. Ara hushed her, patting her hand again as they walked on.

As part of the daily walking routine, they began to speak French, Ara's little boy stumbling between their legs as his mother raged about the wars that men made. Kate was surprised by how much she knew about contemporary conflicts across the world when most of the camp conversations were about the fighting they had just escaped, and survival.

'How do you know so much?' she asked in a pause.

'I listen when I'm at the MSF centre,' said Ara.

'So do I,' said Kate. 'But they don't have those sorts of conversations when I'm around.'

Ara laughed. 'They do not think that I am around. I am invisible to them.'

'What do you mean?'

'They think that I do not understand what they are saying, so it is the same as if I am not there,' Ara said.

'But they must know that you speak French?'

'No, that's my secret. They know I speak English, but not French. *N'est ce pas, chou chou?*' she said, squatting down beside her son.

'*Oui, Maman,*' the toddler replied.

Kate clapped.

The whole of Ara seemed to smile, and the boy beamed up at Kate.

It taught Kate never to speak in front of people in a way that might make them feel invisible or irrelevant.

Without them she was not relevant—she would not be there.

MOLLY AND KATE.

April 1979.

Tom called out goodbye, and Molly heard the front door closing carefully behind him.

He feels guilty about leaving me.

She listened for a while, waiting.

The house was silent. All she could hear was the sound of her daughter, the still-unfamiliar wet sucking sound, milk bubbles popping at the sides of her mouth.

It was beautiful and terrifying.

Up to this point, everything had been controlled by other people. She had left the hospital with Tom, three days after the birth, just the two of them. The neonatal nurses had taken over for the next three weeks while Molly and Tom went to and from the hospital. All Molly had to do was express her milk, the odd plastic cup latched to her as she pumped.

'You'll have to try and imagine that it's baby,' the ward nurse had said as she first presented Molly with the pump. 'You'll need to sit up.'

Molly sat wrestling with the cup.

'Oh, go on, show her how to do it,' Susie barked from the next bed, her baby firmly attached to her nipple.

The nurse perched beside Molly.

'Don't be embarrassed. There's a reason it's called the milking shed up here. Have you ever milked a cow?' Susie laughed.

'Loads of times. I'm a farmer's daughter.'

'Well, you'll be a natural, then. Ignore your nipple. Just milk yourself.' She was still laughing.

Molly flushed as the nurse demonstrated a slow downward push on her own well-covered shelf of a bosom.

'Look,' Susie said, extracting her nipple from her baby's mouth.

The baby was crying as she flipped her hand, making a wide 'C' shape with her thumb and index finger. She eased down from the top of her full breast, closing the curve towards her wet nipple. Milk squirted in her baby's face. The crying stopped and the burbling began as the hot little face latched on to Susie again.

Molly stared, feeling utterly incapable.

'Go on.' Susie's tone was gentler than usual.

Molly took a long breath.

There was nothing but pain at first, her breast heavy, swollen and tender.

'Just think of her,' Susie encouraged.

Molly closed her eyes to create the image of that tiny face again. Her milk began to come through in a thick, sticky, yellowish dribble.

'What's wrong? It doesn't look like milk,' she squeaked.

'It's the first hit, the goodies to plump them up,' Susie said, smiling.

'It's colostrum, Molly, your first milk. It's supposed to be like that, full of protein. Just what baby needs.'

'She's called Kate,' Molly said.

Tom and she had not talked about it, fearful of something happening, of tempting fate.

'Kate. That's lovely. Nice and easy,' the nurse said.

'Who's that after, then?' Susie asked.

'Not sure, but it sounds right,' Molly said, fiddling with the cup of the breast pump.

She did know why. Katherine Hepburn was her heroine, particularly for her great love affair with Spencer Tracy. He had called her Kate, his wild, red-haired, blue-eyed Kate.

Molly hung on the utter romance of it.

She had thought about it while she was pregnant, wondering whether to say something to Tom. He might have laughed at her and then she would have felt silly.

At this moment she didn't really want to admit to her new friend and a nurse that she had just named her child after a film star who had had a love affair for twenty-seven years with a married man.

Susie and Molly's friendship thrived on a diet of teasing while Susie breastfed and Molly expressed milk. As Susie's husband came up with increasingly elaborate reasons as to why he could not come in to see his wife and baby daughter, the two women found a shared dark trait of humour, whispered between them and triggering giggling gales.

'I think he just took me very seriously when I told him not to come,' she said as Tom hovered over Molly one afternoon, attempting to plump up the solid foam pillows around her. 'He's hopeless in hospital. He passed out with the last one when the nurse handed him over.'

Tom and Molly looked at each other.

'Sorry, being insensitive. You didn't even get that chance for that first gooey cuddle,' she rattled on through. 'I'd warned them how squeamish he was, so they had wiped off most of the goo, but he couldn't handle even the tiniest smudge of blood. I'm hoping that he's messing about off campus because then he'll be oh so attentive when I get home. He'll fetch and carry like mad, and I won't have to have sex with him for months, maybe never.'

Molly and Tom stared at her.

'Have I shocked you?'

'Not at all.' Tom reverted to furious pillow-plumping.

'What do you mean "off campus"?' Molly asked.

'Oh good, that's the nurse we need to talk to.' Tom fled, stopping the nurse and wheeling her back to talk to them about what would be needed at home.

When they first left the hospital, Tom turned to Molly as they drove away. She was silent and pale. She needed distracting.

'Did Susie ever fill you in about "off campus"?' he asked.

'What are you talking about?' Molly snapped.

'You know, when she said it about her husband?'

Molly turned away. 'Wasn't it obvious that it meant fucking?'

He knew it made him old-fashioned, but he hated the word, especially when Molly said it.

This was going to be harder than he had thought.

It was harder still when they brought Kate home the following week.

Both sets of grandparents were waiting, lined up along the hall window, waving as Tom parked.

'Oh God, you didn't tell me.' Molly held Kate tight against her, a tiny, pink woolly tam o' shanter pulled down to her barely visible eyebrows.

It was an ironic good luck present from Susie, rapidly knitted as Molly whispered her fears to her new friend in the evening quiet before she had first left the hospital.

Susie had dug in on the ward, refusing to leave for various reasons that baffled the nurses and the hospital administration.

'I don't care how rubbish the food is; someone else is making it, and this is the longest rest I'm going to have for the next ten years,' she had said as she knitted and somehow managed to spoon very green jelly into her mouth at the same time.

As Molly looked away from the four expectant faces in the window, she wanted to be back with Susie, with bowls of hospital jelly and a routine that had made her feel safe.

'I knew you'd say no if I told you how much they wanted to be here.' Tom turned to her. 'Please, darling. I just didn't know how to tell them not to come.'

Molly stared out of the car window. Raindrops hung along the phone wires above her, lit for a moment by a slant of late-afternoon April sun. Kate opened her eyes. Molly knew that a newborn could not see that far, and yet her daughter seemed to be looking at the quivering drops, her gaze calm and unmoving.

I wanted this moment for us, the three of us, this barely formed family. No one else, no clucking, no opinions.

No fucking opinions.

'Tom.' She turned to him as he gathered the baby stuff that had accumulated around Kate in the hospital.

'Yes,' he said.

'Can you please protect me from your mother? If she tells me what I have to do with Kate, just get her away from me.'

'How can I do that?' he asked.

'Just tell her to shut up!'

Tom could see her face in the rear-view mirror. Her mouth was quivering.

'Laughing or crying?' he asked.

She heard the tenderness.

'Both.'

They looked at each other with small, tight smiles.

Molly's parents left that evening, promising to be back again soon. Her mother stood at the door for a moment, looking past her husband and Tom at her daughter and granddaughter. She gave a nervous little wave. Molly's father put one of his big, safe farmer's hands on her back and, with a solid, nodding smile at Molly, steered his wife out of the house.

Molly felt a painful tug under the healing C-section wound as the car doors closed. She wanted to run after them, with Kate.

'Now it's just this cosy group,' Tom's mother said as the headlight beams swung away.

Molly held Kate tight to her, making her cry.

'She needs changing.' She could feel the anger-flush rushing up to her chest as she hurried away, Kate's crying rising to a wail.

Tom's mother rolled her eyes. 'I'll go and unpack, and then I should probably help Molly. She seems rather overwhelmed, don't you think?' Her tone was knowing, and louder than necessary.

For the first time, Tom felt no divided loyalty but a furious protection for Molly and his daughter. He watched his mother following Molly up the stairs, and he wanted to shout after her, to tell her to leave his wife alone.

His father patted him on the arm. 'Leave it, Tom. You'll just make her worse.'

'Why's she being so cruel?' he asked, surprised by his clarity. 'You know Mum.'

'At the moment I'm not sure I do.' Tom turned.

'Talk to your sister. She's been through all of this with her.' His father followed him.

Tom was about to reply, to push the offer away, but he looked at his father and saw the tension around his eyes. It was not his style to say what he just had.

'Thanks, Dad. I will. Drink?'

'Yes, good idea. Time to wet the baby's head.'

The two men retreated to Tom's study.

$\mathscr{D}$

For the first few days, a flow of visitors acted as a buffer between Molly and Tom's mother. Even so, every time his mother approached Kate, Tom could see Molly tensing.

As the first flush of visitors dwindled, the tension crackled.

Tom was closing the door, thanking another set of friends for yet another set of bootees. Beyond the kitchen door, he could see Molly and his mother. Molly was perched on her toes in her flight posture, leaning against the sideboard, Kate draped against her in a post-feed stupor. His mother was reaching out for the baby.

'Tom!' Molly called out. 'I need to get on the pump.'

'But you've just fed her—why do you need to express?' his mother asked, trying to take Kate from Molly.

'Because my boobs are killing me, that's why.' Molly stamped out of the room, passing Kate to Tom.

'Oh dear, what have I done now?' His mother bent to nuzzle into Kate's soft crown.

'Please, Mum,' Tom tried.

'Please what?' she asked, fiddling with Kate's babygro.

The doorbell rang and Tom left to answer it, Kate in his arms.

Upstairs, Molly pushed the cup of the pump over a still-full breast, swearing as the rolled sides pressed into the tenderness. She could hear Tom greeting more visitors, laughing and thanking them for something.

I'm not a fucking circus act.

'Bitch!' she shouted aloud to the ceiling.

Tom heard and hoped that his mother had not. He was trying to understand why he felt so unsettled in this unfamiliar feeling of being entirely on Molly's side.

And now Molly was alone. Tom's parents gone and now Tom too. As the front door clicked behind him, there was silence. No one else was coming because Tom had to put a stop to the visitors to send the message to his parents that it was time to leave. His father had understood; his mother had been harder to persuade.

Tom and his father were confused that she seemed oblivious to the misery she was causing Molly.

'It's her hormones,' she said too often as Molly left the room, incited by another of her parenting barbs.

Their departure tightly dovetailed with his return to teaching for the first time since he had rushed to the hospital nearly three weeks before. His mother had refused to leave before.

'It's a difficult time for you. We want to help,' she had repeated each time Tom made a desultory attempt to ask for time with his wife and daughter alone.

'But, darling, you're both so tired. I remember that so well, and you can't tell what's right from wrong. We're here to help,' she insisted, the one time he had tried to confront her directly.

All he had asked was that they leave to give him a couple of days with just Molly and Kate before returning to teach.

Molly knew Tom was relieved to get away from the wash of hormones and the warfare that had played out every day between his mother and her.

'Just us.' She looked down at Kate.

She had fallen asleep while feeding, sliding off Molly's nipple, her face pillowed in breast, a trickle of milk at the side of her mouth.

An unfamiliar mix of gratitude and oxytocin washed through Molly. For a moment she could not tell where she ended and where Kate began.

We've made it, and now everyone has gone. Thank God.

She could see herself in the dressing-table mirror: a mother and child, curled together, Kate wrapped in the shadow of her body.

She laughed into the silence because they looked like the stupid t-shirt she had loved at university during her Tao period. Yin and yang, a curving black teardrop wrapped into a white one—linked, interconnected, the one existing only in the presence of the other.

Me and her, light and dark, dark and light, curled together.

Then there was a shift, and the reflection seemed to change. She was looking at a swollen, exhausted woman, one fat, veined breast engulfing a tiny body. The woman's expression was unsure, fearful and blotchy, like her breast and her body, everything swollen and tired.

This is it. I am stuck with this. This is not going to change. It's just going to be me and Kate, a lot. Tom at university all day, the house silent. I can't even go out to get a pint of milk in the village on my own. We are locked together.

Kate woke up, pushing both fists into Molly's breast. She stared up at her mother, unblinking as Molly's tears fell onto her face. She opened her mouth as though to catch her mother's tears. She was laughing, her tiny body still not filling out her skin, her arms wrinkled, her legs, stomach and face too. Above this, there was fine, dark, curling baby fluff, and just vast blue eyes staring straight into Molly's.

'My little old man.' She hugged Kate to her. 'Now get back on this boob, and drink yer milk, Butch Cassidy,' she said, laughing.

She must remember to tell Tom how much Kate looked like Paul Newman.

She looked at the bedside clock.

It would be at least another seven hours until he came home.

KATE.

October 1997.

She climbed up onto the loo seat so that no one could see her, even if they looked under the door.

Pressing her palms hard into the sides of the cubicle, Kate started to take slow, steady breaths, the way she had been taught to. This had been how it was ever since she could remember when she could not breathe, her heart battering, her whole body breaking out in sweat. Sometimes the order changed, but she was tuned to pick up the earliest sign, the first flutter, the tightness in her throat, the prickling.

Her sense of smell heightened as an early warning system of what was to come as though her nose was listening for the signs. The odour volume had been high as she walked into the hall, and into a jam of bodies and thudding music.

She had only recognised one person, a second year she had seen earlier in the day minding one of the music society stalls at the Freshers' Fair. The same girl was now wiggling on someone's shoulders, naked except for a tiny pair of denim shorts and huge pink sunglasses. The university crest was painted across her breasts. She waved the t-shirt she had whipped up, aloft, triumphant. Around her, hands reached up, grabbing at her, smearing the images of books and crowns across her chest.

Behind Kate, a wave of people surged to get closer, siphoning her into a place where she could not move, her arms clamped to her by the pressure. She lifted her face to try and breathe.

'Move it,' someone shouted.

She was barged aside by two boys in matching blazers, their ties knotted around their heads, beer mugs aloft and spilling.

'Hey, what about these shiny blue eyes!' one of them yelled, lunging at Kate.

He stank of beer and cigarette breath.

She ducked, squirming through bodies, fixed on the green safety of an exit sign above a door.

Sucking air as she pushed it open, she could smell the loos. There was just one door marked Men and Women.

This was not going to help.

And so she was crouching on the seat, locked in a cubicle, hoping that no one would know that she was there, hiding, terrified and now hyper-ventilating.

She put her head between her hunched knees, her lips pursed to draw in a slow, long draught of breath. As she did, she gagged on the stench of urine and vomit. Jumping off the seat, she yanked it up, dry retching into an already splattered bowl.

Someone was knocking on the cubicle door. 'Hello! Hello! Are you okay?'

Kate was silenced by a flush of hot anxiety.

'Hello?' asked the voice again.

She held her breath.

'I saw what that pissed jerk did just now,' the voice added.

Kate exhaled and unlocked the door.

'Wow! You're really pale,' the girl on the other side of the door said.

In contrast, she was not.

All Kate would remember from that first moment of that first meeting was that this stranger had the most perfect skin she had ever seen.

'I'm Farah,' the girl said, holding out her hand.

They talked for the rest of the evening, Kate perched on the side of one of the sinks, moving aside from time to time as increasingly drunk and incoherent students floundered around the taps. Farah sat on the windowsill, moving only once when a girl in a fairy costume with green hair tried to climb out of the window, muttering about Spiderman and scratching herself like a dog.

They were both hating everything about Freshers' Week. Kate felt like a country hick, Farah a token 'brown babe'. Both felt paralysed by their parents' expectations of their university lives.

Farah's parents had left Iran in 1979, in the same month as the Shah.

'They named me Farah, after their empress.'

'The woman in the fur hat at the airport. My mum loves her,' Kate said.

'Why?'

'I don't really know. Something about her as a tragically glamorous figure. She's got that picture of them leaving Iran, the fur hat and coat. It's weird because it's in a frame as though it's a family picture.'

'She's still the empress to my mother, and her life is completely tragic.'

They edged closer to each other as noise washed in with each staggering figure.

'We'll have to go back out there at some point,' Kate said.

'What's the worst that can happen?' Farah asked.

'We get covered in vomit,' Kate replied.

'Or we get raped,' Farah added.

'Rape or puke, what's your pick?'

Farah leant closer to Kate. 'The gag reflex shuts off arousal, you know?'

'That's gross,' Kate laughed. 'Are you implying that rape would be arousing? Is this the kind of crap they're teaching you?'

'In law, no, but I wanted to do anthropology. My father actually threatened to disown me when I suggested it.' She paused, looking at Kate. 'And you?'

'History and politics. And when exactly did school biology cover the whole arousal-puke-reflex thing?'

'It didn't. I found out. It's a kind of insurance policy,' Farah replied.

'What, you mean you can flip it around and make yourself puke if someone's trying to rape you?'

Farah was laughing. 'Now, that's something I'd like to patent. I would be solely responsible for a mass acceleration in women's rights, all made possible by the "Puke-on-Demand", brainchild of child genius Farah Hosseini.'

'Child genius—what do you mean? Aren't you eighteen yet?'

'Yes, actually no, not quite. In two weeks.'

'So, you'd better get on with it. You've got two weeks to patent this, otherwise you can't call yourself a child genius.'

Farah took a small notebook out of her pocket.

'What are you doing?' Kate asked.

'Reminding myself to invent the Puke-on-Demand.'

'It's not exactly forgettable.'

'I have a heavy timetable. There is a lot to do before I leap across the threshold into adulthood.' She pulled a tiny pencil out of the spine of the notebook.

'You really put something like that on a list?' Kate leant over to see.

'Yes, and lists of lists. Then I compile the lists of the lists and create a master.' Farah looked at Kate.

'Come on.' Kate was unsure how to react.

'Come on what? I bet you make lists too.'

'Yes, but only one. Any more than that and I would just get confused.' Kate paused. 'Actually, I do put Post-it Notes all over the place to remind me to check my list. I had the same one on my bedside lamp for the last two years of school: "Get into Oxford".' She laughed.

'Even though we didn't have to do it, I tracked down old entry papers and redid as many of them as I could. I managed to find about ten years' worth.' Farah still had her pencil poised over the little notebook.

'You're joking?'

'No, I'm not. It's one of those fun sidebars around addiction.' She turned a page in her notebook. 'My mother is addicted to painkillers because my father cheats on her, compulsively, hence her need not to feel anything.' She paused. 'As family traits, addiction and obsession seem to be right up there, so I am trying to make knowledge my drug of choice at this stage.' She looked up. 'Come on, then,' she said in a cartoon BBC announcer tone. 'Armed with sobriety, we will now go forth in the knowledge that our reactions are currently ten times faster than anyone else's in that hall of untamed animals. We can run faster and hit more accurately, though probably not as hard. They will have the strength of the very drunk, but we can dodge.' Farah was taking notes as she spoke.

Kate could see some of them.

Blue eyes. Nordic. Wary—but good wary. Interesting, maybe properly eccentric. Laughs easily.

A forming friendship in thirteen words.

FARAH.

Recently. Late November.

'*An aid worker from the United Kingdom has been reported missing in the northern areas of Pakistan. Early information indicates that it is a kidnapping, though this has not yet been confirmed. The identity of the aid worker and the organisation that they are working for are currently being withheld for security reasons. The foreign secretary...*'

'Kate!' Farah screamed at the car radio, her foot jamming on the brake.

A cab driver swerved around her, swearing, finger aloft. 'Fuckin' Paki bitch. Learn to drive.'

Farah knew that it was Kate.

'What have you done?' She grabbed her handbag, throwing things out of it, turning it over, tipping out case files, snatching her phone out of the heap, tapping at the tiny microphone image. 'Molly and Tom!' she shouted.

Stop! They might not have been contacted yet.

'Kate, Kate, Kate...' Farah wailed. Kate's numbers appeared on the screen. 'Fuck off!' She threw the phone back into the heap beside her.

It's Christmas. I can call them. I always do. 'Molly, Tom, just wanted to call for the Christmas check-in.' Don't be stupid. If I know, they know. Just stop. Think this through.

She sank into the seat.

They had not spoken for six months, the longest period of silence since they had known each other.

Nearly seven months ago, Farah had emailed Kate to tell her about her mother's death.

Kate had rung immediately.

'Far, it's K.' The words faded in and out.

Farah was sitting beside her father in the flat where they had lived for almost her whole life. All around them, from every surface, their life in another world looked out over them from silver frames.

Her father held one of the photographs on his lap, one finger resting on the picture.

It had been taken the year before they had left Tehran. Farah's two brothers were plump toddlers at the front of the picture, her parents behind. Her mother's hair rose in a glossy wave. Her orange skirt was seventies-short, held up by braces that went up and over the curves of a tight brown polo neck. She was wearing a pair of knee-high boots that exactly matched her sweater, so shiny that light bounced off them. The frame was engraved with the winged sun, the Faravahar, everything of Persia in one image.

'She loved those boots.' Her father's finger stroked her image.

'Shh, Abba, Kate's calling. I'm just going to take this.' Farah got up and walked into her parents' bedroom to speak, shutting the door.

They had whispered to each other, Farah sitting on her parents' bed, staring at another picture on the bedside table: their wedding photograph.

The droop of her father's Zapata moustache echoed the flop of her mother's white hat, its brim heavy with giant lace daisies that matched the crocheted ones that made up the lace of her minidress.

'She was gorgeous. Why did he always cheat on her?' Farah choked through her tears.

'I don't know Far; men are such fuckwits. They had been through so much…' The line faded again.

'What?' Farah shouted into the phone. 'Hello? K, can you hear me?'

But Kate had gone.

She sent messages, promising to come home as soon as she could, to spend time with Farah, but dates never materialised.

Farah had been hurt and then angry, too angry to tell Kate how disappointed she was. She had wanted her there because she knew that she would not raise her eyebrows at the making of lists, and then the lists of the lists, long columns of things to do in order to keep the pain at bay.

And now those months of anger, disappointment and hurt were just a vast waste of human time and energy.

She could not even remember where Kate had called from that last time. Had she been near Peshawar or further north?

Her mother's death and the hurt of Kate's absence had caused a fog, but she could remember that it was far enough north to be well into high kidnap risk.

She tapped the Siri microphone again. 'Pakistan aid worker kidnap,' she asked. The reports on the BBC and CNN were the same—an unnamed aid worker missing, suspected kidnapped. Dawn's coverage suggested that it had the markings of a 'sell and buy', the kidnapped a commodity capture to sell to the highest bidder.

FARAH AND MOLLY.

September 2001.

'It's a grotesque cycle: my parents left Iran to get away from it, and now you seem to feel you have to play your part in dealing with the hell that was kicked off then.' Farah was tearing tiny holes in a paper napkin, each one the same size.

'Harsh!' Kate laughed in surprise.

'There are some really disgusting people involved. You have to understand this; they are fucking evil.'

'You never swear,' Kate said.

'I know. I'm so angry. Fuck! And now I'm spitting too.'

'I know.' Kate smiled, wiping her face.

'And what makes you so calm?' Farah asked.

'I'm not!' Kate laughed again. 'I'm just using the Farah Hosseini Puke-on-Demand-by-Faking-It method. And I'm certainly not going to be dealing with any mess. I'm just going to learn—yet another worker ant scampering up and down the big old poop pile.'

'I don't believe Molly and Tom are okay with this,' Farah said.

'You'll have to see for yourself.'

'What?' Farah stopped tearing for a moment.

'Come and stay for a long weekend before I go. It's Mum and Dad's idea, just the tight friends, long walks, pub time, a lot of the Hat Game, everything inoculated with very carefully calibrated amounts of alcohol.'

'You're joking?'

'What do you mean?' Kate asked.

'You're choosing drunken episodes of the Hat Game as what might be your last memories on earth with your family and friends?' Farah smoothed out the paper napkin in front of her, a perfect lacework of symmetrically torn holes.

'You are deeply weird!' Kate picked it up. 'No one should be able to tear holes like this.'

'Why not? It's a myth that people can't draw or make a perfect circle freehand, and it's only because Giotto...'

'No, I really don't need the history of art lesson,' Kate interrupted. 'Will you come to Suffolk?'

'You don't really get it about the danger, do you?' Farah screwed up the napkin and threw into Kate's cup. 'It's doesn't matter how few of them there are because right at the heart of this every one of them is a psychopath. This isn't about religion, or any of the stuff they or anyone else craps on and on about. They don't care how many people die. They just want to go on killing because it makes them feel powerful.' She sniffed, wiping excited spittle threads from the corners of her mouth. 'I can say that. You can't. I suppose that's worker ant lesson number one.'

'Are you going to come?' Kate asked again.

'Of course.' Farah picked up another napkin and started to tear more holes.

When everyone was leaving after the weekend in Suffolk, Molly hugged Farah. She held on to her a little too tightly and for too long. Farah was still soft enough from good sleep, country air and the wine at lunch not to pull back.

'Please stay in touch, Far,' Molly said.

'Of course,' Farah replied.

'I don't mean just now and then. Please really stay in touch.'

Farah had done so, regularly.

Routines grew up around the absence of Kate.

Farah went to stay with Molly and Tom on the closest weekend to Kate's birthday for a few years. Susie was usually there as well, with her third husband for the first two years, and then with Mike, her fourth. Some of her children came a few times too.

It became a set routine to play the Hat Game after dinner on the first night. Susie added to the pattern by always arguing furiously with her teammates all the way through, her hands waving about as she struggled to describe the name she had in her hand.

Tom and Farah made sure that they were always on the same team, their method being quiet precision versus Susie's gesticulating drama.

They usually won, and Susie always insisted on opening another bottle of wine and demanding a rematch, just when everyone wanted to go to home or to bed.

As Farah's working life filled, the weekends faded. Instead, Tom and Molly called her whenever they were coming to London. They would plan something that they wanted to see: a play, an exhibition, a concert.

The quiet rhythm of the visits became pools of muted time in Farah's ever-louder life.

The routine around Christmas visits became the most fixed. It was always on a Thursday in early December. Farah would meet them for lunch to give Christmas shopping advice, largely based on how best to avoid the worst of the crowds. A few hours later, they would meet again for a carol service at one of the 'good choir' churches. Amid the human body warmth of fake-fur collars, sugar-spun blonde hair and carols bellowed out together, there was a cheerfulness that lasted on through most of dinner.

Each time, they toasted Kate, ignoring the blip of silence that followed, separating them for a moment until someone said something to push away the question of why Kate was not coming home for Christmas like almost everyone else.

Farah once tried bringing a date to the carol service and dinner. She thought someone else might dilute the sadness that she felt afterwards when she had waved Molly and Tom off in a taxi to get the last train. It was a hollowness that made her want to call her parents. She had once.

'It is very late. Your mother is already sleeping. Why are you calling? What has happened?' her father had asked her.

She had tried to explain.

'You have been drinking,' her father had said. 'Call us tomorrow.' And he had put the phone down.

The attempt to ease her sadness by bringing a date had not worked. She did not try again. It was easier not to have to keep giving context for someone who did not know Kate.

After each Christmas visit, they would send their stories of the day and evening to Kate separately. Sometimes, she sent a short and enthusiastic reply to all of them, and sometimes she did not respond.

There were all the other times when they rang each other too, whenever they had news from Kate. After a few years, they did not need the excuse of updates about Kate. They rang each other from time to time just to chat. The calls had their own rhythm, every few weeks, and a flurry in November about the Christmas meeting plans.

And then Farah's mother died. There had been no calls since, and Kate and Farah stopped speaking.

That was seven months ago.

$\mathscr{D}$

No one had made a call about the December plan.

Could she call after all this time?

She sat looking at Tom and Molly's number illuminating and fading, tapping the screen each time to bring the number back up.

Someone was knocking on her car window, a man signalling to open it.

Farah stared at him.

He shouted, his mouth right up to the glass. 'Could you move, love? I've got to unload. You're in a loading bay.'

She went on staring.

'You all right, love?' His breath was steaming the window.

She started to cry.

'Come on, love, it's not serious. I just need you to move,' he said, backing away from the window, a hand raised.

'Fuck off!' Farah screamed. 'Fuck off, fuck off, fuck!' And then she started laughing.

$\mathscr{D}$

Farah had laughed herself to tears during the Hat Game on the first night of Kate's farewell weekend in Suffolk.

Susie had been trying to describe Atomic Kitten without knowing what it was. She kept shouting 'It's a nuclear-destructing pussy. Boooom!', thunderclapping her hands between her thighs. Even though her team knew the answer, they let her keep repeating it, straight-faced until the wildfire of laughter took over. It became the tagline of the weekend, re-enacted whenever anyone began to be earnest about Kate's departure.

Farah and Kate met once more after the weekend, for lunch two days before Kate flew out. Farah could only stare down at her food when Kate said that she would probably be away for a year. Immediately, Kate went into Susie's Atomic Kitten routine. Farah laughed, but the tears came in as hard and fast as the laughter. Kate told her she was being hysterical.

'Not funny hysterical, the mad kind,' she had said, hugging Farah.

Here they were again now—the same gagging tears.

As the van driver watched from a distance, a hand still raised, Farah screamed and her forehead dropped onto the centre of the steering wheel, the horn blasting.

MOLLY.

Late November.

She had slept badly. It was a while since she had woken up that many times.

Too much chamomile tea just before bed. Good for sleep. Bad for night peeing.

She decided not to drink it any more, or at least two hours before going to bed.

Time to drain it off before sleep.

Tom had been in a deep sleep when she had woken up yet again.

This time it had been close enough to normal waking time for her not to bother hunting sleep again.

She lay rigidly awake, staring at the thin gap between the windowsill and the curtain. She was waiting for there to be enough light to get up and move about without turning on lights.

However deep Tom's sleep might be, he always woke up when a light was turned on, though Molly pottering about in the dark or half-light never woke him.

After all, he had slept through the hurricane of 1987, even when a tree had crashed and splintered through the coal shed beside the house. But he had snapped awake when Molly turned on the light to see what was happening.

As pale light made a long rectangle between the curtain and the sill, Molly's sight adjusted to the gloom.

Tom slept on as she got up.

She was surprised by her energy as she wrapped herself into her dressing gown.

Why am I so awake? Certainly not excited about my birthday? What's remotely interesting about being sixty-five? Kate will ring. That's exciting. Need to go for a walk. Calm down. Make some tea.

She stood at the kitchen window, her hands around the warmth of a mug, a teabag steaming in the sink below her.

As the clock radio in the corner clicked on to 7.57 a.m., copper light crossed the plough in the paddock beyond the garden, polishing the post van as it drove through the gleam of it.

Molly went upstairs to get dressed.

She took her clothes into the bathroom so that she could close the door and turn on the light. The smell from the loo bowl was strong. She put down the lid.

Nocturnal micturition. That's what it's called.

She was pleased that she could remember the term and pulled the chain with a flourish.

'Moll?' Tom called from the bedroom.

Bugger! He never usually wakes up before 8.30 a.m. now. Must have been the bathroom light.

'Everything okay?' he asked.

'Absolutely. I thought I would go for a walk. There's lovely early sun this morning.'

There was a pause. She could hear him pushing his pillows around.

All normal.

Then he stopped.

'Oh! Darling! Happy birthday!'

'Thank you,' she whispered to her reflection.

Sixty-five.

Her hands looked like her grandmother's now, brown splodges across the pale skin. The same ones were creeping across her face.

'Like a bloody Jersey cow,' she told the mirror, prodding her cheeks.

She would try and put on something smarter later, but maybe not until dinner with Susie and Mike. It was supposed to be a surprise, but how could it be when they have done the same thing every year for thirteen years, and on Susie's birthday as well? It was another of the routines and rituals that had come into play after Kate left, even if Susie and Molly chose the myth that it was because of their husbands' lack of imagination.

Molly pulled on her big pants and then arched to hook her bra—four hooks now to hold everything in. She leant forward.

'Flop 'em in.' She smiled sadly.

She looked up, seeing herself again in the mirror, waist up, from the top of her ten-gallon pants.

The edge of the sink pressed into the soft folds of her stomach, her bra just managing to lift her breasts away from where her belly now began.

This had not been planned, this cascading body.

She put a hand under each large cup and hoisted everything up.

'Yes, that's what I want for my birthday, a boob job.' She tried to laugh at her reflection.

She might even ask Susie later.

Tom and Mike would pretend to talk in the sitting room while they watched the rugby highlights with the sound turned down while Susie sat beside her on the sideboard as she cooked, not helping, of course, still swinging her legs like a girl.

Lucky her, with swingable legs. Still slim, boobs dangerously perky—good genes, bugger her! Or maybe she just kept mum about a boob job. I am going to ask. This time I really am.

Molly turned away from the mirror as she pulled up her trousers—no zips, no buttons. The kangaroo pocket fleece prickled with static as she pushed into it.

Just for the walk, better outfit later—promise.

She turned back, pushing her face closer to the mirror.

Her hair was static-spikey from the fleece.

Hair, not bad, and eyes still just about holding up, probably because my face is so fat. What was it that actress said, something about getting a big arse so that your face doesn't cave in? Brigitte Bardot. Can't have been her, she's looks awful. That other one, definitely French, very sexy. Damn! Catherine, that's it, Catherine who? 'De' something. Deneauve! I remembered—victory! *Victoire!*

So, this year's big birthday question: is it better to have eyes that are just about holding up on their own with a sea of blancmange in the middle, or Susie's still tight little bum, lively tits and a face full of rat poison?

Susie had given herself a course of Botox injections for her sixtieth birthday.

At the beginning of the course, she had been thrilled by her French cosmetic surgeon, giggling as she described his palette of cashmere sweaters, the comfort of the reclining chair at his clinic and the intensity of his gaze as he spoke to her. Molly longed to say that he was looking for lines to zap rather than deep into her eyes.

As Susie became more balloon-tight, Molly did not know how to react. The Botoxed look reminded her of overfull udders when the cows were bellowing to be milked.

Then it went wrong, Susie's left eye drooping as though she had had a stroke. She raged, demanding that Molly be her witness in her increasingly furious accusations against the pastille-shaded, soft-wool jabber. Molly did not give her views because she felt that Susie had agreed to be injected with a poison that was a kissing-cousin to hydrogen cyanide.

That's what they used in the gas chambers of the Holocaust, for God's sake, she ranted to Tom.

Molly tried to persuade herself that she was being sympathetic, but conversations with Susie felt unnatural, spooled too tight.

Then Mike shut down Susie's complaints by having a real stroke.

A month later, on a leaf-mouldy autumn afternoon, Molly was sitting beside a pile of magazines at the doctor's surgery. She did not mind the long wait for a flu jab as it meant time with the pile of weekend magazines that would make Tom snarl. The reading rebellion delighted her, and she dived into a long piece about Botox being used to treat ageing cleavage 'crêpe skin'. Plucking out her jersey neck, she looked down.

'Nothing's going to take on that,' she said to the rumpling valley below.

'You okay?' asked the junior receptionist.

'Nothing a large glass of Merlot won't fix,' Molly said, smiling.

She knew the girl from their local pub. She had been working evening bar shifts for a while. Molly liked her. She did crossword puzzles behind the bar and wore the kind of woolly tights that made Molly smile.

She went back to the article, and to the earnest ending. The journalist was trying to redeem herself with the serious point that Botox was also being used to treat spasms and paralysis in stroke patients. Molly thought about telling Susie, except that Botox had become a forbidden subject.

The droop in Susie's eyelid was still there, though nothing was said about it any more. All conversations were about how Mike was doing.

Molly looked down at her cleavage again now in the bald glare of the bathroom lights.

Another five years crêpier still.

Droopy belly, tits and arse, or droopy face?

She pushed down her hair, fluffed by the static of her easy fleece.

That would do for now. She would wash her face and brush her teeth later as well when she changed.

As she turned out the light and crossed the bed, Tom seemed to have gone back to sleep.

As she pulled on her gumboots beside the back door, she knew that it was getting harder to do something even this simple. She felt stiffer.

Jack almost knocked her over as he shot out of the door, trailing his lead. She hung on to the coat hooks, breathing heavily.

No, this had not been part of the golden years plan.

Jack was pawing at the gate, his banner wolfhound tail aloft, whippety ears up.

Molly grabbed his lead.

'Silly bugger. You're so impatient.'

'Morning!' A voice popped up from beyond the lane beyond the garden hedge.

Molly started.

An arm waved as two bouncing bobble hats slowed at the gate. 'It's Sal.'

Sal from the feed store, daughter of a farming family that had worked the same farm at the end of the lane for two hundred and fifty years. Like her father, her brothers and her sons, Sal had windburnt cheeks, and she was strong, direct and kind.

'Hello, Sal. Sorry, didn't see you. I didn't have you as a runner.'

'I'm not, but Jen is back from uni, and it's the only way we get to talk in private away from the boys. This is the new me.' She waved a hand to show the display of lycra and flashy reflective patches.

'Very sleek. And you too, Jen. Welcome home.' Molly tried to recognise the girl under the other woolly hat.

Every dimension of her seemed to have lengthened far beyond Molly's memory of the stubby-legged girl who used to bounce up and down the lane on a spherical pony, trying to keep up with her brothers.

They talked in short sentences, exchanging bits of news while the joggers bobbed in the road and Molly hung on to Jack as he leapt to lick everyone's faces.

Sal and Jen ran on, puffs of breath in the air, their heads close, chatting. Though Sal was more sinewy and Jen now longer-limbed, they were recognisably the same shape.

Molly and Kate had not done things like that together. They had never found an exclusively mother–daughter thing to do away from Tom.

Molly watched the jogging figures, jealous of their intimacy, suddenly wanting to hear Kate's voice, very much.

'Well, happy bloody birthday to me.' She leant down and let Jack off the lead as they crossed into the paddock.

He shot away, putting up three pheasants from among the maize husks, the birds clattering in the sky.

'Stay on the ground when it comes to Boxing Day, you lot,' Molly called out to them. 'And live another day.'

And then, for no reason that she could understand, she began to cry.

Jack turned to look at her. He stopped, watched for a moment and trotted back to her, burying his head in her crotch.

'Stupid bloody dog,' Molly sobbed, cradling his head in her hands.

MICHAEL AND OMAR.

Late November.

'What do you mean by this?' Azad asked Omar. 'Gone to which place?'

'We don't know.' Omar watched as Azad went on splitting chillies with his huge knife, turning the blade to scrape out the seeds with the blunt side.

'Are you saying she will not be here for dinner this night too?' Azad asked.

Omar watched the cook's back.

Azad was entirely dependent on Kate. She was the sole provider for his family. In his mind he was not employed by the organisation but by Kate, only Kate. It would not help him to be told. He would be terrified for his daughter, and for himself.

Omar understood this.

Michael had just asked him to leave the room as the Skype buzz started. It was a call from the London office. 'I am sorry; it's protocol,' he said in a flat voice. 'Could you speak to Azad?'

'She's my boss too,' Omar muttered.

As he closed the door, he felt the split opening up, the 'us and them' of it. Kate was missing, and now he was a brown skin, the enemy, one of those who might be somehow responsible.

Ø

'I thought one of you was always with her on the delivery trips?' the director asked Michael.

'Yes.'

'So why weren't you on this one?'

'We had to go into Gilgit to meet with the chief of police,' Michael said.

'Who is "we"?'

'Omar and me.'

'Why didn't Kate come with you?' the director asked.

Michael had to decide whether to cover for Kate.

She had not followed procedure.

'Michael, can you hear me?' the director shouted.

'Yes, I can.'

'You need to tell me whatever you can. I have to go to the FCO as soon as we are finished, and I need to tell them everything that you know.'

'Have they heard anything?' Michael asked.

The director looked down from the camera for a moment. 'Michael, please answer these questions: Why didn't Kate come to Gilgit with you? Who do you think the last person that she spoke to was? What did you think she was planning to do after the delivery?' Can we start there? Hello, hello, Michael? Can you hear me?'

Michael stared at the frozen image of the director in front of him. He seemed to be wearing a beret. How odd.

Omar had made every effort to behave normally as he walked into the kitchen.

'For dinner?' he asked Azad, reaching past the cook and the chillies to take a slice of white radish from the careful pile beside the chopping board.

Azad smacked the back of his hand with the flat of his knife. Omar dropped the slice.

'Sister fucker!' Omar snatched back his hand.

Azad turned to face him, knife in hand, and then he asked the questions about Kate.

'She is not back yet, and no, she will not be here for dinner.'

'And breakfast?' Azad asked, his gaze direct.

Hard winter sun backlit Azad, framing him. Omar stared beyond him, out through the window. He was still hoping that the jeep might suddenly appear on the road, the driver hunched over the wheel, Kate's familiar upright posture beside him.

'I am not sure,' Omar replied.

'When will you tell me?' Azad asked.

'Soon,' Omar said as he left the kitchen.

He waited outside the door that Michael had asked him to close, listening. There were no voices.

'Can I come in now?' he asked, opening the door.

'Sure, of course. I'm really sorry about that. It's just...' Michael started.

Omar held up his hand. 'No issues. This is how it is.'

Michael leant over the table, pinching the skin between his eyebrows. 'We got cut off. Do you think we should call her parents?'

'He should be doing that part, no?' Omar asked.

'I was going to ask him, but he was asking so many questions, and then we got cut off.' Michael started to get up but dropped back down again. 'We're already in so much shit because Kate broke the rules by not coming to Gilgit with us, going to the delivery on her own, everything.' He turned sideways on his chair, away from the computer, and sank his forehead into his palms. 'Omar, we're really fucked. They didn't give us a manual for this bit. God, what I would do for a drink.'

'I've got some Scotch.'

'What?'

'I know, *haram*, but as you say, we really are fucked!' Omar hit the 'k' with ferocity.

'Could I have some before I call them?'

'Of course.' Omar turned to go.

'Actually no, that's the wrong way round. Afterwards. I need to speak to them first.'

Omar shrugged.

'What do I say?' Michael asked Omar's retreating back.

'You can only tell them what we know,' he replied.

Michael turned back. Though late light had turned the room grey, the low wattage meant that the weak bulbs were making no mark. He stared out at the road. Two sets of car lights lit up figures walking on the road, momentarily seen then gone. He longed for one of those cars to be the jeep, the driver angry and tired, Kate ramrod, riding shotgun.

Michael began to bump his hand against his forehead, trying to find ideas.

He thought of how they had underlined the risks of the work during his interview, earnestly drawing his attention to the small print at the end of a template contract, discussing how they went about risk assessment and the limitations of insurance coverage.

But they had not talked about this. Disappearance had not come up.

Why had he decided not to go home for Christmas?

Omar was standing beside the door, watching the slow beat of Michael's fist against his forehead.

We have lost Kate, and no one knows what to do. No one can be honest enough to say this. No one.

'I've got the Scotch,' he said, waving a small bottle at Michael.

KATE.

Late November.

This was all wrong. No light, no sense of which way was up, small, dark, damp and loud.

Her head was banging against something sharp, and it was as though she was breathing something solid, not air, but just a thick smell that was hitting the back of her eyes and throat, burning her lungs.

Diesel! That's what it is. Or is it blood? Mine? My head, is it coming from there? I'm so thirsty. Can't feel anything. No, can feel my head—hot, burning.

So thirsty. Water.

Her mouth made the shape of words, but there was no sound.

There was something in her mouth, a gag, burning her throat and lungs, but with a sweet taste that had swollen her tongue. An image shot through, as though an old television set had focused for a moment between flickering lines.

She was standing beside one of the delivery trucks. Something, someone, was pinning her arms to her sides.

A scream for help surged through her but still no words came. There was just the push of her tongue against the gag in her mouth, the blowtorch in her throat as she tried to breathe.

Another memory shuddered through.

There was something in one of the hands that grabbed her. It was pushed across her face, suffocating her. And everything collapsed to black.

How long ago was that? Where am I now? I'm going to be sick. Can't. I'll choke on it.

Farah, I need you. What's the opposite of Puke-on-Demand? How to Not-Puke-on-Demand?

She tried to breathe through her nose the way Molly had taught her.

'Slowly, very slowly. Imagine you're sipping hot chocolate and it's still too hot so you have to take very slow sips. In, and even more slowly out again.' Molly was holding Kate's shoulders as her daughter's little seven-year-old body heaved with panic.

'Katie, watch me. You need to watch.' Molly put Kate's hand on her stomach so that she could feel her breath rising and falling in the swell of her belly.

Little Katie felt her mother breathing and tried to copy her.

Molly's voice was just beside her ear, as clear as it had been, the sound of safety jammed into the claustrophobia, soothing her.

She began to breathe through her nose, taking one steady sip at a time.

A rock of pain rose in her throat, contracting and rasping out a single word.

'Mum!'

The effort made her gag.

Can't be sick. Have to understand what is happening.

Her head hit the sharp thing again. Again, the pain drilled down her spine into her pelvis.

She knew now. She was in the boot of a car.

Just as the pain had risen in her throat, another surge bucked her body against the metal above her.

Hands tied, feet tied, gagged. I'm not going to get out of this one.

Still her body went on jerking up against the roof of the boot, battering for survival.

Now that she knew where she was, the sound of the engine made sense, as did the way the car was throwing her around.

Breathe, Kate, breathe.

She wormed herself away from whatever it was that had been hitting her head, her legs crunching further into her belly, her spine cramming against something else hard and bruising, but at least this thing was not as sharp.

TOM AND MICHAEL.

Late November.

'Hello, could I speak with Mr Black?'

'Speaking.'

'This is Michael Newton.'

'Hello.'

'Can you hear me, Mr Black? I work with Kate. Hello?'

'Yes, yes, I can hear you, Michael. I know who you are. Kate has talked about you. Is she there?' Tom asked, surprised by how normal his voice sounded as he asked the question.

'We have a situation here, Mr Black,' Michael replied.

'Oh, really.' Tom wanted everything to stop. 'Please do call me Tom,' he said, screwing up his face against the cramping in his gut.

'Thank you, yes, Tom. Is Mrs Black with you?' Michael asked.

He knew this was not right, the words in the wrong order, a bad script.

Don't ask him if he's sitting down. This is real. Don't screw this up.

'Well, yes, but not here, not at the moment. What do you mean by "a situation"?'

135

There was silence.

'Michael?'

'It was the normal delivery yesterday and...'

The words fell around Tom, floating but without being connected to each other. They were no different to the ones that he had spent his life marking in essays, using in conversations over dinner with his family or friends, with strangers—all meaningless collections of sounds until the brain decoded them.

He did not want Michael's words to fall into place.

Michael paused. He could hear something on the line, a frail, thin noise.

'Tom? Mr Black?'

'Yes,' Tom whispered.

'Are you sitting down?' Michael shut his eyes with embarrassment as he heard himself ask the question.

'Yes, you're right. I should probably sit down.' Tom picked up both parts of the phone and reversed into the wingback chair beside the window. He held both pieces, looking down the garden, over the gate and beyond, to the paddock.

Within the places inhabited in the geography of home, this was Kate's chair. When they had lived in London, it had been in the corner of the kitchen and it had become her chair then, from the first time she managed to clamber up into it herself.

When they moved to Suffolk, Tom had asked her where she wanted it to go in the new house. She had claimed not to care, and yet it became her unassailable sanctuary. It was where she went to become invisible, feet pulled up off the floor, her books and papers spreading out around the chair, lapping out beyond her sacred island as she took shelter.

Tom would watch her from his desk in the study, her head tilting into a book, one hand wound into her hair, tugging in a slow rhythm as she read. At times, she would look up and out of the window, her profile very still and quiet. Sometimes one of them would catch the other watching, perhaps smile, maybe ignore the other, but comfortable in the ease of it, the pattern.

'Thirty-six hours', 'first information report', 'interview', 'FCO'. The words fell out of the phone. Tom held the receiver away from his ear to separate the sounds from the girl in the chair, her face unmoving in the light from the window, just for a few more moments.

'Michael?' Tom interrupted. 'I have a question.'

'Of course,' Michael replied.

They both waited.

'I don't really understand what you are saying. I think you are telling me that you don't know where Kate is.'

'Well...' Michael started, but caught himself. 'I am sorry but no, we don't know.'

There was no reply.

'Mr Black?'

Tom could feel something falling away, as if the centre was not going to hold.

'Mr Black, are you okay?'

'I'm not sure.' Tom's voice was faint.

'Is there anything I can do?'

'Yes,' Tom rasped. 'Find my daughter.'

KATE.

Late November.

She had been sent on a hostile-environment course after her second posting in Pakistan.

Between her first and second, the threat level had become the material of black humour, mutually assured destruction— MAD—nuclear apocalypse, an 'equal opportunities wipeout'. The risk was total.

And then it shifted.

During her first posting, Kate had met a man whose story changed a lot of things.

It had only been for a few minutes, in a hotel bar in Islamabad in the midst of a crowd, all waving to get the barman's attention. Most of them had been sitting through a long, congratulatory presentation on the success of foreign aid in Pakistan, waiting it out until they could get to the bar.

Kate knew who the man was because she had read his articles. He was older than her, but the combination of owl glasses and very clean hair made him seem boyish. It felt easy to introduce herself and to ask him questions. He gave her precise, careful answers, marking off his points about corruption on elegant fingers, a simple wedding band catching the light.

Kate was only a few months into her posting, but there had still been enough time to miss this kind of quick-fire conversation. She felt self-conscious in the warmth of his earnest charm.

When the journalist's wife came to his side, bringing a group that seemed magnetically connected to her, he switched his attention to her entirely. His wife leant into him, her fingers just touching the side of his neck.

Kate made a gawky retreat, stepping on people's feet, spilling out apologies.

She went and sat in the loo for a while, as she always did when she blushed that deeply, her throat constricting as she tried to breathe.

By the time she came out, he and his wife had gone. The bar had seemed emptier, though there were still as many people there. Kate left as well.

He had been kidnapped a few weeks later, and then murdered.

Foreign journalists and workers were no longer exempt.

Most organisations sent people home, either to stay, or to have hostile-environment training.

Kate went home to train.

Every morning of the course, she drove out to an old airbase half an hour from home. She was always early and sat every day, huddled in the car as the dark paled, waiting for everyone else to arrive for the 7.30 a.m. start.

'You'll have to get your soft little arses used to this, you bunch of sissies,' the recently retired sergeant yelled at them all. He was wholly in charge, a stocky little Yorkshireman who seemed to grow when he was shouting at them. 'This is not a bloody holiday; it's hostile-environment training, just in case any of you thought you had come to the wrong place and were looking for the room-service menu.'

He made two people cry during the first morning. Whispered phone calls during the short lunch break resulted in several people leaving. Three slipped away, while a fourth made a very public exit after lodging what was billed as a formal complaint, any formality collapsing into yelled outrage about the brutality of the British Army.

The sergeant did not move during the shouted accusations, nor did he speak.

After the complainant had finished and gone, he asked, 'Anyone else?' He waited as the group shuffled and coughed.

No one left then, but another two had not come back the following morning.

And yet, for Kate, every aspect of the course had made her feel safe.

She learnt that kicking someone in the balls was unlikely to work, unless you were a hundred per cent accurate, very strong and fast. The sergeant taught them how to knock someone to the ground, regardless of how much bigger and stronger they seemed to be. He showed them how to use their own body weight as both fulcrum and lever rather than being dependent on muscle strength. As a last resort defence, he drilled them on the disabling efficiency of thrusting the thumbs into someone's eye sockets.

Though he assured them that he thought every one of them an idiot beyond any hope of effective self-protection, he watched those who were paying close attention more closely. He made Kate repeat some moves over and over until it felt to her that she did not even have to think before using her elbows to knock someone down with a blow to the diaphragm if she was ever to be attacked from behind.

She also discovered that she was good at carrying on when others were giving up. Clawing her way through mud in freezing rain did not horrify her, to the surprise and amusement of the shrieking sergeant.

She wanted to experience things more directly than most of the group, and so she learnt that the first effect of chloroform made her hands and feet feel numb. Then she could not see, and total blackness followed.

The sergeant had one theme that he hammered into them more than any other. They had to try and override their ingrained human survival instincts if they were to have a chance of surviving in most attack or kidnap situations. With chloroform, this meant not resisting once it was taking effect. Struggling would achieve nothing. Avoidance was the best tactic, assessment of threat the best policy and submission often the best immediate tool for survival.

He had another constant theme: in spite of anything he tried to teach them, 'You're all pretty much fucked unless this course was about a year longer than it is and I could rewire all of your brains.'

∽

Kate had come to believe that regular use of the sergeant's survival checks and drills had mapped them into her as automatic responses. She trusted this.

During the delivery she had not sensed a threat. No internal flag had been raised.

It had been the same lorry driver as usual, kicking up the dust as he walked towards her with his particular swagger.

He was alone, wasn't he? And smiling. Odd.

In the cramped dark, trussed up in a car boot, this now seemed important.

Why smiling? To reassure her, to make her believe that everything was normal?

It had worked.

Here she was.

Threat not assessed.

And now what?

The second phase of the course had been on kidnapping.

They were all asked if they were prepared to do a live-scenario role play. Some of them were not sure what this meant, but they still all agreed when the sergeant made it clear that this would be the only way that they could increase their survival chances in the event of a real kidnap.

One by one they were dragged into a room, hands taped behind their backs, a bag put over their heads. Buckets of cold water were thrown over them, and then questions screamed at them as the wet bag sucked against their faces.

A second wave of people left the course after the role plays, one of them threatening to sue the security company for using unnecessary levels of aggression that had caused personal trauma.

'He'd be a fucking sight more traumatised if he had been kidnapped,' the sergeant barked as the rumour about the complaint buzzed. 'You could have asked what we were going to do. You were given the choice of whether you wanted to do it.' He paused and began again, his voice easing down to a growl. 'As you're still here, you might have a better chance of surviving if you can be bothered to stay. I bloody hope so with all the crap that you're putting me through.'

His next lesson was on how little time they would have to humanise themselves to their captors.

'You're a commercial asset to them, a bit of meat, that's all. They don't give a shit about you, so you'd better bloody try and find out their names.'

$$\mathcal{D}$$

How do you find out their names in a bloody car boot?
I know one of them—the gas cylinder lorry driver's name.

$$\mathcal{D}$$

'They're not going to use people you've met or know. That would be pretty bloody stupid, not that some of these twats aren't that stupid.'

When the sessions were in the portacabin classroom, he liked marching up and down between their desks, stopping in front of one of them to reiterate what he had just said.

'We're working on the basis that you don't know them, therefore if you can find out their names and use them, your chances go up. Around ten per cent of people kidnapped manage to escape or persuade their captors to set them free. My intention here is that you'll have that chance, but that means you're going to have to stop behaving like a bunch of stroppy twats every time it starts getting a bit hairy.' He marched on. 'Got that?'

He stopped in front of Kate's desk.

'On the other hand, using their names might make them jumpier and so even more trigger-happy.'

Everyone had laughed nervously, except Kate.

He leant towards her. 'It's about how you use their names.'

So, not the lorry driver.

Nor his assistant. I know him too, not his name, but I have seen him so many times.

The man who grabbed me smelt of something. It's what I smell of now. Not the chloroform, the other smell.

Diesel.

'Nothing's going to be working. If you've got yourself kidnapped, you've probably been knocked out or drugged. They'll have you tied and gagged. The gagging's the one that really gets people. They think they can't breathe, and that really makes them panic. They haven't gagged your nose though, have they?' The sergeant tapped Kate's nose. 'Breathe through this, slowly as you can. Calms everything down, makes you think better, helps you conserve energy. You are going to need a lot of that if you want to survive.'

Kate breathed through her nose, the sacking sucking in and out in the darkness.

She tried not to grab her breaths and braced against the urge to cry as she clung to the sergeant's and her mother's voices, telling her to breathe 'slowly as you can'.

The car was turning and stopping.

'You're not going to meet your captors at a cocktail party, are you? Not a lot of chit-chat over champagne and posh little things on sticks. It will be violent, and your reaction will be to tense. That's just going to make whatever they do to you hurt a lot more.'

The sergeant was stamping through the cold in front of them in the middle of a winter field. 'We're going to work on overriding that reaction today.'

Leaning into a punch, softening and rolling into the force of it on the cold ground scared Kate. Every time she tried to soften, her whole body braced. The sergeant made her do it repeatedly.

Back in the cocoon of home, she lay in the bath looking at the bruises on her hips and thighs as electric surges pulsed through her whole body. She thought that it was cramp, or the beginning of a flu bug. It was a while before she began to understand that this was how her body digested abject fear, as a series of tiny convulsive seizures.

Her every muscle was bunched as the car stopped. Two doors opened and slammed. Her heart, guts and kidneys clamped as she listened to the footsteps.

They moved past the boot and away from the car. She could hear them talking as they moved away, the words rising and falling in staccato spurts, without being clear enough to understand.

They knew not to speak anywhere close enough for her to make sense of what they were saying.

They know what they are doing.

She pushed back hard again against rising sobs and the gag reflex that came with them.

'Professional kidnappers are the worst. You're just a commodity that they want to sell to the highest bidder. They might want to keep you in okay shape, or that might not matter. You are not going to know, but you have to hope that they want to keep you alive for a trade. That's about the only thing you are going to have in your favour,' the sergeant had told them during another portacabin session.

All day, freezing rain had clattered on the roof. They had all been so relieved it was a theory day that no one complained about the heating not working properly or that one of the two lavatories was blocked, the stink thick in the air. The solace of not being outside, sliding around in frozen mud, had lulled them into a lower level of attention.

Kate knew that she had missed bits, her chin jerking as her head slid forward into sleep. She asked the sergeant afterwards if he had time to clarify some of the points.

'No, I don't have time now, and you didn't seem to have much time today either,' he replied, his head bobbing in imitation of the falling-asleep nod as he threw folders into a battered but well-cared-for army backpack. 'Not sure I could have been any clearer. You're a piece of meat to them, alive or dead, just meat. In your case you'll be a *kafir* lump of flesh too, so that's not going to help, is it?' He raised a hand to her as he stepped out of the portacabin into ice fall. 'More of this tomorrow. Fun, isn't it?'

'I'm sorry...' Kate's excuse about falling asleep flipped away into the dark as the door slammed shut.

She had stayed for a while, trying to write down clear questions for the sergeant, her fingers and brain too cold to get to what she wanted to ask.

As the voices moved away from the car, a dry gurgling rose in Kate's throat. She pinched her eyelids together.

She knew what came next.

'They've got two ways to torture you: physically and psychologically. The pros are going to use every psych trick on you that they can. Nothing fucks us up more than the fear of pain and being left in isolation to think about this. Your fear will exhaust you, and so that's most of the job done for them. So, perhaps you could all be polite enough to stay awake today while I try and teach you bunch of nodding donkeys how you block out the paralysing fear.' The sergeant had been sitting on one of the desks, the day after the ice rain. The heating was working again, bringing with it the full stench of the still-blocked lavatory.

He flared his nostrils with each warm-air wave of sewage, but he said nothing. No one else did either.

'You are almost exactly one and half times stronger than you think you are. So, when you think you're about to give up, you've still got another hundred and fifty per cent to go.'

One and half times stronger. Have to believe it. Have to.

I'm tied up in the boot of a car. I can't breathe. I can't tell whether I am badly injured or just paralysed because I'm probably about to be tortured, raped, killed. Maybe in that order. Maybe not.

'They won't expect you to do what they want. They're going to assume that you are going to resist,' the sergeant said. 'First off, you fight to avoid being taken, but if they've got you, go with it. Be placid, act shocked. You will be, so no bloody acting classes required, though I can only imagine you lot would shine in that department.'

Kate tried to swallow to ease the pain in her throat.

No bloody acting required. Be placid. Do not resist. Listen for their names. Try and get them to use mine. Watch and listen for any family details: parents, wives, children.

'Depending where you get sold on to, some of you will have to deal with a whole load of religious shit, so let's not get pussy about this. Any of you Muslims?'

Two of the group raised their hands. They all braced for the sergeant's response.

'Practising?' he asked.

'At Eid, otherwise not much,' one replied.

The other shrugged.

'Well, you two know what to do, then. The rest of you need to learn to pray. Let them teach you if that's what they want.'

He moved to a space in the corner, where the roof dripped. As they watched he flowed through the fifteen stages of *salah*, his lips moving silently at each point in the circle of prayer. He performed two slow full rounds, his body fluid, almost elegant.

As he finished, he sniffed, wiped his face with both hands and turned back to them.

For the rest of the course, those left paid even closer attention.

A line came.

Make me an instrument of thy peace.

It rose up through Kate's pain, sung at school assembly amid rows of hurriedly brushed hair, collars caught under jerseys and blazers, shuffling feet, rumpled socks. Everyone knew the words. It was the school prayer, repeated every day, never thought about except in RE class, examined under sufferance and then ignored.

Make me an instrument of thy peace.

'They might keep you in the dark for long periods. It will destabilise you, make you weak and disorientated. You'll be confused about what time it is, all your systems always on alert so that you can never sleep. Then wham! They bring you out into the light.' The sergeant had smacked his hands together. 'You won't be able to see a fucking thing.'

❧

That where there are shadows, I may bring light.

❧

On the final day of the course, the sergeant had taken them to one of the hangars beyond the main airfield. Blankets had been laid out in one corner.

'Any of you remember how to do that prayer?' he asked.

One had stepped out of the group and onto the blankets, hands clasped in front of them. Others followed. They waited for a few moments and then one of them raised their hands to their ears.

In silence they knelt together, touching their heads to the blankets, rising, heads bowed, hands clasped.

One of the group did not join in.

'Any particular reason?' the sergeant asked her as everyone else knelt again.

'I'm Jewish,' she said. 'Practising.'

'Well, then you're a dead Jew. It's a prayer. Does it matter who you are praying to when you are praying to stay alive?'

As they began another round, she stepped onto the blanket, head bowed, hands folded.

❧

Lord grant that I may seek to understand rather than to be understood.

Kate prayed to live. And she prayed that it would be fast if she had to die.

It is by dying that one wakens to eternal life.

FARAH, MOLLY AND TOM.

Early December.

Molly was waiting beside the front door.

Farah had rung from the station, and Molly had been standing in the hall since the call, though it took at least twenty minutes to drive from the station.

Tom was in his study, his eyes flicking to the phone beside him.

The Foreign Office contact had told Tom that he would ring at 4 p.m. It was ten to four, but he was ready, just in case.

He could see Molly in the hall, looking at her watch, out of the window, at her watch again, her head jerking with bird movements.

For a moment he saw her as a stranger would, a frightened woman, hunched over by anxiety, half herself, half deaf with fear. He wondered how he would seem to someone who did not know him. Calm Tom, easygoing Tom, careful details-man Tom—the first two gone, the third thing his only safety net now, details his ally.

He realigned the pad beside the phone and reread the questions he had written down. They were all based on what he had been reading about previous kidnappings. The last one was Molly's, just one question:

If you have sensitive information about our daughter, how much can you tell us?

Tom looked at her question again and back at the fidgeting figure in the hall. He had promised her that he would ask it first.

The phone rang.

'Hello?' Tom grabbed it, and Molly darted towards his study.

'Mr Black, this is Mark Fenwick...' Tom could hear a car in the drive.

Molly stepped towards the front door and then back towards Tom and the phone, her hands batting away something in the air.

Tom was trying to listen.

The doorbell rang. Molly did not move for a moment.

'Yes, yes,' Tom said, waving Molly towards the front door.

Farah's whole body was shaking as the taxi turned out of the drive.

She should have driven. No, it was too long to be alone.

She had wanted other people around her, to make decisions for her.

She thought about waving at the taxi, calling him back.

Then Molly was there, her face, her hair, everything about her crumpled.

She looked so small.

Farah started to speak, but Molly engulfed her, clinging to her. They both began to cry.

'...and you'll be speaking with the general there first thing in the morning...' Tom was trying to make notes. He could hear Molly and Farah in the hall. 'Oh, so not the general, then.' He put his hand over his other ear to concentrate on what Mark Fenwick was saying. 'The inspector general of police, I've got it now.'

At every stage of the journey, Farah had wanted to go back, turning back to the Underground as soon as she got to Waterloo, asking at the station when the next train to London was as soon as she arrived, wanting to stop the taxi as it turned into the drive, to ask him to go back, to the station, to London, home. She was scared that she would make everything worse, that she would not be able to offer any kind of hope to Tom and Molly. She had not expected the engulfing sadness that overtook her as Molly clung to her.

And then Molly moved, stepping back as she lifted a hand to Farah's face.

'Far, I was so very, very sorry to hear about your mother,' she said, the old Molly again for a moment, soft but matter-of-fact.

Both gave frail smiles.

Molly was the first to look away.

'Tom's on the phone to the Foreign Office. Come on in. Where's your bag? Have you got a bag? I'm just going to listen in on the call for a moment. Go through and make something, a cup of tea. No, wait, how awful. We haven't seen you for so long. I'll come and make us all a cup of tea in a moment. Good, yes, please just go and flop in the kitchen. Jack's in there. He'll be all over you. I've been hopeless since...' Molly started for Tom's study, her hand trailing aimlessly in the air.

Tom waved at Farah from the study, shushing Molly as she leant across his desk to read what he had been writing.

Farah picked up her bag from outside the door, sniffing hard to stop the tears as she passed the two figures huddled in the study. Leaving her bag on the stairs, she went to the kitchen.

Jack leapt at her, everything flapping.

'Thanks, Jack...' Farah laughed as the dog managed to flip his tongue into her mouth with perfect aim.

ø

'He gets it in every time, even if I'm absolutely sure that my mouth is clamped shut. Dog tongue—lovely! Thank you, Jack. That's the biggest kiss I've had for a year,' Kate had said after another of the dog's very accurate tongue shots.

It had been the last time they had all been together, New Year, two years earlier.

They had been heading out for a walk.

Kate stopped for a moment at the paddock gate.

'I wish I could get home more,' she said, smiling at Farah as Jack launched himself with precision.

Now Farah crouched on the kitchen floor beside Jack, her tears dripping onto his head. He whined and squirmed, knocking her off balance as he shot away.

She grabbed at his tail. 'That's shitty!' she whimpered as she toppled.

'My sentiments exactly,' Tom said as Jack whipped past him at the door.

'Oh, Tom, sorry. I'm a mess.' Farah righted herself, scrubbing at her eyes.

'We're all a bit of a mess here, though Jack remains rudely robust in spite of being under-walked over the past few days.' He helped Farah to her feet and into an awkward hug, holding her in a way that crunched her head into his shoulder. 'Molly's torturing the Foreign Office,' he said, stepping back. 'I think I'm supposed to be putting on the kettle.'

'So am I,' Farah said.

'We can manage to make a pot of tea between the two of us, don't you think?' Tom patted her shoulder.

They moved around each other, Tom filling the kettle as Farah gathered mugs and opened the wrong jars in search of tea. He asked her about the journey, if the train had been on time, how crowded it was, showing outrage about how expensive it was for tea and coffee now.

'It's ridiculous. I keep looking out of that window, just hoping that she might be walking up the paddock.' Molly was behind them in the door. 'She hasn't been here for, oh God, I can't even remember...'

'Moll.' Tom turned to her.

'I know, I know, I'll stop. I don't like that man. He talks to me as though I am both stupid and hysterical,' she said.

Tom looked across at Farah.

'You're rolling your eyes, aren't you? That's not fair,' Molly snapped. 'Now get out of the bloody way and stop pretending to make tea. I'll do it.'

KATE.

Early December.

Why was it so cold?

Parts of her body seemed to have been cut away from the whole.

Her clothes were stiff, chafing in parts, clinging in others. The pain in her skull throbbed, as though it had its own pulse, while the rest of her head felt detached. Every muscle was twisted into an unnatural position.

How long does it take to die—freezing, in pain, dehydrated?

How many hours since she had been standing at the cross-roads, waiting for the delivery, watching for the dust clouds of the approaching lorries? She had been jumping up and down in the cold, fully aware of it as a sensation that was just beginning then to numb her toes.

It had been so easy to do something about it, to warm herself.

She was drifting. For velvety periods, the pain faded into unconsciousness.

I could let go if I wanted to. Just give up.

She drifted, snapping back for a moment with the sense of a warm hum around her, fading again to a roaring sound, as though her lungs were pumping in her eardrums.

Bright light grabbed her back. Shapes were looming above her, sound swelling.

She was being moved, hands grabbing her feet and head, lifting her.

She coiled to fight.

'Freeze! Play dead! Whatever you do, DO NOT FIGHT!' The sergeant's shout came again, as stark as the light.

She froze—a deer in headlights.

'She's dead.'

The voice sounded young and fearful.

'They'll be frightened, those bastards, I assure you. Whatever swagger they're putting on, they're terrified about screwing up and getting killed. The lower down their kidnap food chain they are, the more frightened they're going to be, and that makes people very jumpy on the trigger. You've only got one thing going for you at this stage. You'll be in fight, flight or freeze mode. Everyone's always going on about fight and flight, but not the freeze part. This is the bit you want. Flop, that's you're best defence; rag doll it. And for fuck's sake, you're going to have to learn to keep your eyes closed like you've passed out, not like some kid playing hide and seek, eyes all scrunched up.'

The sergeant had taught them how to be a dead weight, their eyelids closed and heavy.

Can't open my eyes. Mustn't scrunch. Heavy. Dead weight.

The sack over her head was pulling in against her face.

As they lifted her crumpled body, they hit her head against a sharp edge.

'There are times when survival depends on not reacting. That's like pulling off a magic trick. Overriding pain means being a bloody Zen master.'

He had a slab of ice the size of a paving stone brought in. They stood on it until the ice burnt their bare feet, and he was right beside them, his face close to theirs, repeating over and over, 'It's a sensation, not pain, just a sensation.'

Just as they began to feel confident about this new understanding of pain, he warned, 'But none of this is going to help when it comes out of left field. You'll have to just hope that you're so far out of it that you don't react. But here's a bit of good news, at last. Even when you're unconscious, there are still a load of responses to pain: eye-opening, muscle flexion, recoiling. You might get away with a bit of that and still pull the unconscious stunt, but only if you've been taken by pros who don't overreact to everything.'

As they lifted her and hit her head, of course her eyes snapped open and her spine flexed.

They could not see her face under the sack, and they did not react to her arching back.

No one spoke as they carried her.

A cold wind blew against her as they moved away from the car, the feel of it full of unlimited air and sky. She bit down on the urge to try and break free. The effort of it slid her back into silky darkness.

A door was being pushed open, scraping against something. The sound of the footsteps around her changed as they hit a harder surface.

Another door, and then another.

She was flopped onto the ground, a foot pushing her legs and shoulders back against a wall.

A door closed, and then another one.

She was lying on her side as they walked away.

It was that same smell again, the taste of it too, from the jute of the sack.

Diesel.

She gagged.

Help me!

I am stronger than I think I am.

It just felt like a lie, learnt on a course, on an airfield in a safe place that she understood.

I am not strong. I am tied up and gagged on a floor, in a place I don't know, and no one is coming to save me.

She tried to find Molly's and Tom's faces to comfort her, but there was a blank where she wanted memory. She drifted again, the grinding pain at the top of her skull taking her with it.

Someone was pushing her up into a sitting position.

She started to choke.

The same person was rolling up the edges of the sack, very slowly, making sure not to touch her.

Do not react. A stone.

'A stone doesn't do much, does it? Just sits around being a stone. Really smart, stones are. They're around forever while we lot just come and go, make a lot of noise and fuss and then...' He crushed a corner of the ice slab that they had all just been standing on under his heel. 'But stones—silent, watching, cool. Learn from them.'

The sacking had now been rolled up to her nose.

There was a snap.

The hinge of a knife cracking open.

Kate recoiled.

Cannot be like a stone.

The blade came in under the sacking, the flat of it against her cheek, then twisted upwards, away from her skin. The tip of the knife flicked up the edge of the tape that had been holding the gag in place. Then a hand was pulling the tape away from her skin, slowly, painfully. Two fingers darted between her teeth to pull out the wad of the gag, and then the rest of the tape was pulled away.

And suddenly there was air.

The only thing Kate wanted to do was to scream.

'Never, ever scream. It is the most effective way of getting yourself killed. Unless you're throwing it in and you do want to die. So, if you've lost it, if you can't take it any more, by all means scream because that is what will get you killed, fast.'

'I am not going to free your hands and feet,' said a voice in English. 'If you scream, I will put the gag in again.'

'I will not scream.' The sounds came slowly, barely words, forced out of dry lungs and torn lips.

MOLLY AND TOM.
Early December.

T om liked to buy train tickets online, weeks, even months ahead. Finding the best deals gave him surprisingly intense satisfaction.

This time there was no time.

They bought them at the station, during rush hour, at the highest prices.

It was oddly reassuring to Molly that Tom was so red-faced and angry when he saw the price.

For a moment the predictability of his reaction soothed her.

Everything else seemed to be moving, and she felt unsteady all the time. She wanted to hold on to things to keep her balance. She tripped on one of the steps up into the carriage. Tom reached out but missed her hand, nearly falling himself. They stood together inside the carriage door, Molly rubbing her shin as Tom tried to ease her closer to the wall so that other people could get past them. She forced herself not to scream.

They could not find two seats together. Molly bobbed up and down at one end of the carriage, checking that she could see Tom from where she was. Tom found a seat at the other end, and across the aisle.

He sat down and opened the newspaper that he had rolled up tightly before sliding it into an inner coat pocket as they left the house.

'Are you really going to be able to read that thing?' Molly had snapped as she saw the paper.

He had not answered. Now he fixed on the front page, soothed by the familiar layout as he felt his body ease a little with the relief that he had this time away from Molly's emotional rip tides. He opened the paper to distract himself from the guilt that followed on the back of the relief.

I'll read a bit. This is what people do on trains. It's normal. Important to seem normal. Important.

He turned to check on Molly, but he could not see as far as her seat. The window reflection did not reach that far either. As the sidings closed in, the reflections sharpened. All that Tom could see were screens, flicking and blinking, heads bowed, shoulders hunched over them.

Devotees. What a terrible kind of reverence, jammed together but entirely isolated, connected only by fairground tourist reactions to bright and flashing lights. Nothing to share. Not even candyfloss or a bumper car. God, wasn't my first kiss apple-bobbing at a fair?

Tom turned to the sports section.

Molly could not settle.

A woman beside her leant away.

She closed her eyes for a moment.

'Breathe!'

All very well teaching Kate what to do when she inherited the whole bloody panic thing from me, poor baby. She must know that. Never really told her, not directly. She got over it. Clever girl. Really conquered it. Pretending to have it under control isn't the same. It's exhausting. Does Kate pretend too? Does she just fake it better than I do?

What about now? Is she panicking right now, all the time?

Molly's eyes snapped open.

All around her were screens, flickering, flashing and clicking. Horrible, horrible!

She bit into the knuckles of two fingers to stop herself from crying.

For a moment the young woman beside her looked up from her screen. She scanned Molly, frowned and angled herself even further away in her seat.

$\mathscr{D}$

'You know what really does the trick?' Susie had pronounced on the subject of panic, her legs swinging from her usual perch on the kitchen counter. 'A martini—works every time. Vodka martini. Not gin. Something gloomy about gin.'

'I can't whip up a martini when I'm hyperventilating in a queue at the bank, or in the chemist when Mr Lab Coat is full of questions about a prescription that I can't answer. Not exactly a barman to hand then, and that's when it really hits.'

'Oh, I was joking, Moll. I mean, not really joking—a vodka martini really does do it, takes the edge right off. In the absence of that, just put your head in your hands.'

Kate had been in the kitchen with them, stringing beans.

'Susie-wisdom gets it right,' she said.

Molly was surprised. Kate usually contradicted everything about Susie's cocktail-cabinet school of thinking but this time she paused, mid-bean. 'It's the same thing that a mother does when their children are feverish or vomiting, holding their heads. It sends a comfort message to the brain.'

'See!' Susie hoisted her glass, delighted, red wine splashing.

Molly put her head in her hands, her palms pressing into her forehead, trying to push everything away.

'I know how you feel.' It was a man in the seat beside her.

No, you bloody well don't.

Molly looked up as the man clicked off his screen and turned towards her, smiling.

He managed to look both attentive and distracted at the same time.

Thinks he's doing me a big, fat favour.

She tried to smile in reply.

'I'm not going to ask if you're okay,' he said. 'It's just a bad question.'

'What do you mean?' Molly asked.

He shrugged, holding out his hand. 'I'm Mack.'

'Mack,' Molly repeated. 'That's a good name.'

'My grandmother doesn't agree.'

'Oh?'

'She's English. Her son-in-law is Scottish. That's my father. You get the picture?'

'Yes, I probably do.'

Molly looked at him. He seemed so calm, and what he was saying sounded oddly normal.

'Sorry, I'm not very good at small talk at the moment,' she said.

'Fine with me. You're talking to a soldier and chit-chat is seldom our strong suit.'

'A soldier?'

'Of sorts, though most of the lads describe us as sissy soldiers.'

'Why?' Molly asked.

'That's just the backchat for medical officers, or "nut docs" as they refer to my lot.'

'Is that the technical name?'

'Nut doc? Oh, yes.' Mack smiled.

Molly laughed for the first time since her birthday.

'It's what I do when hope's running low,' Mack said.

'What?' she asked.

'Head in the hands.'

'Oh yes, that. I'm sorry.'

'Please don't be. It soothes the mind, back to the mother–child comfort pattern.' Mack smiled at her.

Molly burst into tears.

TOM.

It was just a short paragraph at the bottom of the leader column—the throw-away one that is sometimes based on a rumour picked up from gossip swirling around the newsdesk.

As a country we continue to cinch our belt in the weeds of austerity and yet we still manage to spend £12 billion a year on aid. Of course, much of that is on emergency aid, but should we be increasingly leery about development aid? Those delivering that aid seem to be so loathed in the countries where they are operating that their greatest value on the ground now seems to be as kidnap fodder rather than providers of the real thing...

The words blurred. Tom pushed his head into the seat back.

They can't print that!

'Dad, I don't want to talk to Mum about this. She just goes into overdrive on her bridge-class bollocks gossip, or whether I think the hydrangeas are looking lovelier this year than any other year. She gets so jumpy that I can't carry on.' Kate had been curled up in her chair in front of the window.

There were no books scattered around her any more. It was now where she retreated to when she came home, when Molly was over-telling tales of Susie's Botox saga, the hydrangeas, bridge, or when Tom asked her too many questions about South Asian politics.

'Don't want to talk to her about what?' Tom had asked.

'How bad it could get if something goes wrong.'

'What kind of "wrong"?'

'The bad kind.'

'How bad is bad?'

'And now you're doing it.' She clutched her knees to her chest.

'I'm not talking about bridge or hydrangeas; I'm asking what you mean,' Tom appealed.

'Okay, so, if I'm seriously ill, that's one thing, but attacks on agencies and organisations are getting more common, you know that?'

'Organisations or their staff?' Tom asked.

'Dad! They're the same thing.'

'I just want to understand what you're saying.'

'You know what I'm saying. I mean the media, their reaction, the way they cover these stories. You know what that's like?'

He had known, but they had not talked about kidnap. In their short, uncomfortable conversation, they had not discussed a system if something did happen, nothing about a protocol for messages or who should pass on information.

I didn't protect her.

Tom stared at the page in front of him without seeing.

'Excuse me!'

TOM.

He looked up.

A young woman was trying to push past, one hand wrapped around a little girl on her hip, the other pressed into the seat back in front of him.

'Oh yes, hang on.' He began to fold his paper.

'It's urgent!' She pushed against his leg.

He hunched to one side.

'Thanks.' She squeezed through. 'Could you keep an eye on her while I deal with this?' She nodded her chin to the crumpling face of the toddler on her hip and then pointed to a little girl one seat away from Tom.

She was at the age and stage that meant she had her arms tightly crossed, her bottom lip puffing as she kicked the back of the seat in front of her.

'Of course.' Tom smiled at the woman as she hurried down the corridor, nappy bag bouncing off seats and other passengers.

He turned to the girl.

How old is she, maybe five or six? What am I supposed to do?

'I'm Tom,' he said.

The girl kicked harder at the seat back.

'Can I tell you something?'

She stopped kicking and turned towards him. She nodded.

'Once, on a train in France, my daughter was doing what you are doing at the moment. There was a man sitting in the seat that she was kicking, and he threw a glass of water all over her.'

'Why?' the girl asked.

'Why do you think?' Tom asked.

'He was mean?' the girl replied.

'He said that his daughter used to kick seats, and that someone had done the same thing to her. She stopped doing it after that.'

'Are you going to throw water at me?' the girl asked.

'No, but I thought you might be interested.'

'Why?' she asked, kicking the seat back again.

'I'm not sure,' said Tom and picked up his paper again.

The girl kicked harder.

Tom opened the paper as loudly as he could.

The girl stopped kicking and turned to him again.

'Her bottom smells. It's horrible.'

'I see,' Tom said.

'How old are you?' she asked.

'Sixty-six.'

'I'm six.'

'I'm eleven times as old as you,' Tom said.

The girl looked confused.

'Eleven times six is sixty-six.'

'Why?'

'You probably haven't done times tables yet, have you?' Tom tried to remember how old Kate had been.

'I don't know what that is.'

'Oh, I see.'

'Where is your daughter?' she asked.

Tom put the paper back on his lap, pressing down hard. It was hard to breathe.

'How old is she?'

The air came back in. 'Much older than you,' he said.

'I think my granddad isn't as old as you.' She looked away. 'Do you have a phone? My granddad does. He likes *Angry Birds*. I'm better than he is.'

Tom looked at her.

Nothing to say. I have no idea what she's talking about. She doesn't know anything. She's unmarked, everything just the right now of it. Lucky thing.

He wanted to tell her. He clutched his knees. The paper tore in his lap.

'My grandma died,' the girl said.

Not so unmarked, then.

She was looking at him very directly. 'Her heart stopped working. Granddad couldn't wake her up. She just went on sleeping.' She pulled something out of her pocket. 'This is Lucy.' She held something out to Tom. 'Grandma gave her to me.'

It was a thumb-sized cotton doll, her colours greying from love.

'Thank you,' he said.

'I'm not giving her to you. You can say hello.'

Tom lifted the tiny, mitten-shaped hand of the doll and shook it.

'Hello, Lucy. It is a pleasure to meet you.' He bowed his head.

'You're funny,' the girl said, pulling the doll away and checking her carefully before she put her back in her pocket.

'Looks like you've made a friend.' The girl's mother was in the aisle beside Tom.

'Hang on, I'll get up.' Tom smiled. 'Easier for you to get past.'

'Don't worry,' she said, crushing herself and the nappy bag into the seat in front as she squeezed past, the toddler's feet pushing into Tom's face.

'Well, Miss Stinky's cleaned up for now,' she said, collapsing back into her seat. 'All okay here?' She turned to Tom.

'He's more old than granddad,' the girl said.

'Katie, you know it's rude to ask people how old they are.'

'He was going to throw water on me,' Katie added for effect.

The woman turned back to Tom, and he explained the story of the train in France and his daughter, but the woman was losing interest. '...you see, my daughter is called Kate too,' he said.

'I'm not Kate; I'm Katie,' the girl said.

'Were you christened Kate or Katherine?' Tom asked.

'What does he mean, Mummy?' Katie curled into her mother.

'It's just Katie,' the woman said, turning away.

'Well, it's a lovely name,' he replied, looking back down at the newspaper.

We could and perhaps should ask more questions about what the policy is when it is increasingly clear that aid workers are becoming a dangerous currency. Of course, our government does not negotiate with terrorists or listed terrorist organisations, but aid workers are emotive by the very nature of the work they do...

Tom thumped the seat back in front of him.

'You told me not to do that,' Katie said, watching in fascination.

'Don't annoy the nice man,' Katie's mother said, edging away.

Tom closed his eyes.

$\wp$

'Dad?' Kate had her face lifted to the sun coming through the window.

'Yes.'

'I know I don't really get what this is like for you and Mum because I haven't had children, so I don't know what that particular kind of anxiety is like. I do know, though, that there is a big, fat, selfish element to what I'm doing and how you both tolerate that part of it.'

'Oh, Katie...' Tom started.

'Please don't call me that, Dad. I really do hate it. It's so twee.'

'Sorry,' he said.

She laughed. 'Especially when I'm doing the whole *mea culpa* thing.'

TOM.

He said it again now, eyes closed, head pressed into the seat back of the rush-hour train from Ipswich to Liverpool Street.

'Sorry, darling. I am so sorry.'

Katie's mother edged further away from him again, moving her toddler to the other knee.

MOLLY.

Molly stood up, sat down and then got up again.

'We're not getting in for a while,' Mack told her.

'I know. It's silly, isn't it?'

'Not really.'

'You've been so kind.' She sat down again. 'It must just have been as though you had to start clinic hours early. I am sorry. I'm just being a silly old woman. You've been so kind.'

'Oh, don't worry. There's plenty of shark in me, I have such teeth, dear...' he half said, part sang.

'Mack the Knife!' Molly clapped.

'Yup, that's me.'

Her hand relaxed a little on the armrest.

'It was all because of Bobby Darin,' he said, smiling.

And Molly smiled too. 'He was so gorgeous. Do you know how deeply in love with him my generation was?'

'Oh yes, I can absolutely assure you I know. I wear it tattooed into my soul, my passport, my driving licence.'

'Oh, as in Mack the Knife? I thought Mack was because of your Scottish father.'

'Less of the heritage and more my mother's obsession with Bobby D.'

Molly laughed.

'All right, darling?' Tom was in the aisle, leaning in.

'Oh yes... This is Mack. He was telling me about his mother's obsession with Bobby Darin, hence his name, Mack, like Mack the Knife.' Molly could feel that she was flushed.

'Oh, I see,' Tom said, nodding towards Mack. 'We're nearly there.'

'Good. That's good.' She started to gather up her things.

'I think we should take a cab,' Tom added.

'Mack's in the army. He was in Afghanistan.' Molly reached for Tom's hand.

'Oh.' Tom backed away.

'He's a psychiatrist,' she said, smiling at Mack.

'How interesting. I'll just go and get my coat,' Tom said as he turned.

For a moment they stood on the platform outside the train door, Molly agitated, Mack calm, Tom ushering them both out of the way of the rush. The goodbyes were tight and made more so as the push of the crowd forced them to move down the platform abreast, but separate, Mack checking his phone, Tom and Molly looking straight ahead.

Molly waved to Mack at the barrier as he went towards the Tube.

'Why don't we take the Underground?' She turned back to Tom.

'It will be easier in a cab,' he said.

'Why were you so offhand with him?' she asked.

'In what way?'

'You were quite rude.'

'I didn't mean to be. I was wondering about cabs.'

'He was being terribly helpful, and you were just rude.' She set off towards the Underground sign.

Tom caught up and took her arm. She kept walking.

'We're not supposed to say anything to anyone, you know that. What did you tell him?' He did not let go.

She was trying to shake him off. 'I don't care. He was sensible and, oh Tom, for God's sake, he's in the army.'

'It doesn't matter who he said he is; we were told not to talk to anyone, so why a total stranger?'

'Because...' She turned to him, her face folding. 'I can't do this, Tom.' She sagged against him.

His arms wrapped around her. 'We will.' He kissed the top of her head. 'We can do this, Mouse.' He had not called her that for years.

They held on to each other as the crowd spilled around them.

MOLLY AND TOM.
The FCO.

There was a simple wooden hatstand in the corner. Everything else was so grandly overarching, the domed ceilings crusted with the gold of greatness long gone.

Only the hatstand was on a scale that Molly could grasp, its design spare, the grain of the wood smoothed into elegant curves. She had not seen one for years.

Does anyone hang their hat on hatstands anymore? Does anyone wear hats?

She looked at Tom. He was holding his trilby on his lap. She got up.

'Where are you going?' he asked.

'To hang up my hat.'

'Is that a euphemism?'

'No, here's a hat, and here's a hatstand.' Molly pulled off her woollen beret and hung it up.

Her hair just above her forehead was standing on end. Tom wanted to smooth it down. He smiled at her instead.

'Mr and Mrs Black?' A young woman was standing in the doorway.

'Yes.' Molly stepped forward.

'Thank you for coming in,' the young woman said, her expression and tone flat.

Molly drew herself up.

Don't say it's a pleasure, Tom. I'll kill you.

'It's a pleasure.' Tom held out his hand to the young woman. 'Tom Black.'

'Yes,' said the young woman, smiling, tucking a folder under her arm to shake Tom's hand.

The file fell.

Tom bent down to help.

Stupid man!

Molly watched them, squatting, gathering papers, Tom apologising.

What are you doing? They've lost our daughter, and you're apologising about a bloody folder. What's wrong with everyone?

'Mum!' Kate barked, dumping a bulk-sized bag of dog biscuits on the counter at Sal's, the farmer's daughter's, feed store. 'Are you going to spend the rest of the day saying that you're sorry, or can we move this along?'

Molly was crawling around on the floor beside the counter. She had bumped against a display of lamb feeders, scattering them. Sal did not mind, but Molly was apologising repeatedly.

Sal was laughing. 'Molly, it really doesn't matter. It's fun putting them up, like Christmas-tree decorating with rubbery nipples.'

Kate and Sal poked the nipples at each other, laughing, while Molly went on picking them up.

'Why do you do it, Mum?' Kate asked as they humped Jack's bags of food to the car.

'Oh, stop bullying me, Kate. It's our generation, women, I don't know. It was just beaten into us to say sorry whenever in doubt.'

'But Mum, what about all your sixties-libber stuff? The endless sorry-fest doesn't make sense if you were womaning the barricades from uni on.'

They drove home in uncomfortable silence, Molly resisting the urge to apologise again.

Tom was still on his knees as the young woman hopped up, the folder closed and back under her arm.

Molly bit the inside of her cheek.

The young woman was blushing.

Really stupid to have dropped the file. Who shakes a hand that vigorously? Hope he didn't see anything. I'm not even allowed to read it. Shit! Please doesn't ask me what's in the file. I know she's going to ask me.

'Sorry about that, Mrs Black.' She held out her hand to Molly as confidently as she could. 'Please do come with me.'

Molly bent her head to follow. She moved at speed, close behind the young woman, her town heels beating a march on the vast tiled central court of the Foreign and Commonwealth Office.

'Stop marching about, Mum.' Kate was lifting the bags of dog food out of the boot. 'It's just not a good look,' she called out as Molly stomped across the drive.

'Stop criticising me; it's exhausting,' Molly shouted over her shoulder.

'Hello, darling. She's right. You are marching,' Tom said, holding the kitchen door open. 'What's the matter?'

'Oh, fuck off.' Molly slammed the door.

'It's what you do when you're upset,' he said quietly.

'And I suppose I wasn't meant to hear that? Very helpful. Thank you both very much.' She stamped on across the kitchen. Turning, she caught Tom and Kate exchanging a look she knew so well. 'You two take patronising to a stratospheric level.'

They were so alike that sometimes it hurt enough to make her shout.

Molly was marching now, the crack of her heels angry on the tiles of the durbar court.

Tom caught up with her. 'Hang on. We've got to go and get those contact details.'

She strode on.

'Molly, come on, please...' Tom's voice softened as he blocked her route.

'What?' she stopped. 'Please what? Please stop making a scene? Stop being upset? What, Tom, is it you want me to stop being?' They were standing in front of a statue, a Gurkha, upright, solid, standing to attention, a boy's face in bronze.

Tom tried to take Molly's hand, but she was already pushing out through one of the doors.

He looked around. A few people were watching, one walking towards them as though to help. Tom followed Molly out, a hand in the air and a mouthed sorry to the approaching figure.

'Why don't you want the help they're offering? We must have a liaison officer. We need whatever hostage support they've got. Can't you see that?' Tom was now shouting at Molly.

She stopped under an arch and swung around. 'They don't know anything, Tom, fucking nothing. We know more than them. I don't want to speak to some bleeding heart. This is about us, and Kate. I'm not interested in someone else's sob story and what we can learn from it.' She was standing in the shadow of the arch, slices of hard winter sun on either side of her.

Tom could not see her properly.

'Mr Black,' someone said, close to Tom.

He turned. A man was standing in the shadow of another arch. He stepped out into the light. It was the man from the train.

'Mack!' Molly wailed.

'Easy, Molly.' Mack put out his hands to steady her.

'Easy, girl!' Her father's words to the heifers.

Molly straightened.

'Why are you here?' Tom asked.

'Molly told me that you were coming to the FCO. One of our boys was taken in Afghanistan. His family had a bad time trying to deal with this lot.'

'But aren't this lot your lot?' Tom's tone was cold.

'Not really.'

'Did you follow us?' Tom snapped.

'Tom!' It was an animal shriek.

Tom took a step towards Mack, his arm extended, the hand open.

'I'm sorry. We really are not ourselves.' He patted Mack's shoulder.

Molly glared at him.

'Let me try that again. I am certainly not myself,' he said.

Mack smiled. 'How could anyone be themselves?' The two men gave each other scant smiles. 'But no, I assure you, I didn't follow you. I'm just across the road, so to speak, at the MoD. Molly told me about your appointment here.'

'Thank you.' Molly smoothed the hair spiking out around her forehead. 'I'm sorry. We must look a sight. We're both a mess, that's the truth. Tom's right.' She reached her hand out to Tom. 'Bugger it, I left my beret there.'

Tom looked at her hand for a moment before wrapping his own around it.

'I can go back and get it,' he said.

'Sod it, they can have it.' She shook her head. 'I'll buy a new one, a better one.'

'What about some breakfast?' Mack asked. 'Bet you didn't have any before you left this morning. Who can face porridge before dawn?'

'A condemned man.' Tom's smile was deeper now.

Mack looked at his watch. 'It's going to be more on American brunch timing?'

'What a lovely idea. Kate introduced us to that. It's the weekend treat when she's here: croissants, eggs Benedict, the whole thing.' She squeezed Tom's hand. 'Very good coffee, of course. That's vital.'

Well, if you feel like a bit of a walk, there's a very comfortable place up on Piccadilly, about twenty minutes from here.'

Molly looked at Mack. This was probably how he talked to his mother, no, something more formal than that—perhaps a distant aunt. It made her feel so old.

'We had a part-plan to meet up with a friend of our daughter's after the FCO,' Tom said, 'but...' He paused, looking at Molly. 'Breakfast, brunch, whatever it is, it sounds a good idea,' he added.

'We're meeting her at Green Park Tube, Tom; that's on Piccadilly. That sounds near the place. Is it near, Mack?' Molly asked. 'I'm sure we can call her, can't we, Tom?'

'Of course, yes. We'll call her.' Tom rummaged in his pockets. 'This is a good idea. We're all desperate to speak to someone who knows what they're talking about, someone who is helpful and doesn't want to just try and shut us up.' Molly was speaking fast.

It was not the time for Tom to point that that this was what Mark Fenwick had just offered to them in the meeting, the opportunity to speak to someone who had been through the same thing, who would know how to advise them.

He found the phone in an inside pocket. It was off. He turned away to switch it on.

'Yes, that would help,' Molly said, nodding to the phone as she took Mack's arm. 'Lead on, Nut Doc.'

Tom called Farah, pressing his mouth against the phone as he spoke slowly and clearly, as though talking to someone across a crowded room.

'Yes, it's not far from Green Park station. Keep going and The Ritz is on the other side. That's the side you want to be on and it's just up from there.' Tom tripped and dropped the phone.

They had crossed Whitehall and were heading towards the bridge in St James's Park. Mack was distracting Molly by playing guide.

'...people get confused about it. Joseph Nash was the architect of the FCO building, all that pomp and circumstance. The Nash who designed a lot of this park was a different one, John Nash...' Mack's words drifted back to Tom.

The little screen of the phone was grey, and now cracked. Tom pushed it back into a pocket and followed to the bridge.

Farah tried to call back. Each time it was just the automated message telling her that the number she was calling was switched off.

'Dad, really. What is the point of having a mobile phone if it's turned off all the time?'

Kate had just found Tom. He had been waiting for her in the wrong place for half an hour.

She had been trying to call him.

'It's really not much use sitting in the glove compartment all on its lonesome.' She extracted the phone from its hiding place.

'But it runs out of juice so quickly,' Tom replied.

'Come on, old timer, you wouldn't unplug the phone at home after every phone call, would you?'

He could not follow her logic. The phone at home did not need to have battery power.

'You're being bossy,' he tried with a faint smile.

Kate interpreted the smile. 'Sorry Dad. Pakistan is turning me into a terrible martinet.'

'Kate the Terrible, Harridan of the Hindu Kush.' Tom laughed.

'Sod off, Dad!' But Kate was laughing too.

He knew his joke did not even qualify at the edge of funny, but she had indulged him. He knew that she probably would not have laughed if Molly had come up with the same feeble line.

There were times when it just was unfair.

Ahead of him, Mack and Molly were almost across the bridge. Tom reached for the phone again, looking for signs of life.

Light swelled up through the screen. Shoving it back into his pocket, he hurried on.

A man stepped into his path.

'Please, photo?' said the neat Japanese man, bowing his head as he offered his phone to Tom.

'Oh, yes, of course.' Tom took the phone, waving at Molly, though she was facing away from him in the distance.

The man and his even more fastidiously turned-out wife stood side by side on the bridge, close but not touching. Both stared straight ahead as Tom tried to centre them in the picture and sharpen the focus.

Kate and Tom had spent most of a day finding their way around his phone once she had established that turning it on and off was about as far as he had reached with the technology. He had only really been interested in the camera, and she had taught him to focus, zoom and adjust the exposure. Now he could not remember how to do any of it. But as he looked at the couple on the little screen of the man's phone, the picture focused automatically, the couple clearly contained within the rectangle. Behind them willows wept into the lake, the sharp winter sun dazzled and light bounced around the wild array of Horse Guard's domes and spires.

On the other side of the blue bridge, Molly turned back.

'What the hell is he doing?'

'Looks like he's taking someone's picture. Shall we wait?' Mack replied.

'Bloody man!' Molly put her hands to her mouth. 'Sorry, Mack. All I seem to be able to do at the moment is scream or cry.'

'Either is fine,' said Mack.

She crumpled again.

KATE.

Early December.

I s it dark? Can't tell.

Chloroform-induced nausea rolled through again.

This time Kate could throw up with heaving relief, the gag no longer there. The physicality of vomiting hauled her onto her knees, her chin to the floor, feet and hands still bound, the survival reaction yanking her into a position that would stop her from choking on her own vomit.

As the retching eased, she lay down again, some part of her relaxing with the sense of having expelled some of the poison she had been forced to inhale. She rolled onto her side, away from the stench. As she did, she was surprised by laughter. It rolled through in the same wave as the nausea had before.

God, throwing up is my current comfort. Great. Who'd have thought!

ↄ

'Stop! Dad, I'm going to be sick.'

Tom had tried not to slam on the brakes. It was so hard not to overreact to the pain in her voice.

'Okay, darling. How long?'

It was their drill. Kate would shout; Tom would check how long they had before she knew she was going to throw up.

'Two-minute warning.'

'Oscar Kilo,' he replied.

It was a system that went back to the very beginning of their shared lives, just like 'breaking step' when crossing Albert Bridge. It was part of the family language, the knowing of things that did not need to be explained. Just as Tom and Kate knew that Molly marched when she was in pain, Kate and Molly knew that Tom used the military phonetic alphabet when he was worried. His father had done the same, the safety of military routine helping him to limp back into family life when he had come home from war.

'Oscar Kilo,' Kate repeated as Tom braked, her hand bracing on the dashboard.

After the laughter came tears, relieving the painful dryness in her eyes.

Kate tried to breathe more slowly.

Here it was, the worst thing that could happen.

This is it. I am in it, right in the thickest shit of it.

She could feel the tears, trapped by the blindfold that had been tightened over her eyes when the sack had been taken off.

The dark was not night but blindfold black.

'Assess, assess, assess.' The sergeant had made them blindfold each other, checking closely to see that each one was in place, squeezed tight against their eyes.

'They're not exactly going to ask if you're comfortable, are they?'

He made them march around the airfield apron, one hand on the shoulder of the person in front, zigzagging until they lost all sense of direction.

'You've been blinded, so you are going to panic. Not helpful. You need to watch your breathing so that you don't start hyperventilating. And you have to listen very closely so that you can judge distances around you.'

He walked away from them. They were learning to read sound, and they could tell from the echo of his steps that he had walked them into one of the hangars.

His voice boomed from a distance. 'Assess, assess! Notice everything, abso-bloody-lutely everything. I've got one more treat for you.' He tied their hands and feet together and then roped them to the side of the hangar. 'I'm not going to hurry back, so you'd better get used to this.'

Kate had leant against the hangar side, comforting herself with the sound of her own breathing, the rhythm of it, as she had throughout the course. It gave her perspective, and she had been surprised when the others began to follow her example.

Quietly, she had become the group's leader.

But not now. There was no one to lead as a buffer to her own terror.

She forced her eyes up under her eyelids. The pressure of the blindfold made it seem as though they might burst.

There was no gap at the top.

Squeezing her eyes back down, she found a thread of light at the bottom. Her nose bisected the two tiny blocks of light. They were fanned out into even more minute sections by her eyelashes. She tilted her head back, trying to see. It hit the wall behind her.

White pain jerked her forward.

The strange laughter came again, rocking through her.

'Nothing wrong with laughter. It can be an analgesic. I can only imagine that you lot know your way around most pain meds, so you'll be glad to know about this little perk. Though best not to laugh in front of them. They may think you're mad or heading that way. If they're not pros, that's going to make them very jumpy. There's also the risk that they may decide a mad hostage is not as valuable as a sane one. You can assume that screaming and laughing in front of them is not a good idea. Got that? Laugh when they're not there, or cry, whatever floats yer boat. It will keep you as close to sane as any of you lot are likely to be at this stage.' The sergeant had been answering a question about involuntary reactions. 'You know they say that the three strongest human drivers are sex, laughing and crying? Don't expect the first in any variety that you're going to want, but the second two won't hurt as long as you do them on your own time.'

'Why's it so important not to cry in front of them?' asked someone.

'See if you can work that one out, genius. You lot really are going to be dead in the water,' he snarled, though his eyes laughed.

Dead in the water.

Assess, breathe.

Not dead yet.

Kate rolled carefully so that she could move without hitting the wound. When she sensed there was enough distance from the wall, she tipped her head back to find the pale sliver at the bottom of the blindfold again.

Everything was blurred, even such a thin shred of light. She waited for the detail to filter in, at first at the sides of her nose, the dark hazing of her eyelashes. Beyond these, a spread of floor emerged.

It was blank concrete marked with her bile and blood. She could tell which was blood. The patches were smaller, darker, like those left by a wounded animal limping past.

If only I could limp away. I'm not going anywhere. Don't waste energy. Self-pity is tiring. Pointless. Without point.

She used her bound legs as a lever against what she now knew was the concrete floor, edging herself around a little so that she could see further with her crack of vision.

There was just more concrete floor stretching away beyond her thread of vision.

But there is something else, something on the floor. What was it?

As the form of a metal bucket came into focus, there were footsteps and a voice.

A man was asking someone to open the door.

Kate braced.

MICHAEL AND OMAR.

Early December.

They were all waiting.

Azad kept coming and going, knocking each time, something he never used to do. Every time, he came with the excuse of asking Michael if he would like to have something: chai, then lunch, chai again, and then again.

Michael had been waiting for four hours, barely moving.

Azad knocked again.

'Come in, Azad.'

'Dinner?' The cook stayed in the doorway.

'Yes, of course.'

'Time?' Azad asked.

'Oh, not sure. When they've been, I suppose?'

They both looked out to the road again.

Azad retreated.

Michael had rung the deputy inspector general of police's office several times, and each time he had been told the same thing. They would be leaving in just another five minutes. They would be there very soon.

He had been measuring time by the blocks of light edging across the side of the building as the sun travelled.

The richest light of the day was now sliding over the bougainvillea, turning the flowers wild. Twilight would soon dull the saturated colours.

They would not come once it was dark.

Kate loved the bougainvillea. Sometimes she would pick a small branch of it and put it on the dashboard.

Michael had labelled it as one of her pretentions when he had first seen her putting the flowers in the front of the car.

It had been the day after he arrived, when they went to get a SIM card for him.

He had been irritated by the pile of forms that had to be filled in: three proofs of identification, his address, proof of residence at that address, two referees, copies of his visa, work contract, immigration entry stamp.

Kate had spoken on his behalf because they had not seemed to understand his use of Urdu. He had squirmed in the long pauses when he could not find the right words and felt angrily frustrated when Kate filled the gaps, using both Shina and Urdu.

Afterwards, as they drove through the city, she had she pointed things out. He had sat sullenly by.

Though it was all new to him, there seemed a uniformity to it—everything watermarked by seasonal downpours and crusted with dust, the official buildings all similar cement blocks, so many of the streets layered shacks, and greyness seemed to pervade everything. Every architectural effort of the city was dwarfed by the vastness of the Karakorams all around, even the great central mosque and the lunatic suspension bridges that leapt out across ravines into nothingness.

Now it was as though Michael was remembering someone other than himself, another man, a boy.

He could see Kate clearly again, sitting in front of him in the jeep, the bougainvillea she had picked on the dashboard, her hand reaching to push it back into place each time the driver swung the jeep around the roads, the madly pink flowers sliding from side to side.

That man, that boy, had not even believed that Kate sat in front because of car sickness. He had labelled it as just another power-play pretention along with the bright flowers.

He put his head in his hands.

Stupid, stupid man.

Azad stopped Omar as he walked past the kitchen.

'Anything?' the cook asked.

'I have been in Gilgit, getting supplies, nothing else,' Omar replied.

The cook was standing in the kitchen doorway, blocking the way.

'But people must be talking. Someone must have asked you, or said things to you?'

'Nothing,' Omar said.

Five days,' Azad said. 'And now five nights.'

'I know.' Omar put down the box of supplies.

'It was lower than freezing last night.' Azad hovered over the box.

'I know,' Omar repeated.

'Dinner?'

'Yes.'

'Time?'

'As usual,' Omar replied.

'He is still waiting.' Azad flicked his chin towards the main part of the house.

'They have not been?' Omar asked.

'He has been waiting all afternoon.' Azad bent and picked up the box from Omar's feet as several sets of car lights chased down the grey behind them, flashing across the bougainvillea.

Michael was standing on the veranda, struggling into his coat as three jeeps pulled up.

Running down the steps towards them, he tripped and stumbled against one of the group. Two officers jumped at him, pulling him away from the deputy inspector general of police.

'No issues.' They were waved away by their senior officer. 'It was just a tumble.'

Michael held out his hand. 'Sorry about that. I'm Michael Newton. I'm glad to meet you, Superintendent.'

'Farhana Shah, and it's Deputy Inspector General.' The neatly solid deputy inspector general of police smiled at Michael, though she did not shake his extended hand.

Omar came out onto the veranda. Light fanned from the door behind him, picking out breath in the freezing air.

'Too cold already, *naar*?' said Farhana Shah, her words made into mist.

'Absolutely, come in. Please, come in,' Michael replied, backing away, relieved that the deputy inspector of police had not shaken his hand. It was now shaking in his pocket. He knew that she was The Deputy Inspector of Police, but he had still made the mistake.

No one seemed sure of the order in which they should enter the house, the deputy inspector general's cadre holding back, waiting as Omar held the door.

'Please.' He waved the deputy inspector general in with a flourish that looked overly theatrical to Michael.

Farhana Shah acknowledged the gesture with a nod and entered.

Azad was waiting just beyond the door, his head bowed in respect. His daughter was half-hidden behind the door frame on the other side of the room. Her face was wide open, astonished, as she stared as this very important woman. The deputy inspector general crossed the room and bent towards the girl. They exchanged whispers. The girl giggled, enraptured.

Azad looked on, beaming.

'Chai, ma'am?' Omar asked.

Michael knew he should have asked first. He stopped himself from grabbing a chair for Deputy Inspector General Shah, knowing that he had to let Azad do his job, particularly now with his daughter watching, in front of their honoured company.

'How kind, yes, tea.' The deputy inspector general turned to her officers. She was waiting for something.

One of them flapped a hand at Azad. The cook scurried to him, carrying a chair from the dining table. The officer took the chair and placed it just behind Farhana, close enough to touch the back of her knees. As she felt the chair, she sat and settled herself.

'So, gentlemen, I would like to convey the good wishes of The Inspector General of Police to you. He would be here himself, but he has been delayed with some other very pressing matters.'

Azad looked to Michael and Omar for the next instruction.

Michael pulled another chair from the table and sat down near the deputy inspector general.

Omar wondered what could be more important than the kidnap of an international aid project leader.

To stop himself from clenching his fists, Michael folded his arms and crossed his legs.

Farhana sat straight, her feet squarely on the floor, her hands on her knees. She looked around the room slowly, scanning Azad's neatly folded bedding stacked in one corner, the disorder of papers and files on the dining table, the scatter of IT—laptops, phones, tablets.

'I can imagine this is a very troubling time for all of you people,' she said, turning back to Michael. The tone was softer.

'Thank you,' Michael acknowledged.

'Have you spoken with Miss Black's family?' she asked.

'Yes, we have.' Michael tried and failed to sound confident.

Farhana nodded. 'This will be very hard for them, very hard.' She shook her head slowly, a hand lifting to check her tight bun below the back of her beret.

They sat in silence, the sound of one of the officers clicking a nail too loud. They could hear Azad in the kitchen, two rooms away, the clang of pans, the whoosh of the kerosene as he lit the stove, the grind of a mortar and pestle.

The deputy inspector general cleared her throat.

'*Pukkah chai*, how nice,' she said, as Azad's pounding continued.

Again, there was silence.

'I am sorry to have to ask this.' Farhana shifted in her chair. 'But I am afraid we will need to take some of Miss Black's possessions.'

'I see,' Michael said, looking over to Omar.

'Of course,' Omar added. 'We can help you find what you need.'

'This will not be necessary, but it will be helpful if you could guide my men to her quarters.' She patted her hair again as she replied.

Michael unfolded his arms.

She's got a shit job, and now she's having to deal with an arsy foreigner. I can pretend all I like that I'm not one of those, but the truth? Yes, of course I'm expecting preferential treatment. I want her to do something right now. I don't care what else they've got going on.

$$\mathscr{D}$$

'We don't mean to do it; it just happens,' Kate had said on that first trip to Gilgit with Michael.

She called it '*firangi chuteri*'. Foreigner fuckery.

'It just happens every time we say "them" and when we talk about "us". It just slips in to the way people speak. I don't think anyone means to do it, but it's just there, an unspoken expectation that we will be treated differently.'

They had been in the phone shop, and the owner had waved them to the front of the queue. Michael had been embarrassed when Kate accepted the offer. He had tried to stay in the queue, but Kate had thanked the owner and everyone else in the queue for their patience.

'It's rude to refuse. The offer is a kind of hospitality. We should accept it gratefully and understand that it is a combination of old-world hospitality and laying down credit for the future. It is both graceful and an act of survival.' Kate had watched Michael's reaction. 'I don't care what anyone says because we're all guilty. Everyone pretends that they don't do it, that they don't expect to be treated differently, but they do—every bloody single one of us.'

Enraged, Michael strode away as soon as they left the phone shop.

Kate ran to catch up with him.

'I'm going to tell you about someone I know. She's been here for nearly sixty years and she has been doing the same thing all the time: protecting a threatened tribe. She's mad as a snake, but also practical and effective. She's a Scot and as tough and dour as a granite cliff. She's given every ounce of herself to defending these people who exist on the edge of extinction because they are always being persecuted for being *kafirs*, infidels, ingrates, take it whichever way you want.' She looked very directly at Michael. 'I'm not being preachy, Michael. This is just someone's story.

'She did not marry, no children. This has been her whole life. These people are everything to her. She's over eighty now, her entire adult life spent fighting for this tribe. But she says things about people here that sound horrifying. Her younger self probably would think so too. This is what happens. It is how people adapt to the harshness. It's not right, or good, but we all get a bit rough around the edges. This battered old war horse says stuff that would probably disgust you, but she's only talking in the same way that we all complain about our families, husbands and wives, our friends. I'm not trying to defend it; it's just that we all do it.'

Michael had been so sure that he knew how to protect himself against that kind of roughing of his edges. But here he was, expecting the deputy inspector general to change the rules for him.

He turned to her. 'Of course. Let me show them to her room.'

'It can wait for some time.' Farhana Shah smiled at him. 'Let's have chai first.'

Omar moved another chair from the dining table, put it beside Michael and sat down. As he did, the officers around the deputy inspector general watched him, waiting for him to bring them chairs as well.

He did not.

The man flicking his nails sighed and then went to get one for himself, dragging the chair across the floor. The others followed, moving as though in slow motion.

Farhana Shah smiled as the slow chair dance played out. Michael smiled back at her.

Yes, she's got a crap job, and she is doing the best she can. What she must go through doing her job in this patriarchal shithole.

They sat in silence again, waiting. Azad came in with the chai and a large plate of steaming *pakoras*. He had made them as soon as he knew that the police were coming, waiting all afternoon for the first sign of their arrival before heating up the fat until it began to spit for the pakoras to be dropped in.

'How lovely.' Farhana Shah clapped her hands. 'May I?' She leant towards Azad's beloved samovar, polished to a pale end of sunset.

Azad stepped back, proud but confused that she was asking to do his job.

Michael watched as she wove together the roles of mother and boss.

Yes, she was very clever.

Cardamom, ginger and cloves steamed from the samovar, mixing with the hot, fat, crisp scent of the pakoras.

'How long have you been in this posting?' Farhana asked as she passed the first cup to Michael.

'Not long.'

She shook her head again. 'This is a most terrible thing at any time, but all the more so if you are still learning the strings.' She paused. '*Naar*, this is not right. What is it that am I trying to say?' she asked.

'The ropes, learning the ropes?' Michael replied.

'Of course, thank you. Where does this expression come from?' she asked.

'I'm pretty sure it came from the navy—young sailors and the ropes for the sails, though they call them sheets, I think.' He stopped because the deputy inspector general had cocked her head with a question.

'Sheets is another word for ropes. They have to learn which ropes are needed for which sails...' Michael's voice tapered away.

'Oh, I see.' She clapped again. 'We do not have too much need of ropes, sheets and sails in these parts.'

Everyone laughed, slowly and deliberately.

Omar nodded to Azad to hand around the pakoras.

It was Omar who led the officers to Kate's room once they had drunk and eaten chai and pakoras loudly.

He stood by the door until they opened the drawer where Kate kept her underwear. They left it open, staring in each time they passed. Omar slammed it shut as they waved him back to the door. He pushed back in again when they started to go through a little leather album of her family pictures.

'Leave those,' he snapped.

'We need this for identification,' one of them replied, picking up the album, turning the pages with latexed fingers.

'These are her pictures from home, from England, her family.' Omar grabbed the album from the officer. He snatched it straight back.

'Fingerprints!' he shouted at Omar.

'Are you trying to tell me that the kidnappers came here and went through her family photographs to make sure that this was the right person from the kind of family that would be able to pay a ransom?'

'What is this?' The deputy inspector general was at the doorway, Michael at her shoulder.

The officer shouted his explanation louder than Omar's.

Farhana took the album from the officer and put it back on Kate's desk beside a photograph of Molly and Tom leaning on the paddock gate. Jack was beside them, his front paws on the top bar, tongue lolling as Molly laughed. Tom was smiling, his head tilted a little to one side, the way he did when he was talking to Kate.

She picked up the photograph.

'Sweet people. Very hard for them being so far away,' she said in English, turning to Michael.

They should not leave their homes, these people. What do they expect in this place? Walking targets for ransom, every one of them. Her parents look like they have some money, well dressed, that English way, the Captain Grey way.

The fretwork of fine lines around Farhana's eyes softened as she turned to Michael.

Captain Grey, a man of linen jackets, pale, crisp shirts, elegant shoes and a strangely shy humour for a UN officer. She had worked with him when she had been posted to the Democratic Republic of the Congo. It had taken six months to find out that his first name was Tim. They had spent seventy-two hours together without sleep, trying to negotiate with kidnappers, unofficially. As they had waited out the ragged time between calls, the exhausted tension allowed a little ease with each other.

'By the way, this is pretty rude, but I don't even know your first name,' he had said. 'I'm Tim.' And he had held out his hand to shake hers in the pallid silence before dawn, two days into the negotiation.

Farhana patted her hair and cleared her throat.

Before the shouting had begun, she had been talking to Michael about Kate's family. She had asked him, very directly, if he thought that her parents might try and find a way to negotiate directly with the kidnappers.

Michael did not know Kate's parents, and he had no idea what to say.

Would they?

Farhana put the picture back on the desk.

Unless they negotiate, that poor mummy and daddy are going to be grieving for their daughter.

The deputy inspector general's mother cried every time she went home on leave, and she cried again every time she left, weeping for all the things she could imagine happening to her daughter in the world of men.

'We will keep you informed, of course.' The deputy inspector general was standing beside the jeep as her men stacked Kate's papers, laptop and books into the back of another vehicle.

'Please,' Michael replied.

'Please what?' she asked.

'Sorry. I mean, yes, please. Do keep us informed.'

'If the inspector general has some time, we will come again tomorrow. Please make yourself available,' she said as she pulled on her gloves.

'What time might that be?' Michael asked.

'I will call to tell you,' she said. 'Thank you for your assistance,' she added.

Michael echoed her thank-you.

And they were gone, the lights sweeping away.

'All very polite.' Omar stamped in the cold beside Michael. 'Of course, they won't come back tomorrow.'

'I was rude, wasn't I?' Michael began to shiver beside him. 'I just didn't know what to say at the beginning. She's good, though, don't you think?'

'She has to be. That means ten times better than any man. She had a whole series of high-profile postings before this, the UN and so forth. If she was a man, she would be running the whole region, but she just gets this dark corner.' Omar wiped a nose-drip on his arm.

'Yes, she was telling me when the fuss started.'

'What fuss?'

'The rude officer.'

'*Behen chut.*' Omar sniffed.

'Yup.' Michael huddled deeper into his coat. He hated the expression 'sister fucker' but at this moment he did not mind.

'I don't know what else I could have said. They will not come tomorrow. It's all lip service. They're always going to treat me like a servant, but if they think you are challenging their methods, they will not help us. If they do come—and they won't—but if they do, perhaps act a little stupid?'

'I can't do anything much except stupid,' Michael said. 'But not quite so stupid as to wonder why we're standing out here in the freezing cold.'

'I want to have a cigarette.' Omar took a packet from his pocket.

'It's too cold; smoke inside.' Michael moved to the door.

Omar stayed where he was, his face lit in the flare of a match, followed by the soft crackle of an inhale through tobacco.

Kate had made the rule of no smoking in the house. When she wanted to smoke, she went to great lengths not to be seen, especially by Azad and his daughter.

Only Omar was open about his habit.

'She smokes too,' Michael said from the doorway.

'I know.' Omar squatted down to keep warm.

'Did you know she climbs up on the roof so as not to be seen, even when there's ice up there?' Michael said. 'Mad woman.'

Omar smiled into the dark.

'Can I have one?' Michael asked.

'But you don't smoke, do you?'

'I do when it's this bad.' Michael ducked down beside Omar. 'I told her mum I would call after the police had been, in case...'

Azad watched from the kitchen as another match flared in the dark. He wanted to know why they were not doing more, why they had not asked the powerful deputy inspector general for help, for a search party, for something.

'In case what?' Omar asked Michael.

'In case there is any news.' Michael choked, coughing cold air and smoke.

'But there isn't any.'

'I know, but that doesn't mean I can't call her.'

'What can you say?'

'I have no idea,' Michael replied. 'But I might have to beg some Scotch off you afterwards.'

'No need to beg.'

'Thanks.'

Omar knew that Kate smoked on the roof, even when the narrow walkways between the corrugated green tin shone with high winter ice. They had smoked there together. She would bring the cigarettes and two glasses, one in each pocket. He brought the Scotch.

They would hunch together against the cold, their cigarettes crackling into bright buds as they inhaled. Once, he had lost his balance as Kate passed him a glass. His foot had already been numb from squatting on the ice, and he had fallen against her, both of them bumping down onto the tin. Shushing each other, they waited for any sound from below. None came.

Omar giggled with relief. Kate's shoulder was pressing into his belly, but he did not move. She looked up at him, her finger still to her mouth. He nudged it aside, leaning towards her. Her skin wrapped around him.

KATE.

Early December.

'Are you comfortable?' It was the same voice that Kate had just heard outside the door.

She did not mean to laugh. It just burst through. 'Perfectly, thank you,' she replied, the bubbling in her voice upending her.

'This is a good thing,' said the man.

She could tell that he was smiling as he spoke. He smelt of jasmine. She sensed the physical presence of him as being small, even delicate.

'It seems you have caused yourself some injuries,' he said.

Caused myself!

'Yes, I think so,' she said, swallowing both bile and a scream.

'I will send someone to clean these for you,' he continued.

She did not reply.

'Do you have any questions?' he asked.

'No.'

She heard a quick inhalation, barely audible, the briefest sign of surprise.

'Good, this is all, then.' His hands slapped on something.

Kate flinched.

His legs. He must be kneeling—the slap of his hands on his thighs.

He was almost noiseless as he got up.

Kate braced.

'I will take your leave then,' he said.

Who was this man with his softly spoken English, scented with *ittar* of jasmine, the inducement to the angels to watch over him, to ward off darkness?

Her physical fear of him horrified her.

Why had she forgotten to ask him for water?

She was so thirsty, the pain in her head blurred by the nauseating giddiness of dehydration, her mouth bitter, spitless.

She tried to shuffle further away from the stink of where she had retched. Every part of her hurt as she lay down again.

✍

'Good cop, bad cop. It's an old trick for a very simple reason— it works. They'll probably have a go, particularly you lot heading for South and Central Asia. Most of their stuff is still a straight steal from the old KGB interrogation playbook.'

'Isn't it the FSB now?' one of them had asked the sergeant.

'Not when they started out on this. Yeltsin was probably in kindergarten at the time, or whatever the Russians call that. They didn't have to try and make themselves look better to anyone then.'

To be clear, he had taken them through good cop, bad cop again on the last day of the course.

'Take your own notes because we can't put this in a handout, but this is the stuff that works.'

Kate rolled her swollen tongue around the gritty stickiness in her mouth.

'They'll usually start by softening you up after all the smash and grab of getting you in the first place. They'll probably offer you something you have been fantasising about through the delirium—water, tea, something like that. You'll all be prone to that, you room-serviced lot. Part of you will want to trust them, to believe that this is how it's going to be—that they're going to be civilised about it. So, just forget that.'

Forget that.

Kate tried to ease the parts of her body that had been locked in gripping cramp since the boot of the car.

She could see Miss Platt, her ballet teacher. She was in one of the pale, wraparound dancers' cardigans that she always wore. It was what she used to say, standing over Kate as she rolled on the floor, grabbing her toes in her little pink ballet shoes.

'It's cramp. Kate. Don't worry. All dancers get it. Breathe in to where it hurts and then a big breath out. Open your mouth; let it go. Yes, that's it.'

Always wanted one of those wraparound cardigans, so pretty.

Kate was drifting again.

AZAD AND NOOR.

Early December.

He named her 'light' because he needed as much of it as he could find after she was born.

Noor had been born at home, so no one knew that her heartbeat was weakening as her mother went into labour. She had ruptured as Noor crowned. By the time they got to the hospital, six hours away, Noor's mother had lost so much blood that she never regained consciousness. She never saw her child, though Azad held both her and their newborn baby on his lap all the way to the hospital, the baby still covered in creamy vernix and sticky blood as her mother's life pooled around Azad's feet.

He had sung to his wife and daughter. At first it was *suras* and prayers, but as his wife's skin became powdery and his daughter's eyes still did not open, he sang again the songs that his mother had sung to him as he became both father and mother to his tiny daughter.

When Noor was seven, he had started to work for Kate.

The little girl had attached herself to Kate within hours of their arrival, traipsing around after her as Azad unpacked their few things. While Noor shadowed his new employer, he laid out his knives on the kitchen table before putting anything else away.

As they fell into the daily rhythm, Azad was grateful for the time Noor spent with Kate. He would watch them together, sometimes turning away, his chest tight with the memory of what he and Noor had lost.

He knew that Kate smoked, but he found himself appreciating that she tried to hide the fact. He did not approve, of course, but he respected her for not smoking in front of him, or the child.

Everyone loved the girl, for her tumbling enthusiasm and the speed with which she picked up on things. By time she was nine, she spoke much more English than her father. She would mimic people, pinpoint-accurate in her ability to cut through posturing or sulking.

The house felt less alive when Noor was not around.

Now, in Kate's absence, she was following her father about. She had already asked him four times where Kate was. He kept telling her that she was away, but Noor kept asking. He told her to stop, handing her a small spoonful of fresh *masala* to taste.

And then the deputy inspector general came.

'Was it about Kate Ma'am?' Noor asked after the deputy inspector general and her coterie had left.

'I do not know,' Azad said, his back turned. He had promised himself never to lie to her face again.

Noor had worked out early on in her life that adults turned away when they were lying.

'Why did they take away so many of her things?' Noor was shelling peas for her father, lining up the empty pods methodically, the way her father lined up his knives.

'I do not know,' he replied.

'Are you telling me lies, Baba?'

Azad turned to his daughter. 'I do not know what to tell you because I do not know myself.'

Noor ran her thumbnail down the centre of a pod, popping out six perfect peas. She closed the pod, lined it up with the rest and slid off her stool. Azad had made it for her—just the right height for the high stone work slab that ran the length of the kitchen.

'I will go and do my homework now,' she said, walking past him.

'Noor?' he called after her.

'Yes.' She turned in the doorway.

'I am not lying to you.'

'Okay, Baba.'

'I do not know what is going on.'

'But you do know that there is something wrong. I know this.' Noor was standing very straight, her face flushed.

'What is the point of me telling you if I do not know anything?' Azad stepped towards his daughter, and she took a step away.

'It was a lie, Baba?' Noor turned.

'*Beti*, Noor?' he called after her.

He knew not to follow her.

Noor often did her homework in Kate's room. In winter, it was warmer than the kitchen, particularly during the times when Azad was not cooking, and the light was better than the flickering bulbs in the kitchen.

Kate had always encouraged her. She liked the soft sense of the girl in the room, the lull of it as she tapped away on her laptop and Noor bent over her various workbooks, her hand wrapped tight around a pencil.

This was where Noor went now. She stood outside the door for a moment and tested the handle. Opening it very carefully, she held her breath, longing to see Kate's back leaning over her desk.

'Hello, Noor. Come on in. Is this for homework or to read?' she would ask and then make space for her at the end of her desk or reach for one of the books that she stockpiled for Noor. They were books Tom and Molly had handed down to her: Lewis's world beyond a wardrobe in the frozen forests of Narnia, Tolkien's hairy-footed clan, the boy prince who travelled from an asteroid to understand the world. Noor liked the prince the most, and the fox that he befriended.

'Would I be able to do that if I met a fox?' she had asked Kate when they reached the part where the little prince tamed the fox.

'I should think so,' Kate said.

She had loved the fox when she was a girl too, the mournfulness of him in his deep love for the little prince.

Noor tiptoed across the room, climbed onto Kate's bed and reached onto the shelf for the book. She curled up and propped the book in front of her on Kate's pillow. She began to read again.

Azad knew where to find her when she did not answer his call for dinner.

Omar saw him in the corridor outside Kate's room.

Azad smiled apologetically as he opened the door, showing Omar the girl huddled on Kate's bed, the book dropped to the floor, one of Kate's shawls wrapped tight around her.

He closed the door again.

'She knows I am lying to her,' he whispered.

They looked at each other.

Omar cleared his throat. 'Is there someone in the family that she can go and stay with for some time, just until...' His voice trailed off.

'Are you telling me that I must send her away?' Azad asked.

'No, but wouldn't it be better for the girl?'

'My sister is my only relative who is not many days' journey from this place, but she is still far. Noor would not be able to go to school,' Azad added.

'I didn't think of that.' Omar put a hand on Azad's back, and they retreated.

'She must be very troubled by all of this,' Omar said.

'As we all are.' Azad went back to his pots. 'I will bring dinner. Five, ten minutes.'

Omar stopped as he went back past Kate's room. He stood listening at the door, the little girl's soft breathing clear and even in the quiet. He waited there for a while, reassured by the sound.

TOM AND MOLLY.

Early December.

'Can I have it?' Molly grabbed the phone from Tom as a doorman waved them into a lofty brasserie.

'But I don't think we can use it in here,' Tom replied.

All around the packed tables, he saw Savile-Row-suited men in spare cuts, the wool cashmere smooth. He felt too tweedy and in the wrong place. He wanted to leave.

'I feel very old and very country,' he said without meaning to say it aloud.

Mack was talking to one of the front-of-house staff, a smooth-skinned giant, his hair cropped as tight as his suit.

Mack turned back to Tom. 'Style over content.' He smiled. 'Do you know how much they wish they could carry off "country"?'

'They can't. They're too...' Tom stopped.

'Too scented and pompadoured,' Molly finished for him.

The corners of the polished giant's mouth flicked.

'I don't care. Let's just sit down. Michael said he would call after the police inspector had been. He was supposed to be coming early afternoon, so he could call any time now.' Molly peered at the phone's screen. 'It's not even on, Tom. How did you speak to Farah?'

She did not want to be there either.

Tom was right. It was a bad idea. Too many people, sound bouncing off the hard black-and-white floor, the clatter of cutlery, forks in mouths and on teeth, spoons in bowls, knives on plates, everyone busy chatting about their busy lives.

I can't do this.

She started to ask Tom if they could leave.

Mack saw her colour changing, her eyelids fluttering, a hand to her chest. He moved to her side.

'Let's sit. We've got a table.' He held her weight and whispered, 'Breathe, Molly. Slow and steady.'

Molly nodded, heavy against him.

The very tall, smooth man mobilised. Everything was suddenly moving, people, waiters and waitresses stepping aside as he led the way. Mack steered Molly with Tom hard behind.

'Tom!' Farah's voice called from behind.

Tom turned.

She was at the entrance as Molly was led further into the chattering room.

Tom wanted to leave.

Was that what Molly had been about to say? Too much, too fast, too loud. Why did he bring us here?

'Farah!'

He turned to her, his arms raised, trying to hold on to something. He felt the ground shifting as though it was giving way. Farah took his hands, embracing him as he wavered.

Tom saw the room as though he was suspended from the high ceiling, the black-and-white floor closing in on him, people's heads nodding, shaking, the dance of waiters and waitresses, bright aprons, black trousers, like the floor, black and white. There were Molly and Mack at a table, Molly with her head in her hands, Mack pouring a glass of water, holding it out to her, his mouth moving, words of comfort. And he saw Farah, her thick, dark hair half-caught in her collar, her head twisted to one side at a strange angle against a man's chest, his chest.

He saw himself, a thin, scared old man in a hairy suit.

And then he was back, his arms tangled with Farah's coat and hair.

'How was it?' she asked.

Her words seemed so slow, emerging as though bubbles, deep underwater. Tom squinted, trying to understand what she was saying.

'Tom?' Farah waved her hand in front of his face.

'Yes.'

'Are you okay?' she asked.

You need to smile, to be reassuring. Molly's down. Can't both fall apart at the same time.

He straightened, trying to fill his suit.

'Yes, yes. I'm about as okay as I can be.'

'So, how was it?' she asked again.

'Not great. Molly took against the Foreign Office.'

'She's not alone.'

Tom kept smiling. 'Come on. I'd better introduce you to Molly's toy boy.'

'I'm afraid she's finding ways to blame you,' Mack said, a croissant flake on his chin.

Farah was with Molly in the Ladies.

'I don't understand,' Tom said.

'It's a way of distracting herself.'

'I shouldn't take it personally, then?' Tom forced the question to sound less enraged than he felt.

'How can you not take it personally?' Mack's tone was reassuring.

'The constant hair trigger is exhausting.' Tom waved a finger at Mack's chin. 'That's enough. You're trying to shrink me.'

Mack got the croissant flake with the tip of a finger and popped it in his mouth. 'I wouldn't dare, and you're safe. They're coming back now.'

'So, I just have to try and not be offended by her attacks?' Tom asked.

Mack nodded.

'Well, that all sounds terribly easy.' Tom's smile was faint.

'Irony, the very foundation stone of English resilience. That and the longbow.' Mack smiled back.

'Indeed. Didn't have you pinned as a history buff,' Tom added.

'Hard to go through Sandhurst without taking in the glory of Agincourt and Crécy,' Mack replied.

Both men had got up from the table out of habit as Molly and Farah came back. Tom could see that Molly had washed her face and put on some lipstick.

'Are you taking the train back now?' Farah asked as they stood on the pavement outside the brasserie, her arm wrapped through Molly's as people pushed in and out past them.

Tom and Molly both started to speak at the same time.

'We were going to pick up a couple of things,' Molly said over Tom. 'For Christmas.'

'I've got to head back now,' Mack said, reaching out to Farah. 'Good to meet you.' He bowed a little over her hand as he took it and then shook Tom's vigorously. He turned to Molly who hugged him to her.

Tom and Farah smiled at each other, Tom with an eyebrow raised.

'You've got my number,' Mack said, as though speaking to all of them. 'I will see who I can talk to. Please do call me any time.' He walked away purposefully.

Farah, Tom and Molly turned towards the Underground.

They parted by the ticket machines, heading to different lines, pulled by the rush of people.

'Christmas shopping! Such hell,' Tom shouted as they were sucked into the surge, waving to each other over the sea of heads bent over and plugged into headsets.

Tom and Molly did not speak from Green Park to Oxford Circus, only one stop, but it was a fat silence. Tom wanted to take her hands, but they were stuffed firmly into her coat pockets.

He lifted one of his to put it behind her shoulder, but she gave him a cold look and he dropped it down.

When they emerged at Oxford Circus, the light seemed already faded, the day closing in under thick cloud.

Molly looked up. 'That must be snow.'

Tom tried to remember what the weather forecast had been. He had not really listened to the predawn burble on the radio, deafened by dread about the day to come.

'Well, is it supposed to snow?' Molly asked.

'I'm not sure, darling.' He took her hand and led her away from the Underground entrance crowd, stopping in a small space in front of a shop window.

Beyond the glass, a huge sack filled the display, suspended from above, a gush of presents spilling onto a pile below.

'I don't think we can face this, can we?' he said.

'I promised Susie that I would try and get to Selfridges and pick up some goodies. They're coming for dinner. I don't want to cook. She did her whole Susie-bossy number that we shouldn't be alone tonight, mainly because she thinks I will just pick on you.'

Tom smiled, squeezing her hand. 'Well, she's right, isn't she? Silly old tart.'

Molly squeezed back.

'Shall we tough it out in the food hall, then?' Tom asked.

'I think she...' Molly began to cry.

Tom pushed his arm through hers and held tight.

She had been about to say that she thought Kate would want them to keep carrying on.

'Kate would want us to do this,' he said, giving her his hand-kerchief. 'It's clean.'

She took it and pressed it to her face. 'I bloody know it's clean. I washed and ironed it, or did you think that was the housekeeper fairy in action?' She smiled at Tom.

♫

While she waited at the fish counter, Molly sent Tom to find some of the big, red salmon eggs that they both loved for the pop on the tongue of them—a comfort food.

As he wandered away for a moment, she felt the relief of having something else to focus on.

'What can I do for you?' A young man in a baseball cap and an apron was grinning at her.

Find my daughter!

Molly adjusted her beret.

'Four fishcakes, please, but as much fish as possible. I don't like those potato-stuffed ones.'

'They'd be potato cakes then, wouldn't they?' said the young man. 'But the salmon ones are probably your best bet, about as close as you can get to one hundred per cent fish without flapping.'

'Good. Four of those, then,' Molly said.

That sounded normal.

She held on to the glass rim of the counter, inhaling the cold, smoky sea smell.

Yes, I really did sound quite normal.

Tom was back. 'Found it.' He held out the jar of salmon roe.

They looked at each other, eyes soft.

We can do this. We can pretend to be normal.

Molly took the jar. 'This nice man says the salmon fishcakes are the best ones, so we have a salmon theme.'

The young man flicked the rim of his baseball cap at Tom. 'Great hat,' he said, handing the fishcakes to Molly. 'Salmon cakes for the lady with the gentleman in the trilby, and happy Christmas to two very stylish people!'

They were back out on the pavement, the sky darker still.

'Can we take a cab now?' Molly asked.

Grey gloom was the backdrop as London slid by the taxi window until they passed under the colour chaos of the Oxford Street lights. By the time they reached Park Lane, the lights were simpler, each tree discreetly wound around in white.

A Christmas fair was occupying the whole of one side of Hyde Park, funfair rides flinging up and down above crowded shops and steaming food stalls.

'How are we going to get through this?' Molly asked.

'It doesn't matter if we miss the 3.45; we can catch the next one,' Tom said, trying to read the traffic ahead.

'I don't mean the traffic.'

'I'm so sorry.' He tried to take Molly's hand again, but she snatched back.

'The fishcakes will go off,' she snapped.

'I'm sure they'll be fine for a few hours.'

Molly turned to stare out of the window.

'How disgusting,' she said, looking at the fair.

'It's just people having fun,' Tom said, immediately wishing that he had not.

$$\mathscr{D}$$

Kate had loved funfairs. Even though so many of the rides made her sick, she still wanted to go every time there was one nearby.

Everywhere Tom looked, there were families with children, bright faces bouncing around their parents, some of them bundled up in so many layers that they could hardly walk.

Two little girls were crossing the road just in front of them, weaving through the stalled traffic, their mother running to keep up, their father on the phone further behind, laughing. Both girls were still in their school uniforms, formal green coats with velvet collars and embroidered school emblems, their hairbands matching the collars. Enormous furry reindeer antlers waved from second bands. One of the girls was holding on to her antlers as she ran. Her sister's were sliding off, their mother reaching out to catch them as they fell.

Tom and Molly stared as the little family made their way.

A phone was ringing.

'It's him, get it, get it!' Molly shouted.

Tom scrabbled for the phone.

'Mr Black, hello?' a voice asked.

'Yes, hello!' Tom shouted back.

'Can you hear? Hello, can you hear me?'

'Yes, yes, I can hear you.'

'Hello, hello, can you hear me?' Michael shouted down the line again.

'Yes, yes, I can, but I don't think you can hear me. Maybe call back?' Tom said slowly, spacing the words.

'Fucking Skype!' came Michael's voice, and then the line clicked off.

'What happened?' Molly asked.

'He couldn't hear me.'

'Why are you smiling?'

'He didn't think I could hear, so he had a good old swear about the line,' Tom said.

Molly took the phone. 'Is he going to call back?'

'I'm sure he will.' He knew Michael would prefer to speak to him, but he was not going to take the phone back.

It rang again.

'Hello!' Molly shouted into it.

'Hello, is that Mrs Black?' Michael asked.

'Yes, yes it is.'

'Can you hear me this time?'

'Yes, yes I can.'

'Is Mr Black there?'

'He is,' Molly flared back.

'Could I speak to him?' Michael asked.

'You can speak to me,' she shouted.

'Mr Black, hello, it's Michael. Can you hear me?'

Molly put the phone on to speaker and held it between them.

'Hello, Michael.' Tom tried to keep his voice even.

'Hello, Mr Black.' Michael sounded relieved.

'Tom, please.'

'Yes, sorry. I'm calling now. She finally turned up, but she—'

'What? She's back!' Tom punched the air.

Molly stared at the phone, shaking.

'Mr Black, Tom, Mr Black, Mr Black, can you hear me?' Michael put his mouth next to the microphone, shouting as Molly and Tom clung to each other in the back of the taxi.

'He's still talking,' Molly whispered.

'Hello, hello, yes, Michael. Tell us what happened. Can we speak to her?'

Heavy static buzzed.

'I think we've been cut off. I'm sure he'll call back again. You are clever to know how to do the speaker. Good for you.'

They both looked at the phone.

'You all right back there?' The taxi driver slid the glass divider open.

'Oh yes, we are very, very much all right. Our daughter was kidnapped but she's back...' There was a giggle in Molly's voice.

'Bloody hell, you serious?' the driver asked. 'That's incredible.'

Michael stared at the little blue symbol of a telephone receiver on the screen: 'Call dropped 43 seconds.'

Jesus! They think Kate's back. I said 'she'. They don't know I was talking about the deputy inspector. How did I do that?

He reached out to press the call symbol but stopped for a moment.

What would Kate do? If it was the other way around, if he was the one who had been kidnapped, and this same phone mess-up had happened, what would she do?

She would swear a lot and then she would call straight back.

Michael pressed the blue phone receiver symbol on the screen.

'Hello, Michael, hello, can you hear me?' Tom was shouting again.

Even on the bad line, Michael could hear the wild excitement in his voice.

Fuck!

He took a breath.

'Mr Black, I am so sorry, but I am afraid there was a misunderstanding...' Michael's voice faded.

'Hello, Michael. I'm sorry, can you say that again? Can we speak to Kate?'

'Mr Black, can you hear me?'

'Yes, yes, I can. It's better now.'

'I'm so sorry, but I am afraid there was a misunderstanding. I was trying to say that the deputy inspector general of police came much later than she said she was going to. I was talking about the deputy inspector general. I think you thought I was talking about Kate. I really am so sorry, very sorry.'

There was just a buzzing on the line.

'The deputy inspector general is a woman,' Michael added.

Tom took the phone from his ear slowly.

'Moll, she's not back. Kate's not back.' He lifted the phone again.

'Michael, are you still there? What did she say? What did this policewoman say?'

Molly stared ahead, seeing nothing.

KATE.

Early December.

B oredom.

They don't tell you about that.

Kate was curled up on her side where she always was now in the room, in the corner, her hands untied, ankles shackled, a mess of badly tied bandage around her head and tied under her chin.

They had been warned by the sergeant about tectonic emotional shifts, waves of hysteria, laughter and crying followed by numbed nothingness.

'You've got a bag of tricks to work with now,' he had said, 'except that you won't remember most of it because you haven't had enough time to practise, so it may not be much use to you anyway. Mind you, if it happens, you'll have plenty of time to try and remember.' And he had grinned.

Plenty of time now. Plenty.

And he had missed out the boredom, the wide expanses of it, with the constant backwash of fear underneath.

When her hands had been cut free, both kinds of hysteria surged through.

Two men, their heads and faces bound around in black, had squatted on either side of her, one of them cutting the plastic ties on her wrists and ankles with the same huge knife that had been used to cut the gag. It was too big for the task. The one with the knife grunted with frustration. Kate braced herself, heart cramping. They attached thick metal cuffs and a chain around her ankles before even starting to hack at those ties.

When she felt the tip of a knife against her head blackness fell.

Through the black came the question: how many days was it now since that first meeting with the Pinky-and-Perky double act?

The sergeant had told them to name their captors. 'Stupid names, kids' names, like cartoons: Larry the Lamb for some big, butch bastard. Subversion helps.'

The double act always grunted at each other rather than speaking.

Piggy names fitted.

She could not tell how much time had passed. No one had spoken to her since the Jasmine Man and she had no idea how many days it had been since then.

She needed to find just the right name for him too.

Tom had loved the cartoon pigs, passing them on to Kate from his childhood. She knew all the characters. Basil Bloodhound did not work for Jasmine Man. Ambrose Cat was closer, but still not right. Bertie Bonkers, the baby elephant—that was funny, but there was nothing elephantine about him. Conchita Cow, yes! She could just switch it about. Jasmine Man joined Pinky and Perky as Conchita Bull.

She had her cast.

'These little acts of defiance, like the names, this stuff helps. Doesn't sound like it would work, but it does,' the sergeant had said.

How did he know, this leader of her silent dialogues?

The sergeant was already the main structural point in her inner world, away from the one that she was in.

He had taught them to do that too, the creation of a private world peopled with those who loved and supported them—their team.

If the sergeant was leader, Tom and Molly were team members two and three.

'Pick people and give them jobs on your team. One of them needs to talk sense into you when you're thinking a load of bollocks. Another one has to be the morale-booster.'

Of course, the sergeant was in the talking-sense role. Tom was on morale-boosting.

Mum, not an obvious fit for hand-holding. Farah definitely good for that. Mum, not sure.

Just Mum as Mum?

The next step was to pick out her own place in the room and to mark it as hers. She moved as far as possible from where she had first been thrown down, vomiting in terror and pain. It was at just the point where she could see the door. If she looked along the floor, she could see any movement on the other side through the tiny crack at the bottom, where shadow on the other side of the door traced in a thin line of light.

Her corner was at an angle to the only window in the room. It was small and too high to see out of when standing, unless on a chair, but there was no chair. Yet, at the angle from her corner, Kate could see a portion of sky, the edge of a roof with wooden joists and mud in between, and two branches of a tree.

She knew she was in a village house: the thick, mud walls and roof and small, high windows that keep the warmth in, and the heat and the enemy out. The two branches were still in leaf.

Prickly oak, the tree of Gilgit.

Maybe she was not that far from where she had been taken.

She tried to work out again how long she had been there. The first period had been an incoherent blur of fading in and out. That could have been a few hours, or even days.

And how many days in this room?

She counted five nights.

The first had been spent curled up against the wall in pain, and then a little relief as her body slowly absorbed the water she had been given, just one cup, left beside her while she had been asleep or unconscious.

All that she could remember about that night was the feeling of her blood freezing, her body's constant shivering as it fought the cold.

By the second night, Pinky, or Perky, had given her a blanket. There was still ice in her veins, the blanket a useless weight on top of her. It was more use under her, a thin barrier against the cold floor.

On the third, there was another blanket, one under, the second wrapped around her. Neither gave much warmth, but the wrap of the second blanket felt a little like a cocoon, a place to hide.

Positives, need those. Hang on to them.

The sergeant had warned them about the mind's negative obsessions. Once they had constructed an internal support system, they had to start clawing their way towards optimism.

Two blankets were a lot better than none. A positive.

On the fourth night, Perky, or Pinky, shoved a plate with more food than before towards her.

She could barely eat. Nausea kept overriding hunger.

He shook the bucket at her as well.

Kate stared at him and then the bucket.

'You'll either have screaming diarrhoea, or nothing at all, depends on what kind of guts you've got,' the sergeant had said.

It was nothing at all for Kate.

Were they waiting for her to shit out money or drugs? Did they think she had something inside her that they were after? Had they thought she was someone else, someone who had swallowed something they wanted?

She spent most of that long night wriggling to keep warm, trying to find a way to roll the bottom of her trousers under the cold metal cuffs, to pad them, to keep them away from the open sores caused by her struggle against the hard plastic shackles when she had been in the boot of the car.

On the fifth, Pinky, or Perky, came again to take away her plate. It was still piled with almost untouched rice and watery *dhal*. He signalled that she should push the plate towards him.

The other one hovered behind him in the doorway.

She pushed the plate with her foot the few inches that the chain would allow.

As he crouched to reach for the plate, he took a shuffled step towards her. It was the closest she had been to either of them when fully conscious. He leant forward to take the plate. She could see his eyes between the windings of the black cloth. There was a patch of pale skin at the corner of his left eye.

As he stood to leave, she saw them side by side for a moment. The one who had been near her was shorter, thicker set.

Now she could tell them apart.

Pinky! It fitted with the vitiligo around his eye.

Probably got it all over his face. Not much chance of him getting married—the white stain, *safed daag*, poor boy, tough for him, a curse.

Poor boy! What?

As the door closed behind them, Kate curled into the corner and called down her team.

'Stockholm Syndrome this soon?' she asked out loud.

'Could be that you're just being soppy,' the sergeant said, arms folded, rocking back on his heels.

'Defend me, then,' Kate said to the empty room.

'Stockholm Syndrome and humanising them, not the same thing. It's just going to be harder for you to see them as the enemy if you start thinking about them like you're their friggin' mum,' he said.

'Dad?' Kate asked.

Tom was beside the sergeant, arms crossed too. 'He's right, Kate darling. Harder to see them as the enemy.'

'That's not moral support,' she said. 'And what about if they humanise me?'

'You'll have won.' Tom smiled.

'How?' Kate asked.

Silence.

'Where's Mum?' she asked.

They had gone.

She was sitting in the corner, her head between her knees, talking to the floor.

PINKY AND PERKY.

Early December.

'You were too close,' Perky, the taller one, said as he shut the outer door.

Only Jasmine Man, Conchita Bull, was allowed to speak inside the building.

Pinky pulled the black cloth of his *pagri* away from his face. 'I can't breathe in this thing.'

Pale islands of skin spread across his face and down his neck, an expanding archipelago that had begun with one tiny islet between his finger and thumb when he was eighteen. His beard was as frail as his pale skin and did not hide the patches.

'She could have kicked you,' Perky said.

'I wasn't that close. She's not eating,' Pinky said. 'And she is not shitting, unless she's eating that,' he added, laughing.

Perky did not.

'You know she is mad, this talking thing that she does all the time,' Pinky went on.

'What talking?'

'Don't you hear it? She does it so much.'

'Oh, that. I don't bother to listen.' Perky kicked dust at two goats tied to the tree beside the kitchen. 'Let's eat. I'm hungry. Better not be this shit.' He tipped the food from Kate's plate in front of the goats. They knelt to eat it. 'Watch out it doesn't poison you,' he said, pushing one of them over with his foot.

'Is he coming today?' Pinky asked.

'Who knows? He never tells, just comes and goes.'

'My brother wants to come and see me,' Pinky said.

'Forget that.' Perky whacked one of the goats with the plate as it tried to lick off the remains of the food.

'He could bring some of my mother's cooking,' Pinky added.

'Why does he want to see you?'

'He always knows when I'm lying. He did not believe the story.'

'What did you tell him?' Perky pulled the black cloth from his face, releasing two fists length of full beard.

'That I was going back to teach at the *madrassa* for some time.'

'You, teach?' Perky shoved him, almost knocking him over. 'What would you teach?'

'*Hadith*,' Pinky whispered.

This time Perky laughed. 'Okay, learned *Maulvi Sahib*, tell me what our great cook has come up with tonight.'

Pinky walked ahead, pretending not to have heard.

KATE.

Nine days maybe, plus the ones that got lost. I should be making marks on the wall like in films: seven lines and a crossbar, like a gate, but not a gate, nothing opening, not going anywhere. A week, it must be a week now, with two days lost. Round it up or down, make it a week?

Kate looked around the room, trying to see things that she might have missed, anything.

Nothing.

'What do I do now?' she called to the wall.

'It's not a bloody film,' the sergeant team captain said.

'I know,' Kate said, pulling herself up onto her left hip. 'Getting good at the mermaid wriggle here. Look!'

She stepped herself forward with her hands, and using her shackled feet as a lever, she humped herself forward.

'Why don't you walk?' asked the sergeant.

Kate pointed to her feet.

'There's a chain between them, so take very small steps,' he said.

'I still get head-spins when I stand up.'

'Well done.' Tom was standing behind the sergeant again.

'Hello, Dad.'

'Hello, darling.'

'Mum around?'

'Umm.'

'Farah?' Kate asked.

The team faded.

She slumped forward.

She could cry now. They were out of earshot.

Don't mind them hearing the chat. Might freak them out. Not the crying, mustn't hear the crying.

Keep moving, even if I'm not moving. Keep moving.

Never stop planning. Team captain's orders. Keep planning.

What plan?

How to mark off the days.

She curled and levered herself towards the bucket, the only other thing in the room apart from the blankets and her.

Mermaid. Who am I kidding?

She humped and pushed again.

Darwin's mermaids, big, ugly old manatees, all blubber and tail. That's about right. Columbus's sailors as messed in the head as I am as they ogled their fatty lovelies. And Odysseus's lot, well, dolphins are a lot prettier than manatees. They'd win in a fishy beauty pageant.

She had reached the bucket.

'Look! Can you see them?' Molly was holding Kate by the shoulders as a wall of sea wind pushed them back from the cliff edge. 'You see the Cow and Calf rocks?'

'Yes.' Kate looked towards the hunchbacked outcrops in the sea.

'Now follow a direct line from them back to shore.' Molly took Kate's hand and pointed it out to sea.

Kate could not see anything except for the wind-foamed wave tops.

'Can you see them now?' Molly asked, squeezing Kate's little body back against her legs.

'No!' Kate shouted into the wind.

And then she did. Three seals, their heads above the water, each looking in a different direction.

She squealed, clinging to Molly, jumping up and down.

Kate picked up the bucket, careful not to spill her own urine.

Think I'm more seal than dolphin or manatee. Please not manatee.

Stupid to try and mark the days on the bucket. With what? And at the risk of slopping everything on the floor, maybe even some crap eventually, if I ever go again.

Nothing for a week. Can't be good. In the shit and full of it too.

She looked back at her corner, at the grey bulge of blankets. One of them was fraying along an edge.

I can make knots in loose threads, one for each day.

She dragged herself to the corner again, pushing herself up into her usual position, her back angled between the two walls. Very carefully, she unravelled the longest piece of wool.

Here was something she had not felt for a week, at least a week, an odd excitement, the sense of something.

Of what?

Of hope?

'Got to hang on to hope or you're screwed. If you don't have something to hope for, you just give up. They win, you lose, game over.'

Sergeant wisdom.

She looked at the wool in her hand.

I will knot off the days and of what? Seven knots, seven days gone, locked up, pissing in a bucket, scared shitless. Haven't spoken to anyone since Conchita Bull and his devil act. I will go mad.

She looped the end of the wool around her index finger, rolling and pulling it through to make the first knot.

Is that what they want, that I go mad? What's the point of that?

'Don't ask why. You'll go mad. Keep knotting, sweetie. Think of each one as a very, very dry martini.'

'Susie! Where did you come from?'

'From the reserve bench. You didn't even give me a proper place.' She was in a green cocktail dress.

'What are you wearing?'

'Dressed for the occasion.' Susie was smiling.

'Are you standing in for Mum?'

'She's around,' Susie said.

'Really?'

'Yes.'

'She never makes the team meetings,' Kate said.

'That's between you and her.' Susie left, a pendulum swinging away in her tight dress.

'Mum!' Kate screamed out.

Molly had her hands on her hips. 'I'm not dressing up like Tarty Pants.'

'Mum! You made it, and who said that you had to dress up?'

'What, and let Susie call me the sad-sack lady?'

'Mum!'

'I can wear whatever I want, then?'

'Whatever works for you.'

'I don't want to embarrass you.'

Kate made a thin, animal sound.

Molly had gone.

Kate curled back into her corner, pulling the blankets around her.

SUSIE.
Early December.

'Obviously, I think of them as good friends. I just haven't known them as long as you.' Mike was standing by the front door, looking at the car keys on the hook.

'Seven years, that's enough. How long does it take to be friends?' Susie was shouting from the kitchen. 'You don't want to go, do you?'

'Do I have to answer that?' he said quietly to his reflection in the hall mirror.

'I heard that.'

'Okay, Flappy Ears.' he smiled. 'What are you doing in there?'

'Be there in a sec.'

Susie was standing in front of the fridge, looking at two pictures taken on her last birthday: one at dinner with Tom and Molly, just before the risotto knocked Mike out, and another from lunch two days later in the garden, everyone there, nearly everyone. The boys with wives and children. Dear, dull Cally, her brood, all four of them. Seven grandchildren, three children, two wives—one good, one bad—one husband, me.

Mike looked grey in the picture, his mouth a straight line, his hat pushed forward, adding shadow to his risotto-poisoned pallor. The children and their children, all with their selfie-expressions, glossy and plastic, except for one of the wives, the one Susie called Bad Wife.

Poor thing. So plain. Hates me. Fair enough, not exactly mad about her.

I look okayish, bit flushed. Pissed again. Oh well, it was fun.

There was nothing marking her other son's absence from the table, no empty chair, nothing maudlin. Val was just not there.

No wonder he hates me. Who calls their son Valentine? It was so something or other at the time. Cool, hip? Everything was hip in 1975. Poor boy.

Kate, well, she seemed to understand Val, those two always skulking around in the woods together.

Probably popped each other's cherry.

She smiled at the still very clear memory of them sneaking back one evening. Val was seventeen, Kate fourteen, as always in her uniform of torn jeans and sailor t-shirt, Val in 'hobo-wear' as one stepfather described it—Bill and Cally's father.

Not a kind man.

There they had been two teenagers, scruffy and sullen, avoiding looking at each other.

She remembered the long gap afterwards when they had not spoken to each other.

Of course they had sex in the woods. How sweet and funny. Or maybe not—too quick and sweaty, leaves, twigs and mud sandpapering any chance of sensuality.

Oh, come on! Show me the teenagers who are up to sensual sex.

She pressed a finger to the photograph and then to her lips.

Val's been absent so long I suppose I've got used to it. Now Kate too. Not okay, not okay at all. Really going to need a drink this evening, or four.

She thought about having one now, just quickly, to soften the edge. She was about to call out, to suggest it to Mike.

'Are we going?' he called again from the hall, irritated now.

'Yes, just coming.'

She did not want to go, and Mike definitely did not want to, but it had been her idea. She had pushed Molly.

It's not my child. It's hers. Tom and Molly's girl, funny, sweet, serious, clever Kate.

'At last.' Mike put his arm around her as she pouted to put her lipstick on in front of the mirror beside him. 'Still fancy you when you do that.'

'I'd kiss you, but I'll smear,' she said, pressing her lips together. 'Right, let's go,' she told their reflection.

TOM AND MOLLY.

'Are we really doing this?' Tom asked, standing in his study, still in his overcoat, looking at the answering machine.

Molly groaned from the sofa next door. She was still in her coat as well.

'It's too late to put them off, isn't it?' Tom put a finger over the flashing message light.

Four messages. He did not want to play them until Molly was out of earshot.

'It's Susie. She wouldn't mind,' Molly said.

'Wasn't it her idea?'

'Yes, and we've spent a fortune at Selfridges.' Molly stared down at her feet, soggy from walking through the snow at the station.

'Moll!' Tom was beside her. 'If Jack can't get on the sofa with wet feet, how can you?'

'Well, you've still got your coat on,' she said.

'So have you.' He patted her shoulder.

She reached out and took his hand. 'Tom, I know I'm not doing this very well, and I know you know that...'

He sat down beside her and stroked her hand.

'We're okay though, aren't we?'

Molly looked down.

'I'll go and get Jack,' Tom said, patting her shoulder again as he got up.

Molly did not move. 'I can't face ringing to put them off.'

'I think it's too late. They will have left already.'

'Unlikely. Susie will be running late.' Molly closed her eyes. 'You go and get Jack, and I'll try and pull myself together.'

Tom went back into the study and switched off the answerphone at the wall. The message light stopped flashing.

'Any messages?' Molly asked.

'I haven't checked,' he lied.

'Could you?'

'I'll get Jack first and then check.'

'Is it flashing?' she asked.

'Not sure,' he lied again. 'Back in a minute.' He hurried past her, fiddling with his coat buttons.

Jack was waiting, leaping up at the stable door as Tom opened the top half.

'Hello, fella.'

Jack shot out, turned and leapt up at Tom, tongue flashing, and then he was off, leg raised, hosing down the wall beside the stable.

Tom watched in admiration.

'Impressive, Jack. Been holding on to that all day?'

Jack looked up, leg still cocked.

'No news, Jack. No news.' Tom dropped his head onto his folded arms on the stable door.

The dog finished, shook, curved into a long stretch and then lay down beside Tom. He bent and stroked Jack's head.

The centre must hold. It has to hold, or... or what?

Jack jumped up and settled beside Molly on the sofa, his muzzle on her leg, gazing up at her.

'He knows what's happened,' Molly said.

'I don't want to detract from Jack's great animal empathy, but I think he's just hungry. I'll feed him. Come on, Jack.'

Jack was up and skidding across the wooden floor towards the kitchen and his bowl.

'It's bloody off,' Molly shouted after Tom.

He stopped in the hallway.

Can't lie again.

'What's off?' he called back.

'The bloody answerphone.'

Tom waited a beat and then turned back.

'Moll.' He was standing in the door of the sitting room.

'What?' she snapped.

'I did leave it on. The message light was flashing. I didn't want you to listen to the messages alone.' Jack pushed past him and stood between them, looking from one to the other.

'Oh, go and feed him.' Her tone was softer. 'Do we listen now or wait until Susie and Mike bugger off?'

Tom shrugged.

'Well, they're not going to leave a message on the answerphone if Kate's been killed, are they?' Molly pushed herself up. 'They're not, are they?' She stood up.

'I don't know. They didn't tell us how they would give us messages.'

They stood looking at each other.

Molly looked away first. 'I'll get going on dinner.'

'I'll feed Jack.' But Tom did not move.

'Come on, then,' she said.

They started at the same time, bumping into each other. Tom stopped, stepping back to let Molly through the door. Jack barged between them.

'Bloody dog,' Molly hissed.

Thank God for the dog.

&

'Thank God they've gone.' Tom fell back into the sofa.

Molly was still at the door, waving at Susie and Mike's tail lights with one hand, hanging on to the door frame with the other. She had done what she usually did when she was frightened. She had drunk too much.

Tom had paced himself, though he had given up when it was clear that the others were planning to drink their way through the evening. He caught up in the last hour, irritated by how Susie kept splashing wine into her own glass without offering it to anyone else. The late spurt had just made him feel even more exhausted.

Molly had two bright patches on her cheeks. 'What did you say?' she said, still watching the car lights fading into the dark.

'That wasn't too bad,' he tried.

'That's not what you said.' Molly came back into the sitting room and leant against a chair. Kate's chair.

Tom wanted to ask her to move away, but he was not so drunk that he would say it aloud.

'Come and sit down,' he said.

Jack took up the invitation, leaping onto the sofa and circling before he flopped down.

'No room at th-inn.' Molly's words bumped into each other. 'I want another drink, prob'ly not a good idea. I'll make some herbal muck.' She stopped for a moment. 'That's what Kate would do now, isn't it?'

'It was all delicious.' Tom pushed Jack, making space for Molly.

She looked at the gap on the sofa. 'The fishcakes were dry. I left them in too long.'

'Everything was delicious, and Mike's look of relief when he saw that it wasn't risotto was very funny.'

Molly sat down. 'Rough for him, though. Susie gushing and everyone pretending that there was nothing wrong.' She stopped and turned to Tom. 'But what was that whole silly speech of hers about Kate and Val?'

'Do you think that's true?' Tom asked.

'It's so long ago I can't remember.' Molly closed her eyes for a moment.

Tom hoped she might be falling asleep.

He could clean up the kitchen, sober up while he was doing it, shut everything up, put Molly to bed.

Then he could listen to the messages.

Molly's eyes popped open. 'You know, I think Susie's probably right. Kate was so difficult that summer, endlessly locked in the bathroom, or glumping around, snapping at everyone. I do remember wondering what was going on, but I can't remember if I ever tried to talk to her.' She paused. 'Val was really a number.' She closed her eyes again. 'I can't remember how much more time they spent together after that, can you?'

'I didn't mind Val,' Tom said, still staring at the back of Kate's chair.

'Oh, you! Just because you think he was clever, that makes everything okay?' Molly stopped for a moment. 'Why are we talking about him in the past tense? He's not dead.'

Tom closed his eyes.

Why did she say that? Does she think Kate's dead? Has she had some sixth sense about it, a mother's intuition? Was she starting to grieve?

He wished he was sober and not angry.

But angry about what?

He knew that it was not anger but a creeping fear that Molly was giving up on Kate.

Jack stretched out his legs, making more space for himself, pushing Tom against Molly.

'Stop it!' Tom shouted.

Jack shot off the sofa.

Molly jolted. 'Who are you shouting at?'

'No one, nothing,' he said.

'We can't...' Molly leant her head against Tom's shoulder.

'Can't what?' he asked.

'We can't give up.'

'I know.' He stroked her hair.

'But we do have to try and do better than this.' She softened against him.

'You're right, but the question is how?'

She pushed his hand away and stood up.

It was her hands-on-hips 'state-of-the-nation' stance.

'I've been trying to blame something, someone, the bastards who took her, the Foreign Office, anyone. But most of the time you're the closest thing, so it's you.'

'You mean you think that somehow it's my fault?'

Molly looked at Tom, her head to one side. 'No, of course I don't.' She stopped. 'Rationally, I don't. Irrational, angry me does, though. I don't mean to; it's pathetic, but I just so want something to be angry at, really fucking, screaming banshee angry.'

They were motionless in the ricochet of what she had said.

I've been with this woman for forty-four years, and there are still times when I love her as fiercely as I did when I first met her.

Molly took a slow breath.

He's here. He's still here, now, with me, and all I'm doing is punishing him because Kate loves him so much. Susie's right. I am so shrivel-minded about how much she loves Tom. I am a petty, jealous woman. And I am really so bloody lucky to have this man beside me. Jesus, never marry a sodding saint; it makes you so mean.

She looked up at Tom, and he held out his hand to help her up from the sofa.

KATE.

December.

She needed to get to the bucket, urgently.

As she tried to shuffle, Kate fell against the wall, righted herself, then half dragged, half pulled herself to the bucket.

Her hands felt numb, fumbling at the drawstring of her trousers. 'Kate! Do it!' she shouted.

She crouched over the bucket in a groaning rush that seemed to go on forever.

In a gap, she managed to wriggle herself and the bucket closer to the wall so that she could lean against it.

Another rush, a gut full of it.

She panted, gripping the bucket, and then vomited.

Don't want to get covered in shit. Going to pass out. Don't want shit and puke all over myself. No way to get clean.

'Come on!' she shouted at her legs, willing them to lift her away from the bucket without knocking it over.

The room spun.

For a second the stench from the bucket knocked her back into focus, just long enough to pull up her trousers. She could not have cleaned herself even if there had been water. She managed one small step and fell again.

I need you now. Where are you all? Help me!

A different kind of cold began to seep in, paralysing her body as it crept through her.

She started to haul herself back to her corner as black descended.

She did not hear the door nor see them baulk as the smell of the room hit them.

Even though their faces were covered, she would have been able to see the shock in their eyes if she had been conscious.

They backed away, slamming the door and then bolting the outer door.

They stood, looking at each other, both pulling the black folds from their faces, sucking in air.

Pinky bent over, hands on his knees, vomiting into the dust. Perky was rubbing his face as though his skin had been impregnated by the stench.

Beyond them, the goats pulled on their ropes, straining in the hope of food.

JANAN AND KHAK.

'She's dead,' said Pinky, still retching.

'You said that before. She wasn't then.' Perky leant back against the outer wall.

Pinky stood up. 'What do we do? We have to call him, tell him, ask him what to do now.'

Perky closed his eyes, lifting his face to the sun. 'No, we are not going to call him. We are going to get a doctor. He said we have to keep her alive.'

'How?'

Perky did not answer but turned towards the kitchen.

'Where are you going?' Pinky asked.

Again, he did not answer.

'Should I come with you?' Pinky started to follow.

Perky turned. 'Janan! Don't follow me,' he yelled.

Janan stopped. 'Don't shout. You used my name. He said never to use our names, ever.'

'She can't hear anything.'

'Then you do think she is dead?'

Perky went on walking.

'Where are you going, Khak?'

251

Janan stood beside the goats, unable to move.

They were supposed to stay together all the time. They had to call if there was any trouble. They had to call him right away, no hesitation, fast. He had said this same thing many times.

Khak walking towards the back of the cookhouse. Janan ran after him.

Khak was already in the kitchen, arguing with the cook.

'You have to give it to me,' he was shouting.

'What is this?' Janan asked.

'Shut up!' Khak shouted. 'Give me the key.' He lunged at the cook.

'What key? What are you asking?' Janan tried to step between the two men, but Khak knocked him against the stone sink.

Janan fell hard.

For a moment the only sound was the breath of the three men.

'I need to take the *scooti*,' Khak said calmly, reaching out to help Janan up.

'Shit, man. That really hurt. Let me sit for some time.' Janan rolled off the hip he had fallen onto, leaning back, his head against the cool of the sink. 'You have to tell me what you're going to do about this now.'

Khak spoke carefully, his voice low and controlled. 'We have to get her in front of a doctor. We can't move her, so I am going to get one here.'

'On Cook's scooti?' Janan asked.

'Yes.'

'I have to come with you, we must stay together, this is what he said so many times,' Janan said. 'The scooti can take two, no?' He struggled to his feet, rubbing his hip.

'As you like.' Khak held his hand out to the cook again. 'Come on. Key.'

The cook looked at them both. 'How will you come back with Doctor Sahib? What, with all three of you on my scooti? What are you going to say to Doctor Sahib?'

'Doctor will have his own scooti, maybe a car. Doctors are all rich men. They have cars,' Khak replied. 'We will tell him we have a patient, that he will be paid well for the visit.'

'How will we pay him?' Janan asked.

Khak ignored the question.

The cook shrugged and held out the key. Khak and Janan grabbed for it, and Khak got it.

The cook stood by the door watching, wiping his hands on the cloth that always hung over his shoulder.

He knew that Khak would be the one driving the scooter. He also knew that he had been lying.

He was not going to get a doctor. He just wanted to run away, and now he was stuck with Janan, the trusting idiot. Neither of them knew that the brakes on the scooti only worked when they were pumped, that they did not make contact if squeezed in the normal way.

The back tyre of the scooter was throwing up an arc of dirt as Khak turned onto the dust road. The cook could see Janan clinging on as the spray of earth rose and curled, showering over the side of the road down to the river far below.

Losing the scooti did not matter. It was almost dead, and anyway it was his brother-in-law's.

He did not like his brother-in-law.

He turned away and went to look for his phone. It was a hard, ten-minute walk up the hill to the place he had found where he could get reception. This was not something he had told Khak and Janan, nor the man with no name, the man who always smelt of jasmine.

None of them were local men.

TOM AND MOLLY.

December.

'Tom!'

He heard the shout from his study.

He thought that Molly was out with Jack. But the dog was under his desk, his head on Tom's feet.

'Yes,' he called back.

'Tom!' she called again.

She was upstairs.

'Coming.'

Jack scrambled ahead of him.

'Get downstairs,' Tom hissed, almost tripping over as the dog stopped, crouching on the stairs in front of him.

'No, I'm up here,' Molly called out.

'I was shouting at Jack, not you.'

'Let him come up. Who cares?'

I do. A crisis doesn't mean throwing everything out. Routine, habits, that's what's going to gets us through this.

It was what he was always telling his students as they struggled with finals and relationship dramas, or when a sense of meaninglessness paralysed them.

'Keep going as you always have, same routines, same patterns. You need structure. We all need structure.' He would smile at them kindly, hoping that they were not going to ask any more questions.

It was just Kate who asked the hard questions.

'So, History Dad, you want your students to understand the past in the context of the present?'

Tom had been driving, taking Kate back to university after the Christmas of her first year. He thought that they had been talking about Christmas. Farah had been staying, and he was asking Kate something about Farah's family and the revolution. Her question surprised him.

'Not entirely.' He paused. He liked these conversations, proud of Kate's mind, of how she was playing with ideas, flipping knowledge, getting it right, and wrong. 'In some ways, but rather the other way round. I see the present in the context of history.'

'Okay, so if you had to guess what will have more historical relevance from last year, would you choose Princess Diana's death, Mother Theresa's, the Taliban taking Kabul, Hong Kong going back to the Chinese or Gianni Versace's murder?' Kate looked at her father. 'I'm joking about the last one, by the way.'

'I don't imagine the man who killed him was,' Tom said.

'Wow! Dad, you mean you know who he was?' She laughed.

'Well, you could take almost any of those and imagine it becoming a structural point in a historical context,' he said.

'And in English that means what exactly?' Kate asked.

'Diana's death might become a marking point in the rise of the republican movement. Hong Kong could be the start of a new era of Chinese economic land-grab. I don't think Mother Theresa or indeed Gianni Versace will leave great marks on history.'

'I don't imagine Mother Theresa thought that.' She mimicked Tom.

He laughed and then stopped. 'You know the one that I find hard to grasp though? The rise of the Taliban. As a crusty old historian, of course, I see it as part of an arc of Islamic resurgence, and so back to Farah we go and the starting point of the Iranian Revolution. I just find it terrifying.'

Kate looked at her father. 'That's the one I find the most fascinating. I really want to understand it. It's the biggest story in my life so far.'

'Where are you, Moll?' Tom asked.

'In here,' she called from Kate's room.

He had felt unable to go into her room since they had heard.

Jack was still on the stairs, watching. As Tom turned, the dog shot past him, winding through the half-open door.

Molly was sitting on the bed. She had Kate's greying Snoopy on her lap, one ear half ripped off in a long-ago toy fight with one of Jack's predecessors.

'Hello, darling. What's going on?' Tom asked.

'There's something wrong,' she said, her mouth hardly moving.

A part of him wanted to laugh, to say that of course something was wrong, their daughter was bloody lost in a godforsaken place where they could not protect her.

'What kind of wrong?' he asked.

'I don't know. It's so deep down.' Molly shook her head, hugging the toy to her. Jack poked his head at her to grab for Snoopy.

'Fuck off, Jack,' Molly snapped, batting him on the nose.

Jack reversed back onto the rug beside Kate's desk.

It was the first thing she had brought back from Pakistan, from the camp, bought from a friend of Ara's, her translator. Elongated woven humans and animals floated amid swirls.

Jack flopped onto its mix of square-headed humans, triangular-faced lions and horses with hind legs that looked as though they had been stuck on the wrong way round. Tom sunk down beside the dog, one hand pressing into the carpet, longing for magic, sorcery, for anything.

Molly was looking at him, the old toy's head propped up on the shelf of her bosom.

'It's here.' She pointed to the swell of her belly. 'And please don't ask if I've got indigestion. I can feel it right deep, under the scars.'

The thick smell of dog fart rose from the rug.

'Jack!' Molly hissed.

The dog lifted his head for a moment and then rolled to his side, looking up at Tom, brows raised.

'Could have been me,' Tom said.

'Been eating rotting rabbit lately, have you?' Molly swatted the air.

Behind her was a poster—a young man, his head bent towards the raised face of a young woman. They were kissing in black and white, a grand town hall behind them, a man passing by in a beret, tie and suit, chic but rumpled too.

'So many generations of teenage girls' bedrooms,' Tom said, looking at the poster.

'What?' Molly asked.

'Sorry, I didn't realise I said that aloud. It's the Doisneau picture, every girl's poster lodestar of unattainable romance,' he said. 'Behind you.'

'Oh, that. God, it's been there forever.' Molly turned. 'It's not very Kate now, is it? Actually, was it ever really her? Didn't you get it for her?'

Tom shrugged. 'I thought you did.'

'I did not!' Molly paused. 'Do you think she was in love with Val?' She raised a hand to touch the picture.

'Maybe.' Tom swung the bedroom door to and fro. 'That was particularly disgusting, Jack.'

'Tom!' Molly was urgent again. 'I really didn't think that I minded, but the idea of no grandchildren...' Her voice faded.

It was so long since they had talked about whether Kate would have children. She was thirty-six, living a life so remote from any semblance of family life.

He could not think about Kate as anything except alive.

The possibility, yes, but only in the abstract—the concept of a void, but an unimaginable one.

He looked again at Molly, sitting on their daughter's bed. The world lurched, as it had in the grand brasserie, standing beside Farah, the black-and-white floor shifting beneath him.

Molly watched as Tom swayed.

I shouldn't have said that. Didn't really mean to.

She reached out to him. 'I'm sorry, incredibly selfish.'

'I thought you didn't like babies?' he said.

'Oh my God, you do know I just say that?'

'You seemed very clear about it.'

'It's not them; it's their parents, all the terrible spoiling now and pretending not to hear them when they're making the most awful noise around other people.'

'Isn't there a theory that your own child's screaming doesn't seem as loud to you as it does to everyone else? Tom paused. 'Or is that about poo, that you don't mind the smell of your own baby's?'

'Never worked for me. Don't you remember? I used to have to change Kate with the window open.'

'Oh yes, I do now.' Tom laughed weakly. 'I do remember coming in once and you were hanging out of the window throwing up. Maybe that's where Kate got the throwing-up gene from?'

'So that's my fault too, my legacy to our daughter: a puke gene.' Molly was trying not to smile.

'The brains are definitely mine.' Tom was smiling.

Molly reached out to him again. 'I'm so scared. I don't know how to be, how to behave. You know that I pretend not to like babies. How else was I going to get through not having the chance to have any more after Kate?'

Tom sat down beside her, and she took his hand, in silence, beneath the young lovers in black and white.

Jack barked.

'What?' Molly asked.

'It's the phone. I'll get it in the bedroom.' Tom was already through the door.

Molly was about to follow, but she stopped, picked up Snoopy again and inhaled the toy.

It did not smell of Kate, just passing time's must.

Kate loved you so much, cried into you, hugged you, slept with you more than she ever slept with anyone else, probably told you a million times how much she hated me.

Molly held the greying beagle away from her. 'Grubby Snoopy, keeper of secrets, tell me, where is Kate?'

The toy drooped in her hands.

She could hear Tom next door—he was not using his tight catastrophe tone.

She tried to pick out what he was saying, but it was just a buzz of words as he spoke, with gaps in between.

Please, just a few minutes of not thinking about this, of not being chewed up by it. I want to breathe again, to take Jack for a walk without crying the whole way, to sit and watch some telly with Tom on the sofa. Just not to know, for a few minutes.

Tom came back.

'That was Sal.'

'Oh God, I forgot. I was supposed to go to a meeting about that stupid fuss about recycling bins.'

'She wasn't calling about that. She was watching some documentary about what everyone seems now to describe as "so-called Islamic State", aid workers and journalists, something like that. She wanted to know how Kate is.' Tom leant back against the door.

'What did you say?'

'I didn't know what to say because I don't know who you've spoken to.'

'I haven't said anything to anyone.'

'Farah knows; Susie and Mike know; you told Mack on the train. I'm just not sure who else you've spoken to.'

Molly turned, pushing her face into the pillows, her legs curling in towards her.

'Moll, come on. Scooch up.' He sat down beside her.

'I'm being a baby,' she said.

He patted her shoulder.

'Look at this. You're patting me as though I'm Jack in a strop. I'm a sixty-five-year-old behaving like a four-year-old because this is shitty in ways that I could never have imagined. Whenever I started thinking about anything like this happening to Kate I'd get so angry and direct it elsewhere, usually at you. Poor man.' She batted Tom away. 'Stop patting!'

His hand hovered.

She turned to look up at him. 'What do we say to people?'

'Do we have to say anything?'

'I'm not sure I can manage the whole "How are you Molly?" "Oh, fine thank you. How are you?" I can't pull that off at the moment.' She huddled towards him.

'The social lie would be the easiest way,' he said.

'You're joking, aren't you?' She pulled back. 'Please don't say you're comparing losing Kate with making up some cheesy excuse not to go to a dull county dinner party?'

'Of course I'm not. You know that's not what I meant.'

'You weren't very clear.'

'We haven't lost Kate.' He stopped, sucking in a slow breath through his nose. 'We just don't know.'

'Lost is exactly what she is. We don't know where she is, and she probably doesn't know either, that is if...'

'Come on, Jack. Let's get you and your stinky guts out for a walk.' Tom got up.

Molly lay listening to all that was so familiar: the sounds of Tom moving around the house, talking to the dog, looking for the lead, putting on his coat, the door closing, his voice fading as they walked away.

They were everyday sounds, known but now all heard in another way. Nothing was as it had been.

Kate! Where are you? Come home!

DR FAZLI JADOON.

December.

'Commencement of interview, 11.43 a.m., 22 December, 2014, Interview Room 4, Dr Fazli Jadoon, Medical Superintendent, Government District Hospital, Gilgit.' Deputy Inspector General of Police Farhana Shah clicked off the tape recorder.

'Why do you have to do that?' Dr Fazli Jadoon asked.

'It's procedure, Doctor Sahib.' She looked across the table.

'Is it really necessary?' he asked.

'This is an official interview, so yes, it is.' She took off her beret.

'Then shouldn't you keep that on?'

Farhana folded her beret and put it beside the tape recorder.

Fazli looked around the room: a cement box without windows, the air dank, the walls stained by many things besides underground damp.

'Just one thing, Farhi, before you put that thing back on. I'm not a suspect, am I?'

Farhana looked at her old friend. She smiled. 'We have to be professional about this.'

'Can you answer my question then, please?' he asked.

'No, because it is not relevant to this interview.'

'Farhi, come on.'

He admired her so very much.

There had been a time when he would have liked to have married her, but his marriage had already been arranged by the time they had met.

And now she was being the very thing that he admired in her, her high standards of professionalism.

'I'm a doctor, Farhi. That is all.'

'Shall we start now?' she asked.

He nodded.

'This has not been part of the interview,' she added, picking up the tape recorder again and pressing the button. '11.46 a.m., 22 December, 2014, Interview Room 4, Dr Fazli Jadoon, Medical Superintendent, Government District Hospital, Gilgit.' She put the recorder between them. 'Can you tell me about the call that you received yesterday?'

Dr Fazli Jadoon's assistant was a calm man. His white coat was always cleaner than everyone else's, even when he was controlling the door during the daily OPD, holding back the surge of patients outside, hands grabbing at him to get his attention. He would have to pitch his whole body against the door to stop the crush each time the doctor asked him to bring in another patient.

Dr Jadoon needed a calm, strong man to back up his particular method of practice. All the other doctors at the hospitals, and at all the government hospitals, would have ten to fifteen people coming into the room at the same time. Once the senior doctor, his juniors and the various assistants were included too, it meant that every appointment was carried out in the middle of a crowd.

Most examinations lasted about three minutes. Each patient came in clinging to a mound of notes, test results and prescriptions that had been traipsed around from doctor to doctor, hospital to hospital, in the hope of a miracle cure for poverty and all its accompanying diseases and disorders. The doctor would take the notes, ask some questions, write a prescription, often without even looking up, and the unseen supplicant would be waved away.

Fazli had refused to conform to this model when he returned from his training in England.

At Leeds General Infirmary, he learnt a great many things about being a doctor. For him, one lesson stood above all the others. Whatever the proportions of a public health crisis, it could only be addressed one patient at a time, one person at a time.

Half Fazli's life ago, John Sandman, the officer in charge during the Commonwealth Scholarship interviews, had asked Fazli to bring back to Pakistan what he learnt from the scholarship that he was being given.

It was this that he had brought back.

So Fazli always picked calm, strong assistants to control the waves of complaint that swelled through the door each time it was opened to let in just one patient at a time.

His pristine assistant had not been so calm that morning as he ran into the senior doctors' canteen, scanning the room for Fazli.

This was a man who never ran.

Fazli raised his hand to him.

His assistant was waving his phone in the air.

'A very urgent call,' he said, thrusting the phone at Fazli.

'Aren't they all?' Fazli asked.

'Doctor Sahib, please. It is my wife's cousin.'

Fazli felt a pinch of disappointment. His assistant had never asked for a family favour before. It was something that he respected him for.

He took the phone with resigned irritation.

The voice on the line was choppy.

'I can't hear you.' Fazli held the phone in front of his face, speaking directly into the microphone.

'One minute, please wait,' echoed the voice from the other end.

'I'm waiting,' Fazli replied.

His assistant was at his shoulder, gathering up his white coat and bag, nudging him towards the door.

'What?' he snapped at his assistant, a tone he rarely used.

'Outside, Doctor Sahib. Please speak outside.'

Holding the phone aloft, Fazli apologised to the other doctors he had been talking to. It had been an important conversation about a new admissions system. He followed his assistant out of the canteen, the voice crackling in his hand.

'Yes, yes, I'm still here,' he barked at the phone. 'Just hold on. I'm shifting to somewhere I can hear.'

He was in the mayhem of the hospital car park, vehicles, auto rickshaws, cars, bicycles and people tangling to get to the main entrance.

Two boys in shabby hi vis bibs waved vehicles in and out in no particular order, ignoring the yelling horns all around. Fazli turned to face the wall, cupping his hand around the phone.

'Yes, yes, tell me,' he shouted into it.

'...you know this place?' the voice said.

'The line is not good, what place?'

'The *khud* after Gul, where the bridge was broken in the earthquake. You know this place?'

'I know the area a little, but not the bridge. Why are you telling me about this place?'

'I am saying now, near this place is a woman. She is very sick. You need to come.'

Fazli was about to tell the man that he was handing him back to his assistant to take details and that they would see if it was possible to send an ambulance, but something the man said stopped him.

'Tell me where I have to go when I get to Gul,' he said.

'Did you drive there alone?' Farhana asked.

'Yes,' Fazli replied.

'Would you normally drive on your own outside of the city?' she asked.

'No,' he said.

'So why this time?'

'He told me to come alone.'

Farhana looked up. 'You drove alone on the instruction of a stranger, demanding that you go to a place you had never been before.' She paused. 'Why did you agree to do this thing?'

'He was not a stranger. My assistant knows of him. Is this why you're suspicious?' he asked.

'Not so much suspicious, not that, but I know you, Fazli. You are a very careful man. I don't understand why you were willing to take this risk.'

Fazli stopped for a moment, looking again at the room around him. 'He did not say "woman" when he said there was a very sick woman; he said "*gori*",' he replied.

'Why didn't you say that before?' Farhana asked.

'I hate the expression.'

'White woman. It is just a statement of fact,' she said.

'And you like being called a brown one?'

'It's not the same.'

'Isn't it?' he said. He looked at her directly.

'Are you really telling me that you believe this?' she asked.

'Are you really telling me that you are going to go on recording us bickering about this?' Fazli shook his head at her, smiling.

'They will enjoy.' Farhana clicked the recorder. 'You want some chai, bigot?'

'Why not? Is it as terrible as our stuff at the hospital?'

'Probably worse, mostly sugar with a little water, a tea leaf or two.' She got up and knocked on the door.

It opened, and she put her head through, calling for tea.

The door closed again.

'Are we locked in?' Fazli asked.

'It has an automatic lock.' She was matter-of-fact.

'Why? In case I try and knock you down, take your keys and make my escape from the police headquarters?'

'Come on, please.' She sat down again. 'I can't change the door because I am interviewing someone I know and trust.' She looked across at him. 'Why are you being so defensive?'

'I'm afraid of saying something now that could count against me,' he said. 'And it is not so easy being interrogated by you; you should try it someday.' He stopped for a moment. 'Isn't this a conflict of interest because you know me, by the way?'

'Fazli, it's not an interrogation; this is an interview.' Her tone was sharper. 'And this is Pakistan, not your England-Shingland.'

'Sorry, Madam Deputy Inspector.' He matched her tone.

'Come, we need to carry on.' She picked up the recorder.

'Just one minute.' He raised his hand. 'I don't want this recorded because I want you to understand, but what I am going to say to you is nothing to do with this interview.'

'Understand what?' she asked.

'I wanted to stay in England after studying. They offered me a very good position,' he said.

'I know that,' she replied.

'I know you do, but you do not know this. My reason for wanting to stay was not because of the job but because of someone there, someone I had been working with.'

Farhana looked away, embarrassed for a moment. 'You don't have to explain.'

'I think I do because you seem suspicious that I drove out to this place alone.' He stopped.

'I am sorry for this,' she said.

'May I continue?' he asked.

She nodded.

'I did not tell my family this thing. It was enough to tell them about the position being offered. I thought they would accept this reason, but my father was very clear.' He paused. 'He told me that they had agreed to let me go, that they had helped me by taking loans that they would probably never finish repaying, because I was going to come back here and use the knowledge that I had gained to help this place. Most of all he reminded me that I had been given the scholarship for this reason, that it would be wrong if I did not come back.' He paused. 'Baba made it very clear to me that I would be a traitor to our family, and to my country, if I did not return.' He looked up. 'I am sorry. Am I embarrassing you?' he asked.

'Not at all.' Farhana smoothed over her astonishment.

'I lied to her,' he said.

'What?'

'To this woman.'

'I see.'

'I am not sure that you can,' he said.

She shrugged. 'Perhaps a little.'

'I was not brave enough to say anything to my father, to my family. Instead I lied to her, told her that my father was very sick and that I had to return home.'

There was a knock and the door opened. One of Farhana's men came in with a tray of chai. He put a cup and saucer in front of his superior officer and then pushed a plastic mug across to Fazli.

'Well, he thinks I'm being interrogated,' Fazli said as the door closed behind the man.

'We can swap,' she said, offering her cup to him.

'It may seem so, but I am not trying to make this more difficult. It is strange being interviewed, interrogated, whatever it is you want to call this, by someone you know. Can you agree on this thing?' he asked.

Farhana looked back down at the tape recorder.

This was one of those times when she hated what she did.

'Is that silent assent?' he asked.

She nodded.

'I like chai in plastic cups; this I don't mind, but I would like to be able to finish telling you about Kate.'

Farhana looked up in surprise.

'Yes, confusing. I know we are here to talk about this Miss Kate Black. I am telling you about another Kate, Kate from my England life, another *gori* Kate.' He smiled at his friend.

Farhana nodded. 'But you did not know she was called Kate when you took the call?'

'I did not know she was called Kate when I spoke on the phone; I did not know this when I was driving out there. Listen to me. I did not know she was called Kate Black until you called me. But it was because he told me she was a foreigner. I had a debt to pay.'

Farhana picked up the recorder and put it at the far end of the table.

$\mathcal{D}$

Fazli had not driven on *kacha rasta*, the dirt roads, for years, but the smell of them was immediately familiar, the dust that tasted of hot, dry earth, even in winter.

Billowing clouds of it followed him, filling the driver's mirror.

He had forgotten about 'tail wag'.

It was the expression that his father had used when eighteen-year-old Fazli had sat panting, banished to the passenger seat. He had just had his first unintentional tail wag—a tailspin—in his father's beloved silky green Suzuki Mehran, the pride of the family and badge of his father's earned place in the world.

He could feel the rear wheels beginning that same skimming on the loose surface. He slowed down, every part of him tight with nervous excitement.

Ahead was the broken bridge, closer than he had thought. He braked hard, swirling dirt enveloping the car so that he could not see ahead.

For that moment he felt suspended in a stilling of time, just as it had been when he performed his first surgery, and as it was in his remembered version of when he had first made love to Kate.

She had cried out his name, and he had hushed her because his landlady was disgusted by the idea of mixed-race relationships. That moment was imprinted, the edges still clear and sharp.

As the dust circling the car drifted away, to the left side of the broken bridge he could see the dirt track that he had been told to take.

He took his phone out of his pocket, opening the window to hold it higher, squinting at the screen. There was no cover.

The cook was standing on a rocky overhang above the house. He could see the road below, stretching to its fading point. His family was on the other side of the rubbled knees of the next mountain, just beyond where the road ran out. The narrow track to his village coiled up and away from the broken bridge, above the dirt road.

Crouching down, he watched as a small cloud inched its way along the road from the bridge. It was not the scooti returning. A bike made a different kind of dust, a thinner line. They would not be coming back. This was the kick-up of a car.

He waited until he could see that it was green as the doctor had described. He wanted to be able to see how many people there were. He also wanted to trust the doctor, but even if he was not alone, another person would duck down out of sight.

He could not wait any longer. He knew that he had a little more than five minutes before the car reached the house.

Jumping from the rocks, he let himself cascade down with the scree. He took the crowbar from the outhouse and unbolted the main outside door. In the passageway he stopped and listened.

The only sound was the quietly repeating slap of oak tree branches against the wall in the afternoon wind.

He did not need the crowbar. The padlock was loose, its key still in the lock.

As he opened the door, the stench hit. Lifting his arm to cover his face, he looked in. The sound of the car was close now. He retreated, leaving the door thrown wide. He was running from the main house as the sound of an engine rose over the wind, straining as the little car took on the steepest part of the road just below. Cutting up and behind the buildings, he scrambled back to the overhang and squatted down behind it.

※

'Do you want a break?' Farhana asked.

Fazli looked up. 'No, why do you ask?'

'You seem tired,' she said.

'And that is code for what?'

'For nothing. It is a straight question.'

'Are you saying that the others were not?' He smiled.

He did feel drained and bruised by the feeling of too little sleep.

'All of my questions have been direct.' Farhana shrugged and stretched over the back of her chair, arms raised, back arched.

'You've put on,' Fazli said.

She lowered her arms, crossing them defensively. 'Did you learn nothing from your time away? That is very rude,' she snapped.

'Come on, Farhi. You're the one who always complained about being called "thin and weak" by all the aunties, no?'

Farhana gathered up the plastic and china cups briskly, annoyed with herself for reacting to Fazli's comment. 'It was still rude.'

In his way, he understood.

※

The Kate that Fazli loved had hit him once, batting him away when he had pinched her soft curves and called her 'fatty'.

'Don't ever say that to a woman,' she squealed, pulling away from him.

'But why?' he asked, hands raised in bewilderment.

'It's rude. Women worry about it all the time,' she said, though she took his hand between hers and held it to her.

272

He wanted to explain to her that at home it was a compliment to tell a woman that she was looking curved and full. But instead he buried his face in her belly, breathing in the scent of her, the way her skin changed as he touched her, warm beneath the cool, tiny, golden hairs lifting under his fingers as they traced the shape of her.

𝒮

'Sorry, Farhi—stupid of me. You look well; that is what I meant. You look good, fit, maybe not as tired as when I last saw you.'

'When was that?' she asked.

'At that family Eid party,' he said, laughing.

Fazli's aunt was married to one of Farhana's father's many cousins.

'Oh, that. Was that really the last time? That whole family *tamasha* in Peshawar? That was, what, more than three years ago now?' She shook her head. 'We work in the same town and I only get to see you at an awful family party in Peshawar?'

'Yes,' he replied.

'Why are you so sure it was then?' she asked.

'I know because I had just finished with the divorce. My parents asked me not to come because they were embarrassed by this thing, but that was another whole drama of its own.'

'Why did you come, then?' she asked.

'It was time for me to be with friends again.' He looked down.

Farhana nodded. 'Do you think we can carry on now?' she asked.

'If you like.'

The intimacy of what had been talked about filled the room full of other things that could have been said.

Fazli coughed and Farhana adjusted her chair, straightening her back.

$$\mathscr{D}$$

As the doctor pulled up, he could see three buildings, just as they had been described: a cookhouse, an outhouse and a main house above those, nudged up against the base of the hill.

He parked near the cookhouse and sat for a moment before calling from the car window.

'I am the doctor!'

He waited.

Nothing.

He got out slowly and locked the car but immediately turned back to unlock it.

At the half-opened door to the cookhouse, he called out again.

It looked ordinary inside, tidy piles of things: four plates, four metal cups, three of the plates stacked together with three of the cups on top, the fourth plate and cup to one side.

Four? If the patient was one of them, that meant three others.

Could he outrun them back to the car?

The outhouse door was also open, the inside packed tight with different-sized wooden storage boxes in more orderly piles, a crowbar in the dirt outside.

As Fazli walked towards the main house, he kept his hand on the car key in his pocket.

The main house door was also open, a gap wide enough for him to be able to see into a passageway that was just a block of dark against the bright day.

Why hadn't he picked up the crowbar?

As he turned back to get it, he froze.

There was a scratching sound.

No part of him moved.

The scratching was rhythmic.

Minutely, he tracked the source.

It was coming from the side of the house—a tree, its branches moving against the wall in the wind.

The air came back into his lungs and his eyes began to adjust to the darkness ahead.

There was a right angle of light at the end of the passageway from another half-open door.

'Hello!' he called out in English.

There was only the slap of the branches on the wall.

Fazli took a step into the passage.

'Hello!' he called again.

A thin, animal sound came from beyond the door, forming itself into barely whispered words forced out by weak lungs.

'Help me.'

From the rock, the cook looked on.

He watched this careful man as he checked, paused and listened—almost more like a policeman than a doctor.

But he does not look like a cop. He's dignified, the kind of doctor I would like my family to go to.

He waited until the doctor went into the main house, and then, as soon as he was out of sight, the cook got up. He cut up across the hillside, beyond the main path, onto the sheep tracks, barely as wide as a handspan. He climbed until he was in the place where he could find reception again.

He called his wife and told her that she had to leave the house immediately and bring the children to the old herders' camp on the hill, the place where his grandfather and father had kept the goats and sheep in winter.

She started to ask a question.

'Do this now,' he cut her off, his tone not harsh but urgent.

He knew the man with no name would not know the hiding places in the hillsides.

He was not a man who understood the shape of the land.

'How could you tell this fast?' Farhana asked, pushing the recorder a little closer to Fazli.

'Her skin,' he said.

'What about it?'

'It was mottled,' he said.

'What does that mean?'

'The only part of her body that was exposed was her arm, and I could see from that,' he replied.

'See what?' she asked.

Fazli stopped for a moment.

Her arm had been twisted to one side, the sleeve pulled up far enough for him to be able to see red welts across it.

Pulling his woollen scarf up over his nose and mouth, he crouched beside her, tilting his face away from the stench.

He could see the smudged trail where she had dragged herself away from the filth around a bucket that was against the wall.

He could not find a pulse in her wrist.

The whole of the crown of her head was swollen, pus and blood seeping through dirty bandages that were too tightly bound.

Unwrapping the blanket from around her neck and shoulders, he pulled her jacket and shirt collar aside.

Putting his index and middle fingers to her neck, he searched again for a pulse.

'You know that driver you had, the one with the stain all over one side of his face?' he explained.

'Yes.' Farhana looked surprised.

'It was like that, except it seems more shocking on pale skin.'

'You mean a birthmark?' she asked.

'Yes, it looks like a very bad birthmark, but it's a rash with swelling and blisters.' He paused, thinking. 'The body is trying to push out poison, and the immune system is responding to a fast-moving infection but...'

'Fazli!' Farhana interrupted. 'Do I need a medical lecture?'

'It's so you can understand why I had to get oxygen.'

'Is it relevant?' she asked.

'It is.' He pushed back from the table and turned his chair to one side, stretching his legs. 'Yes, it is,' he said.

He always carried an 'international standard' medic's kit on call. The local standard version was a random collection of greying bandages, tablets and small glass vials of antibiotics, often undated, their rubber seals cracking.

At the same time every two years, Leeds General Infirmary sent Fazli the updated kit, and each time he was delighted again by its pristine state. One at a time, he would admire the entire contents, right down to the standard collection of swabs, butterfly clips, self-gripping bandages, sterile eye dressings, disposable gloves and tweezers. But it was the second layer that really thrilled him: two pouches of synthetic plasma, a small emergency oxygen tank and mask, two half-litres of saline solution, intravenous needles, one spinal needle, catheter tubing, two scalpels and two syringes of epinephrine.

In his focused rush to get back to the car for the kit, he did not even check the hillside, the kitchen or the outhouse. Grabbing the green box, he could not see where he had put the emergency foil blanket pack. He knocked over a box as he rummaged, vegetables that he had picked up before the call. Tomatoes and onions rolled away from the car.

It was only a few hours since he had told his cook that he would pick up the vegetables on his way to the hospital, a simple task now stretched thin into the distance.

With both arms full, he ran back, leaving the key in the lock of the boot, the door open.

Folding the stinking blankets onto their cleanest surface, he propped up Kate's head and shoulders so that he could hold the oxygen mask to her face without having to put the mask's tight elastic around her wounded head. He opened the valve on the tank, a few millimetres wider than recommended, an extra thrust of oxygen.

He saw that his free hand was shaking as he timed thirty seconds. Clenching and releasing his fist, he stretched out his fingers as he looked for a vein in her arm. He had to let go of the mask to tie catheter tubing around her upper arm and to flick the vein on the cold skin of her inner elbow.

'Come on,' he shouted into the silence, searching for any sign of rising blue life under the skin as he held the mask back to her face. 'Come on, come on!'

Kate's head flopped as one of the blankets slipped.

Still no pulse in her wrist.

Nothing in her neck.

'Intracardiac injection, class.' Dr Strang always used to bark the lecture title, bouncing his voice around the hall.

Fazli Jadoon had not liked Dr Strang.

He thought him full of pompous opinions and so beloved of his own thinking that his greatest pleasure seemed to be wandering off point, dragging the students behind him through lengthy stories of diagnostic genius, most of which were his own.

As Dr Strang began on another sludge-coloured February Yorkshire morning, the tiered rows of medical students shifted in their chairs. Fidgeting was a way to stave off both the cold and the boredom of the three hours that lay ahead.

'As an emergency intervention, this method is controversial, but I direct the following to our visiting friends,' Dr Strang continued.

Fazli rolled his eyes at his roommate. Radi Sarkar was another scholarship student. He had transferred from Chittagong Medical College in Dhaka.

Radi yawned back at Fazli.

'Mr Sarkar, you obviously know the subject so well that you can afford to nap. So why don't you share your superior knowledge with us?' Dr Strang crossed his arms and leant forward on the lectern.

Radi stood up, pulled off his heavy, oversized jersey and unbuttoned his shirt.

He rubbed his hands, clapped and blew into his cupped palms, warming them. 'The aim is to get the spinal needle into the ventricular chamber for optimum emergency delivery of drugs, most particularly epinephrine. This is in the event of other delivery systems having failed.' He pushed out his narrow chest. 'There is a risk factor, as it requires an accurate and deep insertion of the needle in the fourth intercostal space in the ribs, directly into the ventricular chamber.' He ran his thumb down the visible rack of his ribs and then stabbed his right index finger between his fourth and fifth ribs, recoiling and coughing from the impact. 'Here, this is where you would be aiming,' he finished.

Dr Strang stared at him.

Radi buttoned up his shirt and began to pull on his jersey. 'As Dr Strang has pointed out, we who herald from backward lands often have a higher requirement for the use of this type of emergency intervention. We do not have so many options to work with.' Popping his head through the neck of his jersey, he bowed to the medical professor and sat down.

Fazli began to clap slowly. It spread until every tier had joined in.

Dr Strang stood back from the lectern, his arms still crossed. Nodding, he unfolded his arms and began to clap too.

Radi and the doctor had not become allies after this, but neither had Dr Strang made things difficult for Radi. He did continue to test Fazli whenever the chance arose during lectures.

Fazli rolled Kate onto her left side, extending her right arm and leg to support her. Bundling one of the filthy blankets into a makeshift pillow again, he then laid out the other one behind the length of her body. He turned her onto her back.

Unbuttoning her jacket was easy, but he had to use a scalpel to cut through the rest of her clothes, her shirt and undershirt. There was no bra to have to cut through. She barely needed one.

There was deep bruising all over her exposed torso. Red blotches were swollen in places, and angry blisters covered the softer skin of her breasts.

Pulling on a pair of surgical gloves, he checked the timing.

Thirty-three seconds.

He closed the oxygen valve back to the recommended level.

Pulling a pen from his pocket, he felt down Kate's ribs, as prominent and easy to see as Radi Sarkar's had been in the lecture theatre twenty-six years ago. Scribbling on his hand to make sure the pen from his pocket was working, he made a small cross on her battered skin, tore the spinal needle out of its packet and pushed it onto one of the syringes of epinephrine.

He stopped, rocked back on his heels and took a slow breath.

Ducking his head to level his eyeline with Kate's ribs, he watched for any movement that the oxygen might have started.

Nothing.

Squaring himself back into a solid squat, he raised the needle high above the pen mark. With the full force of his body, he stabbed and then plunged the contents of the syringe into Kate's heart.

'When are you going to contact her family?' Fazli asked.

Farhana's head was in her hands.

'You okay, Farhi?' he asked.

She looked up.

'You look unwell,' he added.

'I'm not good about needles.' She smiled weakly.

'I know a surgeon like that,' he said, laughing.

'Come on!' she said.

'This is a fact. He always has to leave the room when they are injecting. Then he happily cuts into people: chop, chop, chop.' Fazli cut the air with his hand.

'Stop!' Farhana switched off the tape recorder.

'So, when are you going to call them?' he asked again.

'I have to speak to a few more people.' She looked away.

Fazli looked at his friend. 'You must call them.'

'Of course,' she said, getting up. 'Are you going to go back to the hospital now?'

'So, Madam Deputy is finished with the humble doctor?' He pushed back his chair. 'And yes, I will be going back there now. Are you coming as well?'

'Madam Deputy has finished.' Farhana shook her head with the small grunt of a smile. 'And yes, I am going there as well.'

'You want to come with me?' he asked.

'I'll have to come with my lot. This will be official.' She stopped before knocking on the door. 'Thank you, Fazli.'

'My pleasure,' he replied.

'I don't think it was.' She knocked and paused. 'You are really a good doctor,' she said as the door opened.

For a moment Fazli looked down, his eyes squeezed shut.

NOOR, AZAD,
OMAR AND MICHAEL.

December.

'Noor!' Azad called out for the third time, rubbing his hands under the kitchen tap's very cold water. He shook them hard, irritated that Noor was not answering.

He would have to go and find her.

'Are we eating now?' Omar leant around the kitchen door.

'I'm looking for Noor,' Azad snapped back.

'I heard. I'll get her.' He knew where she would be.

She was in Kate's room, though she was not curled up and reading in her now-familiar blanket nest. Noor was rearranging books.

'By title or author?' Omar asked.

Noor looked at him, hands squarely on little hips, her head to one side.

'Yes, I see, obviously by author.' He smiled apologetically. 'We're eating now.'

She waved her hand at him dismissively.

'That's rude. You come right now!' He was stern.

She put down the books she was holding.

'Sorry,' she whispered.

The girl has become too old.

He turned to leave.

There was a weariness about her now, more marked than in the rest of them, as though her skin was too heavy over her slight body, her gestures bleak. They were all just moving through the days, waiting, but it was as though Noor's childhood was being sucked away.

Omar looked back to see if she was following him. Her back was to him, still intent on the shelf of books, the curve of her narrow shoulders holding back tears.

Michael was already at the table, head bent over a book, pretending to read.

Azad butted the door with his shoulder, dishes in hand.

Noor had been eating with them since Kate had gone. Azad would not join them, but he was glad for Noor to eat with them, as long as she cleared the plates away at the end.

Michael looked up. 'I've thought of something about that last delivery,' he said as Omar came in with Noor trailing behind.

Omar widened his eyes, the signal to stop.

Michael did not notice.

'The stand-off I told you about, about the gas cylinders.'

Omar was shaking his head, but Michael carried on.

A ringer stopped him.

Omar and he grabbed their phones.

'It's not mine. Where is it?' Omar asked.

'It's mine,' Michael said, knocking his chair back as he reached for his phone at the end of the table.

Noor shot across the room to stand beside him as he rummaged for a headset. He moved to the corner, squatting down, his back to the room.

'Hello?' He pushed the headphones hard into his ears. 'Yes, it is.'

He listened, his eyes narrowing.

'Err, yes, I have it. Do you need it now because I can go and get it?' He paused to listen again. 'Can you say again, sorry? We have very bad reception. Hold on. I'm going now, but there's no reception at all in the rest of the house. Can you hold on?' Taking off the headset, he hurried away.

Noor, Azad and Omar stood staring at the phone.

Michael ran back with his notebook. 'It's +44.'

He listened.

'Oh, as in the +44 international dialling access.' He paused, nodding. 'Yes, that's right. 00 44 1472 876232.' He listened as the numbers were repeated back.

'Yes, that's right. Err, and there's something else I thought about that I did not say when we last spoke.' He paused, listening.

'Oh, okay. Will you call, or should I call you? It's probably easier if I call you on Skype because of the reception thing but...' His voice trailed off.

The call had been cut off.

MOLLY AND TOM.

Mid-December.

The phone was ringing.

'Tom!' Molly called. 'Can you get it? I'm washing up.'

There was no reply.

'Tom!'

'On the loo,' came the muffled answer.

'Bugger it!' Molly ran to Tom's study, rubber gloves dripping. The line was dead.

'Shut up!' Molly shouted as Jack started barking in the kitchen.

'Who was it?' Tom called through the downstairs loo door.

'No one there. I'm getting something for this headache,' she said.

She was wrestling with a childproof lid in the bathroom when the phone started ringing again. The lid opened, aspirins scattering, and Molly hurried for the phone again.

'Hello?'

She pressed the receiver hard to her ear, her body hunching around the phone as she tried to catch the faint voice.

'Hello, hello, I can't hear you very well. Can you speak up?' she shouted.

Tom could hear Molly's every word through the closed door, even over Jack's barking.

She kept repeating 'What?' and 'When?'

He leant towards the door, not wanting to miss anything, trying to get his trousers up at the same time.

Awful bloody timing.

It was silent now. No voice, and no more barking.

He pulled the plug.

Hands could come later, upstairs.

'Moll?'

No reply.

'Oh Kate, please, Kate,' he whispered as he grabbed the bannister.

He called out again, leaning against the bottom of the staircase, disorientated, longing again for the moment to be suspended.

Jack was ahead of him, outside the bedroom, scratching at the door.

Tom hurried up after him. 'Shush. Stop it.' He put his hand on the dog's head as he opened the door.

He stood at the threshold, again confused.

'Moll, where are you?'

The door to the bathroom was open, but he could not see her in there.

Jack leapt at the bed.

'Get down!' Tom shouted.

The dog sloped off on the other side.

'I'm here,' Molly said from where Jack had landed.

She was crumpled on the floor, the telephone receiver cradled in her arms.

'Moll?' Tom bent down to her.

She looked up. 'They've found her.'

NOOR.
Mid-December.

Allll around her was noise, people rushing to do things and then forgetting what it was they were trying to do, everyone talking over each other.

There were now four policemen at the house as well. Noor kept looking for the important policewoman, but she was not with them.

Azad had been in the kitchen ever since the call had come to Michael, cooking all the time, feeding everyone as they came and went.

Whenever anyone spoke to Noor, it was with the tone that people use when they are conscious that they should not upset a child, the words supposedly reassuring but just empty to Noor. When she asked questions, it was as though they did not understand what she was saying.

When she asked Michael what was happening, he told her that he had to go up the hill to try and get better phone reception.

'Can I come with you?' she said.

'Later,' he replied, hurrying away.

She asked Omar too. He told her that everything was fine but that it might be better for her to be with her father for the moment.

Her father was busy.

'How will I get to school tomorrow?' she asked as he started to chop another mound of onions.

He did not seem to hear.

'Baba!' she shouted.

'Shh.' He put the flat edge of his knife to his lips, onion juice running down the blade.

'Why?' she asked. 'Everyone is shushing me. Why won't any of you people talk to me?'

Again Azad shushed her.

'Baba, please, school,' she said, her voice lowered.

'Maybe one of the policemen can take you. They seem not to be moving from this place. It will give them something to do rather than just sitting around, eating, taking tea, eating again.'

Noor looked at her father in amazement.

'I can't be dropped at school by a policeman. You know how people will just talk, talk, talk.'

Azad looked at his daughter, just nine, but so much older.

'I can walk you to the bus stop,' he said, putting his hand on her soft hair.

'No! It's all stinky onion, Baba.' She twisted away. 'But you never let me take the bus alone,' she added.

'I will ask Omar to take you, or Michael Sahib can do this?'

'They're not going to take the bus with me.' She started to walk away. 'No one has time.' She slammed the kitchen door behind her.

Azad picked up the knife.

She has become very like Kate Ma'am. A temper on her. Not so good for a woman.

He bent over the onions again, his lips pressed tight, eyes narrowed.

Omar was at the table typing a list, the various policemen drifting around him. They were picking things up, looking at them and asking questions. Omar was ignoring them.

'Was that *tamasha* in the kitchen with you?' he asked Noor in English as she came into the room.

'*Yaar!*'

'What's up?'

'I don't know how I am going to reach school tomorrow,' she answered in English, standing beside him, rocking back and forth on the arm of his chair with the enthusiasm of having finally been heard.

'Maybe one of these nice men can take you?' he continued in English.

'Why are all you people saying this?' she said. 'Baba the same. Tell me, what are people thinking if I reach school with one of these people?' She flicked her head at one of the policemen, his legs swung over the arms of a chair, kicking the back of another.

'Okay.' Omar closed his laptop and turned to her. 'So, what do you want me to do about it?' he said, reverting to Shina.

'Can you take me?'

'I don't think so,' he said, leaning towards her. 'I have to go to Gilgit,' he whispered.

'Why are you whispering?' she asked.

'To annoy them,' he whispered back.

'Can I come with you?' she hissed.

Omar sat up. He had been about to say no, but he paused. 'You would miss school again.'

'I am far ahead in class. Please!' She took his arm in both her hands.

'Let me see. I will speak with your father.' Omar crossed the room, Noor tight in his wake.

The policemen watched but did not move.

MOLLY AND TOM.

Mid-December.

Molly was staring into a suitcase. It was empty except for a torch and a pair of walking boots.

Tom was at the bedroom door. 'I don't think you'll need those,' he said.

'Why not?' she asked.

'The torch is good, but we're not going for a hiking trip.'

'I know that, but it was so wet when we were there before. What am I going to do, totter around in stilettos in the mud?'

'I'm sure people would find that very appealing, though I don't think you've got any, and neither can I picture you peddling around in stilettos. Did I miss a golden footwear moment somewhere across the decades?'

'Probably.' Molly leant down beside the bed. 'And now you have a woman in comfortable lace-up wine gums.' She picked up a pair of deep red, sensibly broad shoes.

'They're ideal,' he said.

'For what, an arse-kicking contest?' Molly gave a little gasp of frustration.

Tom reached out to her. 'You'll be comfortable, and that's what matters.' He paused. 'Are you sure it's a good idea for Susie to drive us to the airport?'

'Of course it's not, but I know I can't face the train and the Underground that early in the morning.' She swapped the hiking boots for the wine gums. 'Mack offered as well, but you saw how Susie was.'

'I really don't think we have to be diplomatic about this, and I do not relish the idea of Susie's predawn driving.' Tom picked up the discarded walking boots. 'You're probably right about these. We could both wear them on the flight to cut down on packing space.'

'Thank you,' Molly said, taking them from him. 'It was just easier to let Susie do it. She desperately wanted to help, and I didn't have the energy to talk her out of it.'

'I know I'd be happier in Mack's station wagon,' Tom said.

'Well, you tell her, then.'

'I will.'

Molly looked at him in surprise. 'Are you really going to?'

'I really am,' he said. 'How long do you think you'll be?' he asked.

'Not long.' She squeezed her eyes shut. 'Tom, I don't know what to pack. What if...?'

'I think pretty much what we took last time will work. Just let me know when you've finished, and I'll come and pack my stuff.' He held out a small box, tied with a white ribbon.

'What's that?' she asked.

'Happy Christmas, darling.'

'Oh, Tom,' Molly spluttered into tears. 'I didn't get you anything. I didn't think...'

'How many times have you bought my present to give to you, for Christmas, your birthday, everything?' He put the box in her hand. 'It was just time for a change.' He pulled her to him as she clutched the little box to her chest.

FAZLI JADOON,
MOLLY AND TOM.

Molly was tugging at the delicate, pearl-studded cross that had been in the little box, winding and unwinding it around her fingers.

Tom was leaning against a wall beside her. He could see how the thin, silver chain dug into her neck as she tugged. His legs felt separate to him, unsteady. He was persuading himself that it was jet lag.

As Fazli Jadoon's assistant walked towards them down the corridor, his white coat was a beacon between the smeary walls.

'Will you come with me, please,' he said, his use of English slow and careful.

He had always found it confusing that 'please' went at the end. It did not make sense. Why say 'please' after asking?

'Where is the doctor?' Molly asked.

The assistant looked at her, his head to one side.

Tom repeated the question.

'To come with me, please,' the assistant repeated, a hand raised to show the way as he hurried ahead of them.

As he pushed the grey swing doors, Fazli Jadoon opened them from the other side, holding his hand out to Tom and Molly.

'I am Dr Fazli Jadoon, and it is my great pleasure to meet you.'

Tom and Molly stopped, Fazli's hand between them.

Tom took it, shaking his hand in a way that no one had since Fazli had been a trainee resident in Leeds twenty-five years before.

'Tom Black, and this is Molly, my wife.' Tom turned to her, his hand to her arm.

Molly was rigid, her eyes wide and fixed.

Though she could hear, everything was slurred. Tom's and the doctor's words sank away as they spoke. A few swam up through the haze: 'sepsis', 'shock', 'failure'.

She was trying to focus on the doctor's face, but her gaze kept dropping to a stain on the pocket of his white coat where his pen had leaked, a black blotch blurring to grey edges.

Molly looked up again.

It's the same colour as the bruising under his eyes. He must be so tired. I know I can't remember if I have ever been as tired as this. Maybe when Kate was a baby.

She gripped Tom's hand on her arm.

'Can we see our daughter?' she asked, her voice distant as though someone else was asking the question.

MOLLY.

That's not Kate.

Molly could not make sense of the shape in front of her. Only the arms were exposed, the skin battered and darkened, as though burnt. The head was covered with a blue surgical cap, the face hidden by an oxygen mask. Tubes, lines and wires ran to and from hanging drips. On either side of the bed, machines flashed and hummed.

They're like something out of *Dr Who*. Too old. Not real.

Molly turned away.

'Tom, it doesn't look like her.'

Tom held her while Fazli moved around the bed, his whole attention focused on the doctor.

The room around Molly divided into blocks of light and shade—the doctor in shade, the bed light, the body dark, around it the machinery pulsing, dark to light.

Ducking away from Tom, she moved to the other side of the bed, the floor shifting beneath her with each step. Molly stared down at a hand on the sheet, searching for something familiar.

I don't know this person. That's not Kate's face. This poor thing is not my daughter.

Fazli was now standing beside her, still talking.

'If you talk to her, she can hear you,' he was saying. 'But she cannot speak at the moment because of the mask.'

Molly looked up.

'I don't recognise her,' she said.

She looked at the doctor, beseeching. 'What should I say?'

Fazli put a finger to his lips.

TOM.

Molly was beside the bed, the doctor at her side, his voice so low that Tom could not hear, though Molly's voice was urgent and loud.

Dr Fazli had told them clearly that even though Kate was moving in and out of consciousness, she could hear.

Why is Molly saying what she's saying? Of course it's Kate.

Kate! We're here, sweet girl. This is how it all began: you barely alive, wired up, hardly recognisable as a being—just tiny limbs under another mesh of tubes, flashing lights, every human function performed by machines. Oh, my little girl, you're back where you started, here but not here.

He stepped past Molly and the doctor and put his hand on the unfamiliar arm lying on the sheet. The skin was hot and clammy, the hand bruised by the cannula. He could see the outline of the fine tube under her skin.

Tom wrapped his fingers around the ends of hers and squeezed, very gently.

The head moved, inflamed eyelids flickering, the light blue of Kate's eyes showing for a moment, stark slivers of sky within deep, bloodshot whites.

TOM.

Her mouth was moving inside the oxygen mask, the other hand reaching across, trying to pull out the cannula.

Tom caught her hand and held it.

He felt Molly's hand on his back, fluttering.

KATE.

Dad!

There was a shape beside her, full of the sense of him.

Are you really here?

Was she speaking aloud, or was it just another silent prayer?

Something was stuck in her. Someone was trying to hurt her.

Have to get it out.

There were hands on her, trying to stop her.

What are you doing? Have to get it out, can't you see?

'Kate! Can you hear me?' Dad's voice.

Have to get him to hear me.

Dad! Help me!

Something was being pulled away from her face. Someone was holding on to her hand. Both were gentle.

Not like in that place.

What place?

That place where she had been.

Where am I now?

'Kate, can you hear me? Can you hear me?'

Dad again, but not as second team member. Real Dad.

She peered out into the world through thin slits between swollen, cracked lids.

'Dad.' She could feel her mouth moving now, a word said aloud, the pain of it all over her face.

She tried to move her fingers under the hand that was holding them. She could feel him holding her, his fingers around hers.

Mum's and Dad's voices.

Safe now.

EPILOGUE
NOOR.
Three days later.

M ichael and Omar were standing in front of her so she could not see how many other people there were in the doctor's room. Noor held on to the back of Omar's coat, peering around him.

The policewoman was there.

She raised her hand to Noor, smiling.

Noor grinned and waved back.

There were two old people, a man and a woman, standing beside the policewoman.

Noor stared. They both looked like Kate, as if she was half of one and half of the other, bony like him, mouth like hers, and it was as though their eyes had been stirred together to make Kate's.

Michael was speaking to one of two men wearing white coats. This man seemed important.

Noor thought he looked strong and kind.

The doctor was answering Michael's question, but she had missed what he asked.

She scrunched the handful of Omar's coat more tightly.

The doctor was saying yes.

Noor looked at him very carefully.

He wouldn't say that if she was dead. He would not do that.

He put his hands into the pockets of his white coat, his face wide open as if he knew everything in the world.

She wanted to ask him why no one would tell her what was happening, but he was talking, giving instructions. He waved Michael, Omar and Noor towards the other man who began to walk ahead of them. They followed his bright white coat down a corridor, through a crowd crushed up against a door, another corridor, another crowd.

And then he stopped at a door with the number 50 on it.

Noor wondered why the 0 was lower than the 5, as though it was trying to escape.

'We're going to wait here, Noor.' Omar leant down, unwinding her hand from his coat.

'Aren't you coming in?'

'You go,' he said, his hand on her back, gently nudging her forward.

The man in the very white coat opened the door.

There was a curtain on the other side that he pushed past, leaving Noor between the door and the curtain.

Was she supposed to stay there?

'Are you coming?' he asked, pulling the curtain aside.

Noor could not move.

The person on the bed looked funny, as though they had been cooked too quickly on her father's *roti* pan, their edges curled and burnt.

They were taking a mask away from their face.

'Hello,' said the crispy person in a voice like Kate's but as though the words were being squeezed from a very small place.

She was trying to open her eyes, but it seemed a huge effort.
'Why have you got a mask?' Noor asked.
'I'm not very good at breathing on my own at the moment.'
'Have you been here all the time?' Noor asked.
'No.'
'Where were you?' Noor moved closer to the bed.
'I don't know.' The cracked eyelids closed.
'Are you going to die, like my amma?'
'I hope not.'
'I put your books in order, by author. I hope you will like it.' Noor leant on the end of the bed. 'Those people in the doctor's room, are they your baba and amma? They look like you. Are they going to take you away? You can't leave. This is your home.'

Kate's painful lids lifted a little. 'Come and sit,' she said. 'Tell me about the books you have been reading.'